TIERNEY JAMES

DARK SIDE OF MORNING

L & D

PRESS

Owasso, OK

ISBN-13: 978-1-965460-10-8 (Paperback)
ISBN-13: 978-1-965460-11-5 (eBook)

DEDICATION

Dedicated to my father who taught me how to tell a story.

Acknowledgments

Jaycee DeLorenzo – It is always a pleasure to work with you in designing my book covers. Your creativity continues to inspire me.

Kate Richards and Wizards of Publishing – Your toughness makes me want to be a better writer. Thanks for your guidance and support.

Paperback Press – Thanks for always believing in me and answering my crazy questions.

CHAPTER 1

Three women alone in a city like Chicago, taking in the sights and pretending their lives are ten times more exciting than is the reality, can let a false sense of security become the mantra of choice. Bright sunshine and clear skies hide the darkness that lies in wait for such reckless behavior.

Lake Michigan, with its glassy blue waters, carried the echoes of Navy Pier all the way to the Museum of Natural History where the women sat on the steps licking ice cream cones, melting faster than their mouths could handle. Anxious laughter floated toward other tourists as they struggled to keep the drips from soiling their identical blue T-shirts proclaiming the Chicago Cubs to be the best baseball team. The idea represented when they dressed in similar outfits in middle school and were not cool enough to know it was a fashion faux pas.

"Hey, the guy with the red shirt made a rude gesture toward us. Must be a Cardinals' fan." Julie bit into her cone, creating such a crunch the other two choked with laughter. Her round face broke into a lopsided grin when traces of vanilla ice cream clung to the corners of her thin lips.

"You're losing your touch, Erica. Usually a man will come over and ask our names while staring at you." Cleo took the last bite of her cone then wiped her hands on the sides of her jeans. Having a friend who reminded you of the cover of *Vogue* could be

"

a real downer at times.

Erica glanced over her shoulder at the man who stumbled up the steps when she winked. "Not a chance." Cleo turned in time to see the man sprawl face down against the granite steps. Her hand slapped across her mouth to cover an amused giggle.

Cleo stood, dusting the seat of her pants as she stared out at the water. "It's beautiful here. See the yacht?" She pointed toward the horizon, but her friends only nodded as they started up the steps. Taking a deep breath, she followed her friends inside. "My dad used to bring me here as a kid."

"Are you sure this is a good idea?" Erica bent forward and kissed her on the temple. "How long has your dad been missing?"

"Three years. Seems longer." The huge T. rex known as Sue loomed before them. Julie asked them to take their picture with the famous dinosaur. "I used to tell my dad I wanted to be a famous paleontologist."

"You mean he didn't try to get you to study Native American culture so you could work together?" Julie eyed the coffee shop and tugged the other two toward the smell of cappuccino and scones.

Cleo shook her head. "Well, maybe at first then, when I entered high school, he said he would rather I go into medicine, which is what I wanted to do in the first place. Said there might be a time people would need me."

"And the rest is history." Erica tugged on her friends. "When were you here last?"

"Three years ago, just before Dad disappeared. I couldn't stay but a couple of days because the hospital was shorthanded. I left him at the hotel to catch a red-eye. He said he was coming here to work after everyone left for the day. Something had him excited."

"Like what?" Julie spied the gift shop. "Can we go in here? My weakness." She headed in that direction, periodically whirling around to walk backward with a childish grin as if waiting for someone to stop her.

The girls went inside, and Julie soon became consumed with souvenirs.

Erica nudged Cleo. "You didn't answer the question. What was he so pumped about? Discover a lost tribe or something?" She lifted a necklace with a feather pendant.

"I don't know." Cleo shrugged. "He continuously said he found an amazing whatever. After years of hearing it, I really didn't pay much attention. All I know is he made it to the museum the night he went missing. The police found no clues. The lightning storm took out the entire security system for two days." She nodded with approval at Erica's choice then helped her try on the necklace. "I wished I'd stayed."

Erica held up three fingers to the sales clerk and paid for the necklaces. "Ridiculous, Cleo. Are you really going to wallow in a pity party for something you had no way of knowing? The outcome would have been the same. Your dad would not have been allowed to bring you here so late at night, and you know I speak the truth."

The truth coming from a no-nonsense person like Erica erased the guilt beginning to well up like a choke hold. "I know. Thanks. All I'm saying is, I wish I knew what happened."

The security footage showed Dr. Daniel Sommers heading into the building then toward the North American Indian exhibit. Lightning flashed through the high windows as he disappeared into the darkness. The cameras went off-line seconds later. The police found her father's car keys. His outdated Chevy remained in the parking lot the next morning. Nothing appeared to be missing from the museum, and no damage to any of the displays indicated anything out of the ordinary.

Several days passed before anyone even noticed Dr. Sommers's car in the parking lot or that he hadn't returned to work. Since he had put in for vacation to enjoy his daughter's long overdue visit, no one thought it odd he hadn't checked in. When Cleo called the museum to speak to him, since he failed to answer her texts or calls, the staff contacted the police. There was no putting two and two together because no two and two existed. Nothing. Not even fingerprint evidence. Dr. Sommers had simply disappeared.

Cleo put on the feather pendant necklace her best friend bought her and helped Julie with hers. She fingered it and wondered, as she did every day, what had happened to her father. The three friends stood in front of a mirror and complimented each other on their new bling.

"Let's get this over with," Erica whispered as they arrived in the North American Indian rooms. "You know all this stuff bores me, right?" She took a seat next to a ten-foot-tall totem pole where a narration continued its informative loop. "I'll wait here. My feet are killing me. Take as long as you want, Cleo." She waved her away as if shooing a fly from her head. "Julie, don't touch that," she ordered as her friend tried to reposition something on the floor next to the totem pole.

"I'm going to the textiles exhibit, Cleo. Is that all right with you?" Julie designed accessories for a high-end boutique in Neiman Marcus. "The brochure claims it came here from France."

Cleo waved her away. Erica stood and stretched like a lazy feline before meandering after Julie. Taking a deep breath, Cleo explored the different cultures of North America. She'd loved the Northwest tribes as a child. Her bookshelves boasted almost every title of Indian folktale. Books were the one indulgence her father had bestowed upon her after her mother died.

Moving into the rooms with the cases of mannequins dressed in various tribal costumes always created a sense of belonging in her. Cleo was only three when her mother died. Her sense of family became these artificial characters dressed as Native Americans. She never told her father she sometimes talked about her problems to them, even in high school. Because he could be totally absorbed in his work at times, Cleo enjoyed telling them about the pranks she and her two friends played on some of the teachers.

Growing toward womanhood, she fancied one case in particular. The Pawnee warrior standing tall and majestic, holding his hatchet in one hand with his bow slung over his shoulder, inspired her imagination. She often told him to pick up the quiver of arrows off the ground before he forgot them. Sounded like a twenty-first-century thing to do.

She moved in front of the case, letting her eyes shift to the warrior in the next one. An Osage male, well over six feet tall and sporting what modern people called a Mohawk haircut. With his face painted red, he bore the visage of an angry warrior.

Cleo cocked her head up at the Osage. "I see you still have an attitude problem, Neosho." Naming him after a river where the Osage lived had seemed appropriate at the age of eight. "You used to scare the dickens out of me. Most kids dream of the bogeyman when they're young. I had you to creep me out." She patted the case in spite of a sign saying *Hands Off.*

Stepping in front of the Pawnee, Cleo sighed with great emotion. "Hello, Wind Dancer. Have I ever told you I'm secretly in love with you?" She peered around her to make sure no one watched or could hear her. "Oh, the things I had you do to me in med school."

A chuckle floated from her lips as she dug out her cell phone and wrote down her number on the memo pad. Holding it up to the case, Cleo winked.

"Give me a call, handsome. I don't have much of a social life, but I promise to make time for you." Staring up into the face of her imaginary hero, Cleo put the phone against her heart. "If only..." She couldn't finish what would never exist. "How about a selfie?" She whirled around, leaned back against the case, and snapped several photos.

Stepping away, with her interest on the photos, a chill prickled along her spine as a new reality zoomed into focus. She stumbled away from the case in horror when the weight of what the phone revealed paralyzed her with confusion. The picture showed the Pawnee, within his enclosure, a hand against the case, beside her, his eyes wide open and beautiful as he stared at her. One raised hand extended as if to touch her hair. Neosho had moved to get in the picture and had raised his club in anger toward the Pawnee. His other hand, doubled in a fist, pounded on the glass for freedom.

With apprehension, Cleo lifted her eyes to stare at the case. Both men stood with their hands pressed against the glass. Still mannequins, but their eyes moved as if human and stared down at her like they had awakened from sleep.

Lights flashed around her. She wanted to run away, but the rooms fell into total darkness. Dim lights in the reconstructed Pawnee earth lodge beckoned her to safety. Gulping down a scream, Cleo ran toward it.

Once inside, the feeling of safety returned. How many times had she climbed upon the buffalo-hide-covered benches serving as beds for the Pawnee and read away the hours? The ever-present smell of sweetness and smoke calmed her nerves. The thudding of her heart forced her to sit down. Usually a storyteller sat at the far end of the lodge and entertained visitors. It must not be time for the program. A hide moved aside at the rear of the lodge and a pregnant woman dressed in buckskins peered inside. Cleo didn't remember there being an opening there. Earth lodges had one doorway.

"Hello?" Cleo stood to face the woman. "Are you the storyteller?"

The woman glanced over her shoulder then to her. To Cleo's surprise, she motioned her to follow, speaking in a language Cleo didn't know.

"I'm sorry. I don't understand." Cleo rubbed her arms at the sudden chill sweeping in from the opening, making some of the items tied to the lodge poles shift slightly. The woman motioned again then disappeared the way she'd come.

Cleo moved to the buffalo hide and lifted it, only to find a solid wall of earth. She patted it softly at first then, with the kind of desperation someone with a mental disorder might display, cried, "No. No. No." She whirled around and escaped out the front then around to the other side of the lodge. Her hands searched with the care of a surgeon for any kind of opening.

"There isn't anything here."

"No. There isn't," quipped Erica as she strolled from another entry point into the exhibits. "What's with the lights being out at the other end? Can this place get any creepier?" She rolled her eyes at the surroundings as if a plague-infested rat might lunge at her any minute.

Cleo collected herself and took deep breaths as her friend turned a pinched expression in her direction. "Are you alright, Cleo? Did you see a ghost? Of course, in this place, that is very possible."

"I want to show you something." Cleo scrolled through her phone for the pictures. "They're gone," she whispered.

"Who?" Erica waved at Julie coming through the double doors.

Realizing what she'd experienced put her in the having-a-nervous-breakdown category, Cleo decided to drop it. "Never mind."

"I'm starving. Are you finished, Cleo?" Julie patted her stomach. "I'm tired of being the chubby friend. You guys need to fatten up a bit."

Erica smirked. "You're not chubby, just short. Besides, you're the one with all the personality. You know everyone or will before we leave." Erica guided her friends toward the exit. "Your gravestone will say, *for a good time, call Julie.*" She laughed as they entered the grand foyer.

Although quiet, Cleo let the echoing laughter sooth her troubled mind. "Let's get out of here. Can we take the water taxi to Navy Pier then catch a cab to my place?"

Her friends agreed the day continued to be too beautiful to pass up such a trip on the water.

The girls joined several others on the water taxi and inhaled the fresh air as they moved offshore. Cleo basked in her memories as the Museum of Natural History faded to a small outline on the horizon. Julie managed to pump information from the other passengers, passed out her business cards, and then talked about their short vacation, while Erica sipped on her bottled water.

The trip soon ended as the taxi puttered into the dock. Cleo watched a man with a limp move toward the exit and assist the other passengers out of the boat. He said something to Julie, making her giggle and blush. Erica frowned and refused help.

Cleo remained seated until everyone else exited. She wanted to feel the rock of the boat and hear the sounds of sea birds flying overhead as long as possible.

"Miss? You coming?" The man with a limp spoke with a French accent. He twisted his lips into what appeared to be a grin. His eyes matched the blue of Lake Michigan on a sunny day.

She stood and wobbled slightly as a wave rocked the boat. Before she could get her sea legs, another wave hit, throwing her forward. The Frenchman caught her and pulled her up straight. They stood nose to nose. Cleo tried to squirm free, but the man held her firmly without much effort.

"Thank you," Cleo said as she watched her friends stroll up the plank.

"It is good to see you, Cleopatra." The Frenchman's tone grew low.

She jerked free and stared at the man. *Cleopatra.* Her father had given her the name as a child. "What did you call me?"

The Frenchman continued to smile, revealing a bottom row of slightly crooked teeth that did nothing to take away from his rugged masculinity. Such men always bordered on enticement for her. Very tan and clean-shaven, Cleo found his familiarity disturbing. His blond hair, with hints of premature gray, curled at the ends. His calloused hands and wiry muscles lent themselves to a man used to hard work. She guessed him to be a few years older than herself.

"Cleopatra. Your father called you the name as a child. No?" The mischievous twinkle in his eyes reminded her of a boy with a secret. Cleo took a step away, but he followed. "You do not recognize me." He shrugged. "I saw you once when I visited the museum with Wind Dancer."

"I don't know you."

"Jacque Marquette. I'm known as the Frenchman."

"Sorry. You must have me confused with—"

"No. I don't. Another time, another place, Cleopatra."

Cleo forced a frown followed by a snarl. "Leave me alone."

The Frenchman reached out and grabbed her elbow stopping her in her tracks. "If I can't get to you when the time comes, then go to the museum. Others will help you transcend."

"Everything alright?" Erica looked down at her from the promenade above.

Cleo jerked free. "Coming," she replied. Then she leveled her glare on the Frenchman. "Touch me again and I'll file a complaint."

The man nodded as he stepped away. "Be careful, Cleopatra. Others may cross over who mean you harm."

Cleo hurried up the ramp to join her friends deciding a trip to a good therapist would be in order as soon as she made it back to work.

Waiting for a cab then traveling to her condo took nearly an hour in evening traffic. Her friends voiced complaints of being tired. Even she felt the excitement of the day cave in around her. The museum hopping and snacking on things normally off-limits to keep their figures added to Cleo's discomfort. Since she'd made late dinner reservations at the Signature Room at the 95th at the John Hancock Center, the girls sprawled across beds and the sofa bed to maybe take a nap and watch the news. They took showers then snuggled in their robes to wait for the steam to clear the bathroom before applying fresh makeup.

"You got your TV on?" Cleo thought Erica sounded as if she were chewing on a crunchy bar of some kind. "It's the Museum of Natural History. Something must have happened after all, causing that power surge."

Cleo stepped out of the bathroom with a toothbrush still clamped between her teeth as the story unfolded. Both friends migrated to her room and flopped on her bed like awkward walruses. Julie pointed the remote volume option then fluffed her pillows behind her. "Maybe we made the news."

"No one can say how the two mannequins disappeared in the North American Indian displays today at the Museum of Natural History. They simply vanished." The reporter certainly knew how to add an air of mystery to her voice. Video then rolled showing police entering and exiting the wing of the museum where Cleo stood earlier in the day.

Next, an informed docent spoke to the reporter. "Can you tell us what exactly is missing?"

"The Pawnee and Osage figures wearing priceless period costumes over a hundred and eighty-five years old. We are hoping they will be returned and this is some kind of sick prank."

The camera refocused on the reporter. "And there you have it. A real-life mystery on our hands."

Erica muted the television and squinted at Cleo. "Did you notice anything amuck, Cleo?"

Cleo shook her head feeling the rise of panic at withholding information from her friends. What would they think about her mental stability? "You know, the lights flickered, some went out. Then I hurried to the Pawnee earth lodge. Creepy, as you always say." She slipped into the bathroom and shut the door.

Leaning against it, she tried to slow her heartbeat. With a quick spit in the sink, Cleo took stock of her pale appearance in the mirror. "What is going on?" she whispered. "Am I having a nervous breakdown? Do I have schizophrenia? Should I tell them what I saw?"

She knew the answer to all of those questions.

No.

CHAPTER 2

Darkness cloaked the city canyons built of concrete edifices. The weather forecast predicted storms later in the evening, adding a layer to the already-ominous expectation of danger. Even the gusts, typical of the Windy City, drove a spike of caution into her heart.

Thousands of lights from honking vehicles created strobes across the highways ninety-five floors below the women eating their dinner in the Signature Room.

"I'm glad we wore cocktail dresses tonight." Cleo still tried to cover her nervousness.

"I like to pretend we have someplace to go afterwards." Erica flipped her hair away from her oval face. "We lucked out with a table by the window."

"I'm breathless at seeing the city from up here." Julie spoke wistfully when she lifted the menu to scan.

Cleo let her gaze drift to the city below, expanding like blankets of diamonds. She wondered if the view brought other voices in the restaurant to a soft decibel like theirs.

"This is incredible, Cleo." Erica caught the eye of a couple of businessmen two tables away. One of them winked, but she returned to the menu. "I've never been here before, even though I grew up nearby. Guess I'll need a better class of man if I intend to come here again."

Cleo tried to shake the dread welling up inside her. "My dad brought me here for my twenty-first birthday then again when I received my acceptance into medical school." She smirked at her wide-eyed friends. "My treat. I am a doctor, you know."

"Yeah, with a hefty school loan to pay. We'll pay for our own." Julie ordered the surf and turf with sautéed baby squash and zucchini in a natural sauce. "I'm in heaven." She rolled her eyes, followed by a moan. "I'm the only one who can afford this."

"She's right. Dutch treat tonight. We crashed at your place, saving us hundreds. If you want to spring for dessert, I'm going to request"—Erica nodded toward a nearby couple eyeing the final touch of their meal— "banana tiramisu."

The evening continued for several more hours. Cleo hesitated to conclude their last night together before returning to busy lives. Erica enjoyed her job as a flight attendant, based in Nashville, Tennessee. Julie lived and worked from Dallas, Texas, but traveled everywhere with her design business. Cleo continued to call Chicago home even after so many years studying medicine. Several prestigious hospitals in other states had tried to entice her into leaving but, at this stage of her life, making another change didn't seem wise.

"Let's head up to the observation floor. I read there's a coffee shop." Julie selected the elevator button. "We've got an hour before it closes according to the brochure." She jabbed a finger at the unfolded paper in her hand.

Of course, Julie headed for the gift shop as soon as they stepped off the elevator. "Get me a latte with skim milk and lots of whipped cream!"

Cleo and Erica laughed.

The day of constant activities weighed on Cleo as their weekend drew to a close. Staring out at the city with warm brewed coffees cradled between her hands, put a fitting ending to their reunion. Their chatter, although sporadic, remained light with friendly jabs and promises to return a year later to do it all again. Reluctantly, the women made their way toward the elevators at the eleven o'clock announcement of ten more minutes before the deck closed. Several families squeezed on with Julie and Erica.

"Oops! I forgot my jacket. Go ahead I'll catch up." Cleo waved them off. She slipped past the cluster of people waiting for the next elevator. The ding of the elevator signaled the remaining tourists needed to leave. Cleo had located her jacket when she heard the slow whoosh of doors closing. Moving to stand before another elevator, she thought of her father and the memories they'd created.

The image of a little boy playing with her in the earth lodge sprang to mind as did one of Wind Dancer standing tall in the display case. She took out her phone and scrolled to her library of pictures. This time she found what she hunted for, except the cases behind her in the photo stood empty. She brought it up closer to her eyes as she stepped into the elevator, and she punched the down button. Looking up, her eyes fell on a tall man searching the observation deck. Dressed in buckskins and sporting a Mohawk haircut, he lowered his red-painted face toward her.

"Neosho," she whispered in terror.

The Osage rushed toward the elevator and slammed against the closing doors. In his scowl and narrowed eyelids, Cleo recognized evil. She curled into the corner hoping the Osage couldn't reach her. When she reached the ground floor, she darted out into the lobby, nearly knocking her friends down.

"Whoa. The devil hot on your trail?" Julie grabbed her around the waist.

"Let's get out of here."

The women headed outside, only to be stopped by two police officers. The squad car parked at the curb had the flashing lights in play.

"Evening, ladies. I'm Officer Cooke, and this is Officer Wayne. If you don't mind we'd like to take you to the Museum of Natural History, please."

"What is this about?" Erica stepped in front of her friends.

"I can't say, ma'am. All I know is your presence is requested by some detective."

Cleo stole a glance over her shoulder into the Hancock Center where people raced from the elevator like they'd been shot out of a cannon. Neosho stepped off last then appeared to survey his surroundings before he spotted her.

"No problem. Let's go." Cleo tried not to appear too anxious. "Come on. Think of it as another adventure." She strode ahead of them, and they all piled into the rear seat of the police car. It merged into traffic as Neosho emerged from the building.

"What?" Erica followed Cleo's gaze out the rear window. "Why are you nervous as a cat? If you're worried about something, then spill it," she demanded. "Are you spooked about returning to the museum at night because of your father?"

Cleo faced forward and pretended to adjust her shoulders. "Don't be silly. I'm fine. Just thought I saw someone I knew at the Hancock."

Both her friends laid their hands on hers in support. "It's going to be okay, Cleo," Julie whispered into her ear.

The drive took only ten minutes with police flashers on and breaking the speed limit, although the driver did not engage the siren. At least a dozen police cars parked in the fire lane in front of the Museum of Natural History.

The officers opened the doors of the car for them and offered a polite and silent escort toward the front doors. Cleo forced herself to slow down and take in Lake Michigan and the city spread out like a fallen sparkler.

Who was the man dressed like Neosho? Why had he run at her with evil in his eyes? She'd thought at first only she could see him, but those people rushed off the elevator for a reason. She focused on her surroundings; she'd returned to the scene of her father's disappearance as well as where the mannequins had been stolen.

"Ladies, thank you for coming. This won't take long. Our lead detective would like to ask you a few questions about your visit this afternoon." Cleo guessed this gray-haired policeman with the expanded waistline and bags beneath his eyes might specialize in a great deal of desk work since his fingers appeared to be swollen with arthritis. She wondered if he chose to be here in hopes of a little excitement.

"I don't understand. How did you know about our visit here?" Erica sounded indignant. She often spouted her lawyer father's velociraptor style of interrogation. Cleo tried to shush her, knowing this kind of exchange might be inappropriate when they had been invited by the police.

"I apologize for taking you away from your last night in Chicago, but—"

"Wait. You knew tonight was our last in Chicago?" Erica raised an accusing eyebrow, her voice icy.

The officer shrugged. "Security takes pictures of everyone

who comes in or out, and you used your credit cards for tickets at the gift shop. Please accompany me to the coffee shop." He touched Erica's elbow, but she jerked away. Stepping to one of the tables on the outer edge of the coffee shop, the officer pointed to the chairs. "You young ladies left a trail a mile wide." He flicked his gaze at Cleo. "You're the one the detective wants to see." He tilted his head toward another young police officer standing nearby. "You other two sit."

"We most certainly will not," Erica snapped, reaching for Cleo's hand. "We stick together."

"Not tonight, you don't." The officer's voice no longer sounded like that of someone who ate doughnuts for breakfast.

"It's okay, Erica." Cleo motioned to the table with her chin. "I won't be long. I'm fine. Don't worry."

"Yeah? Well, just scream if you need us." Erica took on a louder, indignant tone as he led Cleo away. She turned back to give her friend a confident thumbs-up even though she felt anything but.

Footsteps always sounded louder in museums. A few lights from the gift shop and exhibits off the main foyer spilled across the floor, stretching the shadows of the policemen standing at various exits. A few men and woman in lab coats spoke in hushed voices, heads close together. Cleo didn't recognize any of them.

Most of the people she'd known had moved on since her father's disappearance. Some left for museums in Washington D.C. or Canada. A few took jobs in South America or were on digs out West or in Alaska. Losing touch with them had been deliberate. Their voices and praise of her father only managed to keep the flame of despair of unanswered questions alive. So, she'd stopped returning calls or answering notes of concern. Cleo had officially moved on with her life several years before. Her current situation wasn't helping her to keep a tight grip on reality.

"What was that?" Cleo stopped as light flashed through the thick glass doors leading to the foyer where they'd entered. The fan-shaped windows higher up created strobe-like designs as lightning continued to flicker.

"Thunderstorm moving in. That lightning strike was a close one. You okay? Afraid of storms?" The officer stopped to look toward the windows. "Radio says expect heavy rain. Don't worry about a cab. We'll get you girls wherever you want to go when we're done here."

Cleo nodded and moved forward then veered to the left toward the Native American exhibit near the Pawnee earth lodge. When she stopped and took a deep breath, the act of summoning courage felt a little beyond her grasp.

"It's dark, I know." The officer stepped over the threshold. "Give it a second, and your eyes will adjust. The lights are on dimmers so they're at the low point. Oh, there they go."

The lights got a little brighter but not enough they would damage the precious artifacts over time. She already knew the drill concerning the safety of the relics. The museum had become her playground as a child, study hall as a teenager, and even where she learned to fantasize about a Pawnee warrior named Wind Dancer who rescued her from too much work and, finally, grief.

The officer pointed toward the room with display cases. "The detective is in there." He left her standing alone.

Cleo took a deep breath, as if about to take a swan dive into Lake Michigan, before stepping forward. The smell of a natural history museum was always the same no matter where it was located. Some might dislike the hint of mustiness, but, to her, it smelled as familiar as a blanket kept on the foot of her bed. This place meant home, and someone had tried to dirty it up in her psyche.

"Hello?" She fingered her hair behind her ears then twisted it into a bun at her nape. Feeling a few strands slip out and frame her face, she smoothed her hands down the front of her jacket as if that would make coming here easier. "Detective?"

"Over here," came a masculine voice from the shadows.

He stood facing the display cases, but his stance spoke of casual aloofness as he stared into the two empty mannequin cases. He shed the gray suit coat and threw it over his shoulder, like a rucksack a hiker might use. A wrinkled white shirt indicated a man who didn't care about his appearance. Even so, the sloppiness failed to hide the muscles in the detective's shoulders. His hair curled at the ends and appeared damp under the dim lights. The gray was taking over the blond in wide streaks. The angular profile revealed a nose with a bump near the top, which made her wonder if he broke it at work or doing something ordinary men participated in, like a pickup game of football.

"Detective?" She stepped closer when the lights slowly faded again. The detective pivoted toward her, leaving his face in the shadows. "I'm Dr. Cleo Sommers. What is this all about?"

He extended his hand as the light from the display case brightened once again to engulf his face. The vise-like grip, drew her focus to a tanned leathery hand. When she tried to withdraw her touch without success, she lifted her eyes. A shocked gasp escaped her mouth. She stumbled over her own feet as she tried to escape. He tightened his hold, jerking her into his arms.

"Let me go," she demanded, her fists doubled against his chest.

He did so immediately, his forehead pinched in bewilderment. "I'm—"

"I know who you are. Jacque Marquette or should I call you the Frenchman?" Her voice quivered. "Is this some kind of a joke?"

"Excuse me?"

"Today. At Navy Pier. You helped me off the water taxi." She fumbled her jacket close then folded the lapels over since his eyes had dropped to the bare skin above her cocktail dress. "You're Jacque Marquette."

"Yes. I am. How did you know?" He lifted his head as he let a short chuckle escape. "Oh. I guess Officer O'Neal told you—"

"No. You did today at Navy Pier. You're not listening." Her tense tone forced him to observe her a little closer. "You told me to be careful."

"Dr. Sommers, I spent the afternoon in court and nowhere near Navy Pier."

Cleo tried to process the information and realized this man did not have a French accent or a row of crooked teeth like the man at the pier. "He could be your twin," she breathed, as she brought a hand to her throat. "Exactly."

"They say we all have a doppelganger. Of course, it is odd we have the same name." His grin took the edge off Cleo's skeptical attitude. "Guess mine works at Navy Pier." His expression became serious. "I have a few questions about these empty cases, if you don't mind. If you're afraid to be here with me alone, I can call in another officer…"

"No. I'm fine."

"You visited here earlier today."

"Yes."

"No offense, Dr. Sommers, but you and your friends impress me as Macy's shoppers rather than tourists taking an educational tour of the Field Museum, especially since you grew up in Chicago." His lips twisted into a lopsided smirk.

"Why are you questioning us in particular? A hundred-people wandered here on the main level."

"But not in here, according to the security loops."

True. She'd been alone when the lights went out. "I didn't see anything."

"Really? Because, according to this"—he took out his cell phone and retrieved something before showing her the screen— "you stood right in front of these cases to take a selfie. One second, they're here"—he nodded to the empty cases— "and the next they've vanished. The video shows you running, looking over your shoulder. Did something spook you?"

Cleo swallowed hard then shrugged. "The lights flickered then went out. My father—"

"Yes. The famous Dr. Daniel Sommers who disappeared four years ago. I know. I figure you came to pay your respects."

Did her surprise show in her eyes?

"I read up on you before I sent the officers to the Hancock Center. And before you ask how I knew you went there, technology and credit cards leave a big trail. I was also able to retrieve the pictures you took."

"Sounds illegal to me."

"Well, not for cops. We are still able to read texts, emails, and pictures in certain situations. The phone companies are very cooperative." He scrolled down on his phone again. "Can you explain this?"

Cleo hugged her arms. There she stood, grinning to beat the band, with Wind Dancer kneeling beside her. The detective saw it, too? She straightened and met his skeptical gaze with her own.

"What do you want me to say, Jacque?"

"Ah. It's Detective Marquette." He slipped the phone into his pants pocket. "I want you to tell me if you saw these two guys slipping out of the cases, or at least how they got out. We figure they had already moved the mannequins when you came in. They dressed in the clothing and stood until you came by. Probably wanted to scare the hell out of the tourists. Strange you didn't notice how lifelike they were."

This Jacque Marquette could absolutely pass for the man at the pier. Uncanny. "I don't know what to tell you, Detective Marquette," she said with a little bit of attitude.

"I understand you grew up in this museum. Wouldn't you, of all people, notice something amiss?"

"What are you saying, Detective? That I'm withholding information, or maybe you think I stole the mannequins? I didn't see anything."

He sighed and slipped his jacket on. "I think you know more than you're telling. You tore straight to the Pawnee earth lodge like a bat out of hell."

"It was dark. The anniversary of my father's disappearance is approaching, and nothing has been resolved. Couple those things with a very vivid imagination and you would run, too. I don't suppose Chicago PD has any leads on my father's case?" Before the detective could respond, Cleo narrowed her eyes. "I didn't think so."

"Is that what this is about? You want us to reopen the case?"

"I wasn't aware the case had been mothballed." Cleo dropped her arms to her sides and took a step away but turned back to roll her eyes over him top to bottom in disdain. "I think you're stalking me. First at Navy Pier and now here. I'm leaving. And, since it's about to rain, you'd better take care of your leg. This kind of weather can make you limp something awful."

Before she could take another step, the detective moved into her personal space and leveled an impatient stare. All the good will evaporated from his face, leaving a cold, hard expression, his jaw clenching over and over. "How the hell do you know about my leg?"

"You limped at the pier. Nice try." Tilting her head, Cleo watched the detective purse his lips. "But you're not limping. I guess you were faking it this afternoon."

A voice came from the shadows in a French accent. "The Osage is coming. We need to find Wind Dancer."

The detective drew his weapon and pointed it toward the

voice. He tucked Cleo behind him. "Come out with your hands up."

Cleo peered around the detective as the Frenchman from Navy Pier stepped out to confront his look-alike. Cleo whispered, "Hmm. I'm sorry, Detective. Apparently, you really do have a twin. I'm thinking he is as much on the up and up as you."

"Ya think?"

CHAPTER 3

When the Frenchman lowered his hands, the detective waved his weapon at him. "I wouldn't do that if I were you. Get 'em up higher."

Thunder rolled across the museum, followed by a lightning strike somewhere close by. Cleo flinched when another *boom* rattled the display cases.

Cleo stepped to the detective's side and watched him squint at the Frenchman. It must be terrifying to realize the person before you was a mirror image of yourself. The Frenchman wore clothes resembling something to wear on a camping trip in some remote Alaskan wilderness.

"And you are?" The detective's voice held icy calm.

"That is of no consequence." The Frenchman's gaze fell on Cleo, taking her in, head to toe. He extended his hand toward her, palm up, as if wanting her to grasp it. "Cleopatra. It is time to go. Soon the opening will close. We could die here if we don't cross over. Join me. The Osage comes, and I need to make sure you're safe before he finds us." His voice grew tight with urgency.

"Dr. Sommers isn't going anywhere." The detective spoke into his collar microphone as another rumble of thunder rolled over them. "Hey! Officer needed." They all stood for a moment, not moving, but nobody came. "Dr. Sommers, can you get an officer to come in here? They probably can't hear me over the storm." He backed toward the double-door opening, moving Cleo along behind him, his weapon pointed at the Frenchman.

She rushed into the grand foyer and halted so fast she nearly fell forward. Everyone stood frozen in various positions, as if mannequins. The scientists from the lab still huddled together as if talking, the policemen peered out the front door, their eyes narrowed in some kind of bizarre fascination. Her friends sat at a small bistro table on the edge of the coffee shop, facing each other with blank stares. A flash of lightning revealed a single moving figure outside the glass doors in the foyer. He stood over six feet tall with a Mohawk haircut. Neosho, the Osage, had found her. She watched him rattle each door and stopped each time as if confused as to why it wouldn't open.

With an awkward pivot, Cleo raced into the Native American exhibit to find the Frenchman lowering his hands as the detective lowered his weapon and spun around in a circle, agape. The mannequins in the cases surrounding them banged on the glass, shouting in languages she couldn't understand.

Cleo arrived beside the detective. "I hope you figure this out." She looked over at the Frenchman. "Let's go," she yelled above another boom of thunder.

The Frenchman smirked at his detective twin, grabbed Cleo's hand, pulled her toward the Pawnee earth lodge. "You need to stop my brother who is coming through the front doors, to give us a head start."

The detective, in spite of his frown of bewilderment, nodded and headed toward the grand hall.

They escaped into the earth lodge. A fire blazed up in the pit but failed to emit any heat. A wind blew the buffalo hide at the rear of the lodge. He jerked it aside and tugged Cleo forward. "I leave you here. Go through and jump. I can't let the Osage know of this. I will find where he came through and return if I can."

"Jump?" Cleo felt panic rise up inside her. "There is no jumping here. It's solid." Even as she spoke the words, she felt a wind blow through the opening where she'd seen someone wave to her earlier in the day. Hadn't she played with a little Indian boy who came through this opening when she was a child? "I can't."

"Remember to jump forward."

The Frenchman grinned with wicked resolve and shoved her

through. The hide dropped down and she stood in darkness. "No," she screamed patting the wall for the opening. It had disappeared. She banged on black walls smelling of wet earth as something skittered across her feet. She lifted them in a frightened dance of revulsion. Knowing she could be trapped with bugs and maybe rodents did nothing to calm her pounding heart.

She reached out her hands to try and touch another wall, but found nothing, only darkness. Tears welled up in her eyes as terror gripped her ability to think. Would Neosho find her before she could get out of this dark tunnel? What if he did? It had to be better than this.

"Jump forward," the Frenchman said.

"Okay," she whimpered. "Forward it is." She took a small jump but slammed into a human wall. A scream escaped her as her hands went behind her to find the earth lodge wall again. Falling against it, she tried to slow her breathing and the heartbeat pounding in her ears, setting up a roadblock to rational thoughts.

A hand grabbed her arm and drew her deeper into the darkness. The shadowy image of a man with long hair lowered his face into hers before he pulled her after him. No amount of twisting, begging, or slapping freed her of the vise-like grip. The feel of buckskin touched her body as the man halted and jerked her in front of him, while at the same time wrapping a muscled arm around her waist.

Cleo felt crushed against his chest as he patted, what should be a wall, with his free hand. Somehow the pause enabled her to piece together what was happening. He sidestepped two more times without any trouble, dragging her, still pressed against his heaving chest. The pounding motion continued until the third time he used his fist. This time the sound changed. A glow emanated from a growing hole in the wall, lighting up his face.

"I need you to hold tight, Cleopatra." His voice carried the slight accent she'd heard from some Native Americans when her father took her on his summer trips to the reservations. "This may hurt at first. You will feel hot then cold. Do not let go of me." He wrapped what felt like a rope around her waist then around him. "The wind may try to tear us apart. Do you understand?"

Cleo nodded as she dug her fingers into the buckskins then buried her face into his chest. The touch of his palm on the back of her head reassured her somewhat. "Once we are there I will need your help." Cleo stared up into his dark face and realized Wind Dancer, the man of her creative imagination for so many years, held her in his arms. "Ready?"

Before Cleo could agree, the floor gave way beneath them, and they fell into an abyss where darkness gobbled up the light she'd seen only seconds earlier. She would have screamed if the pressure inside her lungs allowed it. One minute her lungs burned with a kind of fiery heat then instantly felt ice cold as a wind tried to drag her free of Wind Dancer. The rope loosened; his arms tightened to the point of cutting off her circulation.

Her arms flew upwards as a scream continued to try and escape her lips. The downward plunge through a tunnel widened, its sides hard like polished stone, until she saw shimmering light beneath them.

The sound of her dress ripping as it caught on something sharp caused an avalanche of fear. She continued to spiral out into open space. With nothing beneath her but air, Cleo reached out, but Wind Dancer no longer held her. Had he disappeared? The flailing of arms and legs could not stop her plunge toward what she imagined a shimmering lake. She crashed into water with ungodly force, knocking her into confusion.

The cold water swallowed her to a depth one feels near death. A momentary sense of confusion caused her to open her eyes into a watery world in search of Wind Dancer. She pushed free of the rope and swam upward toward the light. Something large moved beneath, giving her an adrenaline rush to swim faster toward the surface. Two beluga whales shoved her playfully, eyes twinkling. She spotted Wind Dancer pulling himself out of an indoor pool. He bent down and reached for Cleo coming to the edge. Lifting her out of the water felt as if he possessed super strength.

"I have not ever seen such a fish," he panted, gulping for air.

"It's a beluga whale. I think we're in the Shedd Aquarium. Security will be here any minute. We've got to get out of here." Cleo twisted the water from her hair, nodding toward exterior doors. Of course, security might be frozen there, too. She tried to push against the doors only to discover them locked. "I can't budge them. Help me get these open, Wind Dancer. I think if we…"

Before she could finish instructions, Wind Dancer slammed

into the door with all his strength knocking it off the hinges. She stared up at him in awe as he lifted his hands for inspection. He seemed as surprised as her at his ability.

The belugas chattered and splashed.

"The fish says we must go."

She could correct him later on his use of fish for a mammal. Wind Dancer from the Pawnee Tribe of Nebraska in the 1800s would have no knowledge of such beasts. Yet, he understood the beluga. Astounding.

"I live about five miles away, near Navy Pier," she said. "I'm not sure how we're going to get there."

They circled around to the front of the building. The storm had evolved into distant thunder, while sheets of cold rain continued to fall. Squad cars remained still with their strobe lights on but not flashing. Several officers stood nearby, remained frozen in some kind of time warp. How long had it been?

"Come," he demanded, striding toward a mounted police officer.

"What are you going to do?" Cleo's teeth chattered as much out of fear as from being wet and cold. "Can't he see you? And why are animals still moving when humans can't?"

"I don't know. I will explain what I can later." He lifted the officer from the saddle and sat him on the hood of one of the cars. The chestnut horse followed Wind Dancer and snorted disapprovingly. After he rubbed the animal's neck and mumbled some words, the horse bobbed his head then shied away. With hand outstretched toward Cleo, he nodded at the cars. "Those machines will not work. Can you ride behind me?"

A loud roar of discontent came from the top of the steps at the Museum of Natural History, adjacent to the aquarium. The Osage barreled down the steps.

When Cleo and Wind Dancer approached the horse, the animal shook its head as if he would have none of it. Grabbing the bridle with one hand, he then released it long enough to swing up into the saddle. As he reached down to grab Cleo's hand and swing her up, the Osage rushed toward them with an ear-splitting yell. She dropped Wind Dancer's hand and raced toward the highway.

The sound of galloping hooves echoed on the pavement as Cleo tripped and spilled into a bed of tulips. Rolling over, she crab crawled away from danger. Wind Dancer guided the horse to cut off Neosho. The Osage grabbed the bridle and dragged the horse to the ground.

She feared Wind Dancer would be pinned beneath the animal. He managed to jump off onto the other man, swinging a fist that connected to his face. Both men hit the ground, but Wind Dancer staggered up and whistled for the horse struggling to its feet.

With one fluid motion, he leapt into the saddle and tugged on the reins. As he let loose his own ear-splitting yell, the horse reared then galloped toward his enemy. The Osage did not budge at first then jerked to the side, only to lose his footing and fall, hitting his head against a short concrete pillar.

Cleo stumbled to her feet, and Wind Dancer guided the horse toward her. "Come."

Cleo grasped his hand and he swung her up behind him. Neosho stirred, but she pointed in the direction of Navy Pier then wrapped her arms around the Pawnee's waist. The horse lunged forward, nearly throwing her off sideways. Her knees tightened against horseflesh as her body jarred against the movement of a terrified animal.

<p style="text-align:center">~~~~</p>

Cleo banged on the locked doors of her building. Around them, things came to life. Cars moved at a snail's pace one second then over the speed limit the next. Dodging them proved to be tricky, but the horse did what he needed to. She suggested, to avoid further scrutiny, they free the horse a block away from her place. Running the rest of the way in soggy clothes complicated a speedy progress. The effects of hypothermia from falling into the Shedd Aquarium pool then riding, soaked to the skin, like the wind through remnants of a thunderstorm could kill them if they didn't get inside soon. Chicago wasn't known for warm spring nights.

When the attendant opened the door and wandered away swaying slightly, Cleo tightened her grip on Wind Dancer's waist and guided him inside.

He revived a bit as the elevator door closed and fading gravity lifted them to the tenth floor. He pushed on the walls then banged his fists until she grabbed him around the chest and patted his shoulders.

"It's okay, Wind Dancer. I'm taking you to my condo."

"What is condo?" He took a deep breath and smashed her tighter into his chest. "Safe?"

"Yes. Safe. I live here." The doors opened. He staggered out, but straightened as if ready to do battle. "It's okay. This way." She motioned for him to follow.

They left wet footprints of bare feet. Their shoes would cause a lot of speculation at the bottom of the beluga whale pool. She punched in her security code to unlock the door and stepped across the threshold. Wind Dancer remained in the hall, glancing warily from side to side.

"It's okay, Wind Dancer."

His teeth chattered as he tried to speak, his narrowed eyes filled with confusion. Tugging on his hand, she led him inside and hit the light switch. He fell against the door as if she'd created some kind of miracle. "Lights come on with this." She showed him the switch. "No magic."

He appeared helpless to Cleo as blue lips indicated he suffered the onslaught of hypothermia.

"I never thought I'd be saying this to you, but get undressed. I need to warm you up." Her own body spiraled toward danger, but someone had to take charge of the situation.

She hurried into the bedroom and retrieved a thermal blanket from the top shelf of her closet. Entering the living room, she found Wind Dancer standing in the middle of the floor, dripping water on her new hardwood floors. He turned his head toward her like a robot in one of those lifelike displays they had at Disney World.

"Help me." She tried to lift up his buckskin shirt and only managed to free him when he finally reached down to assist. "Okay. Now the pants." She locked her fingers in the waistband and met his interested gaze when he grabbed her hand. "Don't tell me you're shy. I'm not buying it. Besides, I'm a doctor. I've seen it all." He smiled and let her continue but offered his help here as well. "Oh. My. Goodness. Okay. So maybe 'seen it all' was an understatement." Cleo couldn't help but stare at him in all his magnificent glory. "Where have you been all my life?"

"Museum," he said with such unconcern Cleo shook herself

back to reality. In quick order, she wrapped the blanket around his naked torso then grabbed a dry towel for his long hair. She stood on tiptoe to rub it across his head. "You should get warm. I don't think I can help with your clothes." It sounded so matter-of-fact coming from his blue lips.

No way could she undress in front of a god, so she hurried into the bedroom, disrobed down to her undies, and suddenly wished she'd taken more care to spring for the lace ones instead of sensible cotton. What did it matter? Women didn't wear anything under their clothes in his time. But, somehow, her twenty-first-century attitude beckoned her to at least make an effort. Unfortunately, when she searched through her dresser drawer, it reminded her she'd neglected her sex life for way too long.

"Are you feeling better?" Cleo hugged the blue quilt around her as she spied Wind Dancer standing in the exact spot she'd left him. He stared out through the expansive plate-glass windows at the flickering lights of the city and neighboring building. A stream of light moved along the highway. What must it be like for him seeing all of this for the first time?

"Wind Dancer?"

He turned toward her and let his eyes slid from the top of her strawberry-colored hair down to her naked legs and feet. *Yep. He is definitely feeling better,* she reasoned as his gaze lingered on various portions of her body. He still shivered, as did she.

"We need to drink something warm. I'll make some decaf tea."

He nodded as if he understood.

The condo-apartment complex built each unit with an open concept. So, as Cleo made the tea in the microwave she remained in his view. His brow creased when the timer dinged, but then moved toward the gas fireplace in the corner.

"We need to build fire to stay warm. Starting to rain again."

Not thinking it would be an issue, Cleo lifted the remote control from the counter and touched 'On.' Flames flashed up, like it should, sending Wind Dancer backward until he fell across an ottoman then the floor with the blanket in serious disarray.

"Oh! Sorry." She hit 'Off' and laid it down on the tray where she'd placed the mugs of tea. He continued to stare in horror at the fireplace for a few seconds then at her.

"Here. Let me show you how we make fire."

He frowned at each on-off click, while she tried not to grin.

"You try. Electronic. Not magic, although I guess that is up for discussion."

He relieved her small rectangular object and pushed buttons until he declared he felt safe doing so. "Lights magic, too?"

"As a matter-of-fact, yes." She picked up another device from the couch and dimmed the lights then brightened them. He drained his cup before he took the new toy.

Cleo wrapped her quilt around her a little tighter and leaned against the couch. The sheepskin rug felt warm against her feet, and the tea made her drowsy. As her eyes grew heavier, the lights dimmed to complete darkness and the fire burned brighter. Something whispered in her subconscious that things needed to be done, friends to find and a Pawnee to dress, but someone warm gathered her close, and everything faded to oblivion.

When the first rays of dappled light seeped into the condo, Cleo woke, cradled in Wind Dancer's arms, beneath his blanket. If she moved, he would wake up. Better to lie still and think this through. It had been a while since she'd had a man in her bed, or floor in this case. More like several years. After the last experience, she'd sworn off double-crossing, cheating handsome men who thought they were god's gift to the lonely.

His dark skin offered such elegant contrast to her pale never-in-the-sun complexion. With utmost care, she lifted the blanket to scrutinize the rest of him. Living outdoors with nothing but his survival instincts certainly worked for this guy. She lowered the blanket again and discovered Wind Dancer watching her. Her face grew feverish with embarrassment.

Wind Dancer then lifted the blanket and gazed at her body. He laid his hand across her bra and tugged. "Is this some kind of weapon?"

She felt paralyzed with his hand in such an intimate place. "Some people think so." She chuckled, knowing the response sounded lame.

His hand slid down to her cotton undies. "And this? Another weapon?" This time, she tried to move his hand, which touched her hip, causing her to jump. His smile matched the mischief in his eyes. "You are ticklish." He let his hands explore her entire body causing her to burst into laughter as she tried desperately to remove herself from his touch. His laughter matched hers until he rolled her on top of him. "Thank you for last night."

She tried to remember what exactly he might be thanking her for. Wouldn't she remember if they'd had sex? "I'm sorry. What?"

"You brought me here. I was dying from the cold. You saved me."

"Oh, that," she said in an almost-disappointed tone. "I think we're even. The Osage wanted to kill us both. What did you do to tick him off?" She managed to free herself as she found her own quilt. Standing proved a clumsy effort at best.

He shook his head. "Tick off? I don't understand." Standing up buck naked didn't appear to affect his modesty, but he wrapped the blanket around his body nonetheless.

"He is angry. Why?"

"Where are my clothes?" He searched the room with dark eyes the color of Hershey's Kisses. Moving toward her bedroom, Wind Dancer disappeared.

"Wait. Where are you going?"

"Need to…" He stopped and appeared confused again as he pointed down to his privates.

"Oh. Bathroom?" She led him to her small restroom and lifted the toilet lid before grabbing a cup off the sink. After filling it with water, she poured it into the bowl. He watched her closely as she flushed.

He nodded toward the door. "Understand. Cleopatra, wait out there. Don't need help."

"Thank heavens for small miracles." The words came out a mumble as she closed the door. She resisted rushing in when the shower squeaked on because the intercom from the front desk sounded. With a glance to the bathroom, Cleo threw up her hands and went to answer the call.

"Ms. Sommers, your two friends are on their way up with a police officer."

The doorbell buzzed as she signed off. With a quick dash into the bedroom, she slipped on the yoga pants crumpled in a chair along with the plain buckskin shirt she'd laid over a barstool to dry.

The doorbell buzzed twice.

"Hey, guys!"

"Hey, guys?" Erica snapped storming inside. "Where did you go? We were worried sick."

Julie chimed in. "Yeah. Got any coffee and Danish? I'm starved."

Cleo continued to hang onto the doorknob as Jacque Marquette strolled in with bloodshot eyes and a scowl imprinted on his narrow face. "We meet again," he said so casually she imagined their conversation involved the weather rather than lost artifacts. Could this be nothing more than a big scheme to confuse her?

He raised his chin at the two ladies helping themselves in the kitchen. "I tried to tell your friends one of my officers took you downtown to go through some pictures of known art thieves. Because of our"—he locked eyes with her— "conversation dealing with Indians, identical twins—"

"Oh, yes. Of course, Detective." He sounded as if he might be protecting her.

"Sorry, ladies, but last night my life went a little sideways with the storm knocking out security at the museum again. I handed you off to a few young officers to get you home. When I realized you hadn't arrived here, I sent another car for you. Totally my fault. However..." Cleo watched him pause as he stared at her friends.

She realized their mouths had dropped open and their Danish suspended in midair as they stared at something across the room. When she and the detective followed their gaze to Wind Dancer in the bedroom doorway with nothing but a towel, a rush of heat crept up her neck and face.

He focused on her for what she thought might be guidance in this situation. Rushing to stand in front of him, she caught a whiff of cucumber-melon body soap. "Everyone, this is my friend, Joseph Wind Dancer." All eyes seemed to lose their ability to blink. Their stares bordered on rudeness except for the detective who appeared to be evaluating the latest turn of events. "Ahh, Joseph is a staff sergeant for the Royal Mounted Police."

"Interesting," said Detective Marquette. He extended his hand toward the man as his eyes narrowed in the way suspicious police officers possessed.

"It is good to see you my friend." Wind Dancer grabbed his hand and pumped it vigorously. "I worried you did not make it."

"Yeah. I'm good." The detective spoke slowly, brow furrowed.

Wind Dancer whispered in Cleo's ear. "You're wearing my shirt."

"Oh. So I am." A nervous laugh ensued. "Look in the box in the closet. I think you'll find what you need."

Wind Dancer's eyes went to the two women staring at him from the kitchen, and he frowned before disappearing into the bedroom.

"Honestly, Cleo, you could have let us in on your little secret." Julie took a big bite of her Danish, chewed then continued. "I guess the interrogation went better than expected. Why doesn't anything like that happen to me?"

Erica set her Danish on the counter and moved forward. "Okay. I guess I can forgive you for not coming to get us. You deserve a little fun in your life, considering everything you've been through."

"I think you misunderstand the—"

Erica held up a hand. "No need to explain. It's nice to know you can loosen up a bit. We've both got planes to catch, and there is an officer downstairs waiting to whisk us off to O'Hare." Erica kissed her on the cheek. "Thanks for a great weekend, kiddo. Gives new meaning to 'mounted police,' I think." The joke didn't register with Cleo at first.

"It's not what you think."

"Good. Because my thoughts went pretty bland concerning you." She led Julie out of the kitchen. "Let's get our bags and leave Cleo to her handsome policemen." Erica shifted her eyes to Jacque and winked, which drew zero response.

In less than five minutes, they headed out the door, begging for a full report by the end of the week.

CHAPTER 4

Cleo leaned against the door and sighed. "Why didn't you tell them about the museum?"

"I don't know anything yet," Jacque quipped. "They knew nothing when everything came alive last night. Care to tell me what happened to you?"

"I'm not sure what happened. One minute I entered the earth lodge and the next the guy in my bedroom tied me to his chest. He sent both of us plunging into the beluga pool at the Shedd Aquarium."

"That explains the ruckus over there this morning when the whales were found playing with shoes in their tank. Didn't take long to identify the moccasins from the display at the Field Museum. I need a favor." The detective moved to the bedroom door and stole a glance inside.

"Name it."

"The other fella, my twin…" His quiet tone drew Cleo closer.

"Where is he?" she asked.

"In your ER under a John Doe. I told him to keep quiet and pretend to be homeless, although I'm not altogether sure he grasped the concept. He was shot."

"How bad?"

He shrugged. "He's breathing. He tried to dig it out with his knife. Tough old coot."

Cleo headed into her bedroom as Wind Dancer came out and knocked her off balance. He steadied her with a strong arm around her.

The Pawnee smiled over at the detective. "Jacque, this is the woman I told you about. Cleopatra Sommers." His welcoming expression suggested he believed him to be the Frenchman. As he released Cleo, he pointed at the detective. "Where did you get those clothes? They are strange on you. And your beard is gone. Why?" He stepped away from the two and held his arms out, showing his own new outfit. "Do you wear these clothes, Cleopatra?"

"Please call me Cleo. They belonged to my father." The denim shirt and blue jeans fit the Pawnee much better than they had her father. Besides being a little too tight, the jeans hit him at the ankle. "I kept them thinking I would find him some day."

Wind Dancer opened his mouth to speak then appeared to think better of it. He looked down at the floor. "My feet are cold in this strange place, but the air in here is warm." He shifted his eyes to the detective. "Where do I get moccasins like yours, Jacque?"

"These are boots." Jacque continued to eye the Pawnee. "Cleo, do you have your father's shoes until I can get this character something better? While I'm at it, are you the one from the case at the museum?" His voice followed Cleo into her room.

"Yes. You know this. We talked about it for a long time. Cleo's father sent us. I didn't tell her he is alive."

She managed to find a pair of jeans of her own and a sweatshirt with the Chicago Bears logo on the front. She wiggled into them before returning to the men with the shoes and socks. "These belonged to my dad as well. I hope they fit. Sorry. What did you say about my father?"

Wind Dancer sat down on the floor. He put on the socks and shoes as if he'd done it before. Surprising. "Yes. Fit. I don't like how they feel."

Cleo touched his arm. "Wind Dancer, this isn't the Frenchman Jacque you knew. This is a policeman. Do you know what a policeman is?"

His eyes shifted to the detective and he frowned.

"Your friend is hurt. We need to go to the hospital. Okay?"

He nodded, a kind of acceptance, but stepped in between the

detective and her.

~~~~

The three entered the emergency room, winded and disheveled. Cleo had tried to explain things about the Frenchman on the way. Thanks to the detective's suggestion, she'd ridden in the backseat with the Pawnee. The flashing lights, sirens, and other chaos, a fact of life in Chicago, kept him moving in the seat. He wouldn't wear a seat belt. Between jerking around to see where they'd been, dodging oncoming cars like they would plow into them, he kept grabbing her as if he could protect her. Cleo felt exhausted by the time they'd reached the hospital.

"The John Doe I brought in last night. Where is he?" Jacque flashed his badge at the receptionist.

Her eyes went to Cleo, not him. "Surgery. Two hours ago."

"I thought you said it wasn't bad?" Cleo asked.

They all started down the hall, Wind Dancer trailing behind as he tried to take it all in. "I said he was breathing and tried to dig the bullet out," Jacque muttered.

"Where did he get shot?"

"His abdomen, I think."

"Good lord," she moaned. "You guys wait here. Who shot him by the way?"

"I did," Jacque said straight-faced causing her to whirl around as Wind Dancer realized the weight of his words. "He pointed a musket thing at one of my officers as he emerged from the frozen state. I told him to drop it. The officer tried to take it from him. I tried to intervene by getting in the fray. It went off." His words sounded so callous and cold, Cleo could do nothing but stare at him in disbelief. "I couldn't let my officer get hurt."

"Accident?" Wind Dancer asked as his brow furrowed and his voice deepened. When Jacque raised his chin in acknowledgement, the Pawnee shifted his attention to Cleo. "Go. Save my friend. Accident."

"Wind Dancer, you need to stay with this man. Don't do anything stupid or crazy. Understand?"

"How would you know if I did something like that in this place?" He grimaced.
~~~~

She laid a hand on his arm. How strong he felt compared to most men she'd touched. "I see your point. I'll see what I can find out." She located the attending surgeon and pulled him aside. "Doctor, what can you tell me about the shooting victim?"

He shoved his hands in his coat pockets. "I'm not optimistic for John Doe. We did everything possible. He rested in recovery then was taken to his room. The man also had some infection from some old stab wounds. We tried to clean it up, but he might lose his leg over it. Who is this guy?"

Cleo promised to catch him up to speed later as she rushed out to find the Frenchman. Along the way, she stopped to retrieve the two new men in her life.

Once inside the room, she stepped up to his bed to examine the chart.

She inspected the beeping monitors, checking his stats then laid a hand on his wrist to take his pulse. When his eyelids fluttered open, she spooned ice chips into his mouth, suppressing a twinge of pity at his parched, cracked lips.

"Hello again, Cleopatra. I'm glad I finally got to meet you."

She leaned in, as if nearness could help her understand his thick French accent.

"The other man, the one who shot me…?"

"He is with Wind Dancer."

His eyes widened.

"It's okay. He is safe. The police officer didn't mean to shoot you."

"I know. The Osage?"

She shook her head. "I don't know. He tried to kill us."

"Your father says he is very sick." He coughed, his face twisted into a grimace. "The Osage must be stopped."

She gasped. "My father is sick?"

"I am dying. Bring me Wind Dancer," he whispered.

"I am here, old friend." Wind Dancer's voice made her body jump as he moved to his friend's bedside. Jacque stood nearby.

He shrugged at Cleo then nodded at the Pawnee.

"I'm dying," the Frenchman repeated and touched Wind Dancer's hand. "Do what is needed."

Wind Dancer lifted his hands, palms up then chanted a singsong verse, drawing the unwanted attention of several nurses.

Cleo held her hand up to stop their intrusion, but the flash of the detective's badge halted them outside the door. When the chanting stopped, Wind Dancer lowered his ear to his friend's lips. After a few moments, he straightened.

"Go with time, Frenchman. I will see you beyond someday on the Morning Star if not before."

The Frenchman sucked in a rattling breath and dropped back. As the monitors behind him blared their alarm, hospital staff pushed into the room. They were in charge now, and a badge wouldn't stop them. Cleo tugged on Wind Dancer's arm, but it took Jacque's assistance to drag him out of the room.

The sounds of reviving a heart had never impressed Cleo until she observed the Pawnee's blank stare through the window into the room where doctors and nurses applied paddles to the Frenchman's chest in an attempt to restart his heart. She tried to explain the procedure, but it sounded like voodoo magic even to her trained ears.

"I'm sorry, Joseph." The detective picked up on the fictional name she'd given. Cleo thought for a second the detective actually meant what he said. "I feel like I shot myself. I don't understand any of this. We need to get to the bottom of it."

Cleo heard the dreaded words. "Let's call it. 10:57 a.m." Her heart ached for some reason. Had he known her father? Did he know where to find him? She watched Wind Dancer. If so, maybe he knew, too.

"I have a shift in two hours. Can you take Wind"—she corrected herself as one of the attendants wheeled a cart past her— "Joseph with you, Detective? I can't leave him to wander the streets of Chicago." She fished a credit card from her jean pocket. "Take this and buy him some clothes and shoes. And some"—she motioned around her waist— "you know…he is going commando right now. Probably not a good idea."

Jacque smirked. "Probably not. He can come with me. I've got some paperwork to take care of at headquarters then we'll go shopping." He returned the card to her. "I got this. Least I can do. I've got a lot of questions for this guy."

"Can it wait until I'm there? I'd like to hear the answers, too."

"No. You don't get to make the rules on this one, Cleo." She noticed they'd transitioned to a first-name basis. "I'll swing by and pick you up around nine tonight. We'll grab some pizza and catch up then. Okay with you?"

Her eyes went to the Frenchman's body being covered in a white sheet. "Yes. I need to do a few things myself, Jacque. I'll take care of your twin." She tilted her head toward the body.

~~~~

The Osage emerged from an alley he'd discovered the night before. His head hurt and a lump on his head felt tender where he'd fallen against something hard. He wondered where the woman with fire hair hid. Cleopatra. The name filled his head. How he'd ended up in a dark passage between towering buildings remained a mystery.

For years, he'd watched from the glass enclosure along with the Pawnee, Wind Dancer. As the little girl grew into womanhood, she'd chosen the Pawnee, not him, to share secrets and dreams. When her father crossed over a night long ago, Cleo returned for one last time to grieve. He could tell from her tears and the way she stumbled around the room, where his case stood, she suffered from a broken heart. Police searched the area to find clues. Although he had one foot in the past, the museum taught him all about the future. Some things remained unclear. The meaning of words changed so often he failed to keep up.

The Pawnee had become his enemy long ago. He made his people sick, and now Wind Dancer would pay by taking his precious fire-haired woman to the other side. Finding several ways in and out of this world taught him patience. The pale skin of her body and the sun in her hair would satisfy him in his world. She'd stopped talking to him long ago—until yesterday. Something tugged at him even though she spoke in a teasing fashion. He didn't like to be teased. Maybe she could save the rest of his people as her father claimed. Maybe the little girl he'd watched grow into a woman would come willingly. Either way, he would have to kill Wind Dancer for what he'd done.
~~~~

CHAPTER 5

The day dragged on at a snail's pace for Cleo, in spite of a busy day in the ER. For once, enough help arrived due to the expectation of bad weather and continued gang activity in the area. She kept wondering how Wind Dancer fared with the short-tempered detective. Should she have let them leave together? Time would tell. Time sounded like the key to all of this.

She'd glanced at the news around five when interviews with people at the Field Museum and the Shedd Aquarium took the lead story. There remained more questions than answers as the news media appeared to be salivating over the unexplained events. The patrolman who lost his horse gave little indication of why he had become separated from his ride. He posed with his animal, which bobbed its head up and down. With a humorous thought, she imagined the horse wanting to interject some vital information. Fortunately, the news reported security cameras had failed with the storm. Although Cleo didn't understand why they hadn't worked, she believed it had nothing to do with the storm.

Three text messages came in the afternoon, two from her friends alerting her they arrived home safely with a colorful reference to her Canadian Mounted Policeman. In spite of the X-rating, she chuckled a little, drawing the attention of one of the nurses. The third text came from Detective Marquette.

It said simply, "All is well. No problems. He is very quiet and won't talk to me. See you tonight."

She longed to take a hot shower with cucumber-melon soap in her own home. Getting one earlier in the morning hadn't worked out. The hospital showers provided for long shifts failed to remove the faint scent of the beluga whale. She wrinkled her nose at the sensation of poopy whale water and smelly horse hair that might still be stuck to her skin. After sending a text to the detective to come to the condo, she bugged out thirty minutes early. She managed to make it home in time to take a hot shower then slipped into clean jeans, and a thin sweater. She felt like a new person. A quick towel dry of her hair and a light application of makeup gave her a better outlook on life.

Having no men in her life, other than coworkers, the thought of two coming to visit at the same time made her feel almost giddy. When the detective called to let her know they were bringing pizza up to her place instead of going out, she gave her appearance one last glance in the mirror. Could she really be this excited and flushed? The thought of Wind Dancer returning to her caused a spike in her pulse.

The desk clerk alerted her to her guests. At the ding of the elevator, Cleo resisted flinging open the door and waving like a cheerleader at a homecoming parade. Even when the doorbell buzzed, she opened the door slowly, struggling to still her shaking hand.

Wind Dancer stood in the hallway, beaming at her. Why did he have to be so handsome? Straight black hair to his shoulders, golden-brown skin, darkened she guessed, by too much sun exposure. Aware once again of his lean body she already knew to be hard as a rock, created a feeling of weakness in the knees, and a rising desire to get rid of the detective ASAP.

Maybe it was wishful thinking, but she thought his gaze toward her took on a smoldering edge beneath an otherwise calm exterior. His mouth bordered on being wide, but it was the full lips beneath a straight nose that created a flutter in the pit of her stomach. The nose flared as he took in a breath then released it slowly. The few scars on one side of his face failed to rob him of his rough beauty.

"I'm starving," Cleo declared as she locked the door, inhaling the aroma of luscious tomato, mozzarella, and basil from the pizza box the detective held. The idea of anyone being a match for a Pawnee warrior who probably could chase down a buffalo and bop him on the head with little effort could certainly take down an intruder with little effort. "What kind of pizza?"

"Half veggie—thought you might be the veggie type—and meat lovers for us." He raised his chin toward Wind Dancer. "Right, Joseph?"

Wind Dancer shifted his eyes from Cleo who had begun to wither under his examination. He mimicked the raised chin as Jacque had done. He followed Cleo into the kitchen and began opening cabinet doors, inspecting the contents with his almond-shaped eyes, occasionally inspecting an item then would close it and move to the next.

Cleo removed some plates and glasses. "I don't have any beer. Not much of a drinker. I have water and I think there's some kind of diet soda my friends left."

"Diet will be okay with me. How about you, Joseph?"

"Diet okay with me," he echoed.

Cleo frowned at Jacque. "You don't have to drink that, Wind Dancer, just because he wants it."

"My buddy says he wants what I have." Jacque opened the pizza box and leaned in to sniff.

Cleo rolled her eyes. "I'll have water. Maybe I should pour you some water, Wind Dancer."

"No. Diet is good," Wind Dancer insisted.

The Pawnee took a deep drink and began to sneeze. Had he ever had carbonation before? Or caffeine. He strode around the condo holding a piece of pizza.

"You need to sit down and eat, Wind Dancer." The detective pointed at a chair.

"Cle-o," he said, as if toying with the sound of her nickname, "you should call me Joseph like he does." He pointed his half-eaten pizza at the detective. "No one will suspect I'm not from here."

She and Jacque choked on their laughter.

"Yeah. Well we're going to have to work on that." Jacque chewed then took a swig of soda. "Joseph and I had quite a day." The detective faced Cleo. "Joseph here learned some new things on how to fit in with the underbelly of Chicago's frequent flyers at the precinct. Show her what you learned."

Wind Dancer sat down at the table and wiped his hands on his jeans. When he raised his middle finger on both hands, she gasped and glared at Jacque. Wind Dancer's smile faded.

"Wind—I mean, Joseph, you can't show people that. It is an insult. You are showing them you don't like them or you wish them bad luck. No respect."

"Bad luck?" Jacque chuckled. "Never heard that before." He grabbed another piece of pizza. "Cleo is right. Those guys at the station didn't like you putting them in a headlock when they mouthed off to one of the officers." His grin appeared. "They weren't thanking you for your guidance. Probably a good thing Chicago's finest had your back."

"I understand." He nodded. "I will remember this."

Cleo crumpled a napkin after dabbing at her mouth. "Joseph, when I was with your friend in the hospital he talked about the Osage but also about my father. He said 'Your father says he is sick.' Did he mean he knew where my father is and he is ill? Do you also know something about my father?"

Jacque laid down his pizza and chewed his last bite a little slower. "You never mentioned you knew Cleo's father. Do you?"

"Yes. Of course." Before it could sink in, he continued, "He is my friend. Like the Frenchman."

"My father is alive?" Cleo couldn't contain the surprise in her voice. "Where is he?"

"The other side of the earth lodge. It opens into my world. Sometimes it closes and nothing can get through."

"What the hell is he talking about?" Jacque rubbed his nape and shivered.

"It is where I come from. Like the Frenchman. Your father found this passage four years ago. I came upon him, nearly dead after falling into the river. When he revived, he teach me, sorry, I mean, taught me about this world so I could come see you." His eyes softened for an instant. "I told him we are friends and the many things you told me."

Under her breath, she mumbled, "Hopefully not everything I told you."

Wind Dancer raised an eyebrow. "No. Not everything."

"Are we having a moment or what?" Jacque snapped. "Let's

stay on topic." He rubbed his hands on a napkin. "What the hell are you talking about? The other side sounds like something Stephen King would write about."

Wind Dancer cocked his head. "I should meet this king. I do not like the president very much. He makes promises then breaks them. Maybe a king would be better."

Cleo opened her mouth to speak but stopped when Jacque held up his hand to her. "Are you telling me there is some kind of parallel universe or something?"

"It is not exactly parallel because it is in the past. This means it already happened." Wind Dancer stared at the pizza as if examining his next move.

"I'm aware of what it means. How does that work?" This time the detective shot a questioning glance at Cleo.

"How should I know? Worm holes? Magic? Voodoo? Hocus pocus? But I know it exists. The Frenchman threw me through the wall. There was an opening earlier in the day." She told him about the encounter with the woman in the earth lodge trying to get her to come through. "I was terrified because I saw Wind Dancer and Neosho moving in their case." She then told the detective about the Osage coming after them. "I'm not sure why he is so angry."

"He comes for you. You are a healer. He knows this. When you talked to me, he could hear. He wants you to save his people. Your father knew this. He spent the last few years teaching me everything about this world in case I ever needed to come across or if you came in search of him."

"My father is alive," she sighed, dabbing at wet eyes.

"You're believing this stuff?" Jacque dragged another piece of pizza onto his plate then one for the Pawnee. "Guess you're not as smart as I thought. Sounds pretty desperate. And I'm not sure Joseph here, and Neosho aren't escaped inmates from the Minnehaha Insane Asylum."

"You sound incredibly racist, Detective Marquette," she said with a huff drawing a concerned frown from Wind Dancer. Reaching across the table she patted Wind Dancer's hand as he reached for the pizza. "I believe you, Joseph. So, tell us. What did your friend mean about my father being ill?"

"Your father isn't sick. He strong. When the Frenchman said to tell you he was sick he meant Neosho. Many Osage die from sickness. Your father thinks Neosho might be sick, too, or will be soon." He swallowed and pointed to the pizza box. "This is good. What part of this do you hunt?"

"Mostly just the name of the restaurant," Jacque spoke with his mouth full.

"I don't understand." He gulped the last of the diet cola from the two-liter bottle then burped. Jacque laughed then he also burped.

"Stop it. Both of you. You're disgusting."

"Sorry, Cleo. Just trying to make the guy feel at home." Jacque closed the empty box. "Bad manners, Joseph. Women don't really like men to burp."

"Understood. Sorry, Cleo." He reached out and grabbed her hand. "We need a safe place so we don't get sick and he doesn't try to take you."

"You keep talking about getting sick. What's wrong with him?"

"He will have small holes in socks."

Jacque frowned. He held up both his feet to show his mismatched socks with holes in the heels. He'd left his shoes at the door as had Wind Dancer. "Guess I already caught it, then."

The Pawnee furrowed his brow as if bewildered then shook his head. "No. Not socks. Holes in body." He pointed to the side of his face where a number of scars trailed down to his chin. "I very sick once. Almost died. Your father saved my people by moving me far away to get well. They didn't get sick. Neosho met the same white men as me. Your father say they carried this sickness. Neosho let them stay with his people. We did not. They got sick and many died."

Cleo jumped to her feet as she grabbed his face and inspected it closely. "Oh no," she moaned.

"What is it?" Jacque leaned in to inspect the Pawnee.

"Neosho is carrying smallpox."

CHAPTER 6

Jacque stood as if in slow motion. "Smallpox. The disease."

Wind Dancer lifted his eyes to the two-people towering over him, grave concern etched on their faces.

"Yes. Your father said we must stop him from coming here. Neosho tried to get your father to help, but he is not the right kind of doctor. When your father realized what Neosho intended to do, he tried to stop him. He got away and headed here."

"How did he know of the opening to this world?" Cleo's voice dropped to almost a whisper.

"We all know. Every tribe in the cases at the museum know this. Only the Pawnee have a way in, and it is the earth lodge. The other tribes have not found this."

"Are there other openings? The Frenchman sounded like he knew of someplace else."

"Sometimes the opening moves from the lodge to another place. That is why we fell into the fish pool."

Cleo laid her hand against her forehead. "Why didn't Jacque and I freeze up like the others? Or the animals?"

"There is a space between light and dark, good and evil. This holds great power. The opening in my world poured out enough magic to protect you. As to the animals, they are not affected by such things. Everyone knows this."

"Magic?" Jacque shook his head and let out an exasperated

sigh. "Let's focus, shall we," the detective snapped. "Are you sure this Neosho guy has smallpox?"

"His village became sick after the white men called surveyors left. I think they acted like soldiers. Very hard men. Neosho not sick when he left the case, but your father said this sickness would harm you." He reached out and touched Cleo's cheek then withdrew his hand. "I could not let such a thing happen. I will find and destroy him before he infects you. Don't be afraid."

Jacque propped his hands on the table. "You don't understand. He could infect the entire city within a matter of a few hours." He looked over at Cleo. "Have you been vaccinated?"

"Yes. When I traveled with Doctors Without Borders."

"We need to contact the Center for Disease Control and Homeland Security immediately."

"The trouble is there are only about seven million doses of vaccine. There are almost three million people in Chicago alone. If Neosho is walking through the streets with a fever, he could be infecting hundreds of people. We've got to find him."

"First responders, health care professionals, teachers, and the Field Museum employees who were there last night need the vaccine ASAP." Jacque fumbled for his phone.

"Yes. If they have been exposed, then the vaccine will offer some protection. It is doubtful Neosho approached any of them, though. Do you remember?"

"He was one bad-ass Indian. The Frenchman caught up with me and tried to take the officer's gun. I believed he planned to kill him. I think maybe this Neosho character was searching for something, maybe you, then headed outside. So, no, he probably didn't interact with any museum people or your friends. The coffee shop is located too far from where your friends waited. If he touched them before they got on the planes, this could be spreading beyond our control."

"To be on the safe side, how about making up something to quarantine them. Then you'd need to get a plane manifest, to see who else was on those planes," Cleo added. "Think of the web of infection because Neosho got too close."

Wind Dancer watched each of them talk, shifting his eyes each time one of them spoke. Finally he stood, becoming imposing as a frown darkened his face. "A plain is where we hunt buffalo. Will this kill the buffalo if we do not stop it?"

Cleo reached out and touched his shoulder, realizing how strange all of this must be for the Pawnee. Cleo fingered her hair behind her ears. "No. The buffalo will be fine. You need not worry about them. This is a different kind of plain. I will show you pictures later. In the meantime, I need to run a blood test on you and get Jacque vaccinated." She refocused on the detective. "Make your calls, Jacque, after I run blood work on Joseph. I have a feeling we're going to need to answer a lot of questions. This whole parallel universe idea isn't going to fly unless you can prove it to the CDC and Homeland. They'll lock us up and then it will be too late. I know a volunteer at the Museum of Science and Industry who used to work for NASA. He'll believe us. He worked on this kind of thing for years."

"How can I help?" Wind Dancer raised his chin in a take-charge gesture, his beautiful, chiseled face lit by her modern chandelier.

"I need to run some tests on you. Would that be okay?"

"Yes. Whatever you need."

Jacque slapped him on the back. "You're a good man, Joseph. Sorry about your friend. I really didn't mean to hurt him." His phone buzzed. Lifting it to his ear, he listened then shifted his eyes to Wind Dancer. "Impossible."

Cleo felt herself go on alert as he shoved the phone inside his shirt pocket. "What is it?"

"Apparently, the Frenchman just walked out of the morgue."

~~~~

Neosho didn't like this land. The noise made his head hurt, and the smells confused him. Yet he understood from watching through the glass for so many years this land meant the future. Nothing harmed the white man, it seemed. They survived while his people lay dying of blisters on their skin or high fevers. Medicine of the white man would stop the sickness. He would take it to them and Cleopatra, too. When he told her how Wind Dancer caused his people to die, she would follow.
~~~~

The strength in his body increased when he crossed over to this world, but he still got tired. Could the sickness be causing him to feel the weight of fatigue? He would find Cleopatra and force her to heal him so he could return to his time. Killing his enemy, Wind Dancer, might have to wait. But the Pawnee was sure to follow if he took his woman. This pleased Neosho as he rested his head against a headboard of a narrow bed.

A man with a Bible saw him wandering earlier and told him of a shelter for men. The man took a few steps away from him as if frightened at first. But, as he stroked his Bible, he appeared to become calm. Neosho let the skinny man show him the building then led him inside. After some words and writing on paper, the man directed him to a tiny space where he could sleep for a while. He had been roaming aimlessly since the night before when he crossed over. At least he didn't have to worry about the Frenchman finding him. Neosho had watched as the man with the gun shot him. At first he thought he saw double. Did the Frenchman have a brother?

He wanted to think about this more, but his eyes became too heavy. Tomorrow, he would find the woman. He inhaled deeply, remembering how she smelled. Soft. Clean. Unlike this place. She wouldn't be hard to find.

~~~~

"You're joking. I checked him myself before they took him down." Cleo folded her arms across her chest while shifting her weight to one hip in a show of defiance.

"There's a guy with a knot on his head and an attendant who watched him stroll out all calm and collected, who will disagree with you."

"They were high on something."

"Maybe. But the officer who drove up as it all went down is a straight-up guy."

Cleo unfolded her arms to steal a glance at Wind Dancer, who had begun flexing his hands. "Joseph, did you hear what Jacque said? Could your friend still be alive?"

"No. Look at this. I am very strong here." He picked up the plastic two-liter bottle and squeezed it flat. He met her gaze and
~~~~

grinned ear to ear. "I am powerful."

Jacque picked up the same bottle and folded it in half. "Dude, anyone can do that. Even the doc here, who probably couldn't lift a ten-pound bag of potatoes."

Wind Dancer frowned, and his eyebrows met over his nose in a confused state. "Hmm. I thought the same about you, Jacque. Yet, you fold this bottle like reeds of grass." He picked up the bottle and examined it.

"Anyway. The Frenchman. You say he couldn't be alive?" The detective snatched the plastic bottle from the Pawnee.

"No. He is a ghost now. Like a witch or skinwalker the Dine talk about."

"Skinwalker? Dine?"

Cleo stepped to the detective's side as Wind Dancer explored the condo. "The Dine is another name for the Navajo. Skinwalkers are like witches. They can make you do bad things or steal your soul and a number of other things not very pleasant. I'm guessing my dad told him all about the Navajo since his secondary focus after the Plains Indians included Southwest tribes. He worked with several universities." The sound of a pop didn't immediately distract her or the crumbling of an unknown substance. "If the Frenchman is alive, maybe he is going after Neosho on his own. If he is a skinwalker, then he will have a heightened sense of smell, sight, and strength. If we find him, then he may lead us to the Osage."

Something hit the floor and they looked up. Wind Dancer stood crushing the black stones she'd collected at the beach. The size of softballs, she'd picked them up after seeing the same ones in a home interior store for a small fortune. Shipping them saved her a boatload of money. Wind Dancer picked one up then crushed it between his fingers before letting the pebbles pepper the floor. Both the detective and Cleo moved toward him, mouths parted in astonishment.

"Jacque, can you do this, too?" Wind Dancer possessed the curiosity of a child. "I could never do this on the other side. This must be why there are so many of you and you could not get sick from the smallpox. Your people are very strong."

"Joseph, I can't crush rocks. Something has happened to you to make you this strong." He stared at the Pawnee with more than a little concern. A slight tremor made his voice stutter. "Let me say again, I'm really sorry I hurt your friend."

"The Frenchman moves among us. He will find us then we hunt the Osage."

"You knew he would return to life?" Cleo remembered the chanting and prayer-like words he'd spoken over the Frenchman as he faded toward death.

"Yes. Of course. I said the words to make it so. Only for a short time. Then he will leave."

"Yeah? Where will he go?" The detective took the last black stone from the Pawnee's hand and replaced it in the wicker bowl on the mantle. "Don't be doing this kind of thing in public. It will freak people out."

"Understood." He stood taller as he rolled his shoulders. His eyes narrowed to slits, and his mouth thinned to a straight line.

"I should go, Cleo. I've lots to do before this all hits the fan." Although he spoke to Cleo, the detective never took his eyes off the Pawnee. There appeared to be a new revelation in his voice, his eyes, and his stance. "I'm thinking if I take this guy in, locking him up won't do much good. And I'm not real comfortable leaving him here."

"I will protect Cleopatra. You don't need to worry about her."

Jacque shifted his eyes to evaluate Cleo who stood small and fragile all of a sudden. "Cleo?"

"He can stay here. It's better we don't lose track of him. What's the problem?"

The detective took her elbow and led her to the kitchen in hopes the Pawnee wouldn't hear. Although, with his heightened strength, it was a reasonable assumption his hearing had gone supersonic as well. "I don't trust this guy. He's a walking weapon. Who knows what will set him off if things get dicey." He stole a curious glance over his shoulder at the Pawnee who folded his arms across his chest and watched them with the expression of a man who had eaten a green persimmon. "Besides, I don't like the way he keeps watching you. Do you have a gun?"

"No. Don't be ridiculous. He would never hurt me."

"Cleo, a man like that doesn't look at a woman like you and think about crushing plastic soda bottles. He didn't talk much today, but when he did, you were the topic. Clearly he thinks you two have some kind of relationship."

She wondered how she felt about the events concerning Wind Dancer. Part of her wanted to throw herself into his arms and explore the possibilities. The other part wanted to be careful not to fall for another scoundrel who would shatter any self-respect she had left.

"I can handle Wind Dancer. You do what you need to then let me know what is going on. I suspect we're going to have to move fast once the CDC and Homeland gets involved. I'll leave a message for my friend who can help us with this parallel universe stuff, and we'll meet up in the morning." She stopped at the bedroom door. "There's a couple of freezer packs in the fridge. An insulated lunch box over the sink. I'll get a blood sample from Wind Dancer for you to take. Taking this to the hospital would raise too many questions and get me in a lot of trouble. When you talk to the CDC, tell them to bring at least a thousand doses of vaccine. I'll vaccinate you guys tomorrow, and your men."

~~~~

Jacque nodded at Wind Dancer then yawned. He motioned for the Pawnee to join him. "Joseph, buddy, about Cleo…" He set about doing what Cleo requested. "Hands off. Understand?"

Wind Dancer lifted his hands with the usual bewilderment. "You want me to take off my hands?"

"No. I mean you can't be touching or trying to make her your squaw or whatever you people do in your world."

"This sounds very condescending, Jacque." He arched an eyebrow above his stone-cold face.

The Indian knew a lot more English than he gave him credit for. "I don't want you scaring Cleo. She's a nice lady, and there is lots of work to be done. I know you like her, but she might not feel the same way."

"She does. You can trust me."

The detective exhaled as he jammed the freezer packs in the lunchbox. "Jeeze Louise. No touching," he growled. "Promise me."

Wind Dancer smirked and patted Jacque on top of the head like a child.
~~~~

"Promise what?" Cleo said rushing into the room with a small medical kit.

"Nothing." The men said in unison.

CHAPTER 7

In the room next door slept a Pawnee warrior from the nineteenth century. After showing him where he would spend the rest of the night, Cleo thought she'd noted a slight hint of disappointment in Wind Dancer's eyes, but he didn't complain or voice his preference to be in her bed. A wave of relief mixed with "what if" jumbled up in the pit of her stomach. To have the man of your dreams step out of a museum case, into your life, and then save you from a monster with smallpox would make any heart melt.

All those years growing up in front of him, she loved him and even talked about the future when no one else would listen or had time to notice. Wind Dancer had never wavered, not that he had a choice. Relationship after relationship failed or never got off the ground creating insecurity regarding matters of the heart. Seeing Wind Dancer in the flesh gave her some new insight to why those romantic interludes had failed. The only man she'd ever loved lived not only in a different time zone, but a parallel universe.

At a light tap, Cleo held her breath then threw the covers to go to the door. She'd locked it so when she twisted the knob a soft click popped. With only a crack to peek through, she saw Wind Dancer in the faded jeans once belonging to her father. He stood naked from the waist up, with his long black hair falling down his chest.

"I couldn't sleep, Cleopatra, and yet I am tired."

Cleo opened the door a little wider forgetting she wore only a long football jersey. "Probably all the caffeine you drank with the pizza. Let me give you some acetaminophen and a glass of water." After she brought him the necessary meds, he prowled around her room with a kind of dark observation creasing his forehead. "The pill will take about twenty minutes to make you feel better. Want to talk for a while?"

She knew she should flip on some lights instead of letting the city glow seep through the one small window to make an eerie kind of romance.

"Yes." Wind Dancer sat down on her bed. He bounced a time or two as if getting the feel then scooted to the middle. "Come." He stretched out his hand. When she didn't take it, he patted the space where she'd lain minutes earlier. He rubbed his hand across the area as if he could still feel the warmth of her body. "Please, Cleopatra. I mean, Cleo." The disarming smile beckoned her, and she crawled up on the bed then propped some pillows behind her. "Would you like for me to tell you about your father?"

"Is he well?"

"Yes. And he is very proud of you. Once I brought him to the museum case, hoping you would come." He readjusted his position, moving up next to her, and rested his head against the headboard. "This is a much better way to sleep than where I come from. I think, though, it might make a man soft."

"After my father disappeared I couldn't bring myself to keep returning to the museum."

"I missed you." His breath moved her hair when he moved his head toward her. "Now, here you are. This makes me very happy." He smiled as he looked away.

You have no idea what I'm feeling. "Why didn't my father return?" She needed to change the subject. Talking about her father threw imaginary cold water on the possibility of becoming physical.

"For a while, he wasn't strong enough. Then"—he slipped his arm beneath her shoulders and then down around her waist— "he fell in love with my youngest sister. They have a little boy. Another child is on the way."

A bolt of lightning could not have made her jump more as she twisted to face him. "My father has another family?" She felt awe and betrayal as she remembered the pregnant woman who tried to get her to come through the wall of the earth lodge. The chances existed the woman might be her new stepmother.

"Yes. You sound angry." Wind Dancer tightened his hold. With her only inches from his face, he continued. "I like how your eyes flash when this happens. I can feel your breath. It smells like the sweetgrass of the prairie after a rain. You are more beautiful in person, Cleo."

She felt like a balloon someone pricked with a pin, letting all the frustration escape at an alarming rate. "I think maybe you aren't here to talk."

"No. But Jacque thinks I should talk more not touch. Is this true?" His lips whispered against hers. Those dark eyes appeared to flame with longing as his hand pressed against her back so she melted against his chest.

"I. Don't. Know." In the flesh he was so much more than she ever imagined all those years chatting with him through the case at the museum. Her heart pounded, desire welling up inside her. Their lips touched as he grinned, and in his hands came up to her hair. As he closed his eyes, he slumped into her. She jerked away. "Wind Dancer?"

His dead weight filled her arms. He drifted toward a sleep state. "Who knew acetaminophen would tranquilize a universe-jumping Pawnee?" She gently shoved him away and watched him scoot down onto one of the pillows. His hand gripped her arm and one finger played against her skin. "Don't go," he whispered, dreamlike. "Cleo?"

She covered him with a blanket. "Yes, Wind Dancer?"

"I love you." His deep breathing signaled he drowned in slumber with such peace, Cleo could do nothing but sit and stare at him. She didn't try and resist such masculinity as she placed a kiss on his mouth, beckoning her to taste a new life rising within her.

"And I love you, Wind Dancer, more than any woman should. I always have," she whispered.

~~~~

Even before the ragged men stirred, Neosho rose moving through the building with peeling paint and the smell of body odor.
~~~~

White men stank. Why didn't they bathe? He would never understand this. With so much water a few miles away and a river meandering through the city, surely it occurred to them they should clean themselves. These men repulsed him. They shuffled their feet and mumbled things he did not understand. The men on the street and at the museum did not resemble these people.

A bearded man who stood as tall as him, covered with what he knew to be tattoos, handed him a cup of hot liquid.

"Have some coffee, friend. Doughnuts over there on the table." He pointed to a large box down the hall. "There's a chill in the air this morning. Springtime weather in Chicago is wishy-washy. By the looks of ya, you might need a coat." His eyes traveled up to the Mohawk haircut. "I think I saw a couple of caps in there, too. The wind off Lake Michigan can be brutal even in spring, although I think the weather said we're in for a warm-up."

Neosho recognized the smell of coffee. The hot liquid warmed his body. He gobbled three doughnuts, liking the sweetness. As he grabbed a fourth, he shoved past the bearded man to inspect the box of coats. He dug through, throwing what he didn't want on the floor until he found a green one with a large letter on the back.

"I think you picked a new one. Notice the letter G? Means Green Bay Packers. People around here are Bears fans. Probably why the thing has never been worn."

Neosho frowned as he detected some contempt in the man's voice.

Neosho inspected the coat after listening to the bearded man. He slipped it on and then dug through the box until he found a matching sock hat. Placing it down over his ears, Neosho had no idea he resembled a crazed Packers fan come to wreak havoc on Chicago. "I will take these."

"Suit yourself. I guess you can handle yourself okay." The man eyed Neosho from head to toe. "Those moccasins might not be the best. Someone brought some boots in yesterday. You're welcome to try them out."

Neosho wiggled his toes, feeling the damp cold seep up from the concrete floor into his feet. He followed the man in silence as they entered a small space behind the counter where he'd checked in the night before. Sitting down on the floor, he tugged to remove the moccasins then measured them against the bottom of several pair of boots.

"Are these Green Bay shoes, too?"

The bearded man chuckled. "What? Are you, like from outer space? No. They're from Wal-Mart. Brand new, too. Take'em."

Neosho tried to wiggle his toes in the hard shoes then made exaggerated steps to try them out. "They make noise. How do you sneak up on your enemy?"

The Osage watched the bearded man pale. Did he sense something unusual about him? Would he be a problem?

"No enemies here. You don't need to be afraid."

"Not afraid." His voice sounded deep and intimidating. "Neosho afraid of nothing." After he spun around with a jerky movement, he stormed around the counter to survey the foyer leading out.

"Should I reserve a room for you tonight?"

The Osage ignored the question and lumbered toward the exit. He heard the noise box with pictures come alive with news of the museum. The tattooed man called after him about the moccasins he'd left on the floor. Neosho looked over his shoulder at the man but failed to comprehend the man lifting something black to his ear and saying words about 911.

~~~~

Jacque called early the next morning. "I'm sending a car for you guys. The place is crawling with the CDC. Homeland, too."

"I need to contact my work," Cleo told him.

"Already taken care of." He paused. "Everything go okay with our guy last night?"

"Yes. No problems."

"Glad to hear it. You better prepare him for what is about to happen. These guys are serious as a heart attack."

"I'll see you soon, Jacque. Thanks." She clicked off her cell and discovered Wind Dancer watching her from the bedroom door.

He'd taken a shower and dressed in new jeans that actually fit him. The black T-shirt reminded her of a bad-boy poster she'd seen in a bar. All he needed was a motorcycle with a skull stenciled on it. His feet remained bare, but he held a pair of cowboy boots in his hand. She backed away, offering a weak grin, but he continued
~~~~

toward her.

"I woke this morning and you had left," he said.

"I slept in the other room. I thought you might rest better."

"Are you afraid of me, Cleopatra?"

She thought about his question for a minute. "A little. It seems impossible you are here and really in my life."

Closer. "I will protect you from Neosho. We will solve this problem together. Then you can let me into your real life. I want to be a part of your future."

Cleo melted when their eyes locked. "You don't really know me, Wind Dancer. I might not be the person you think I am. If you decide to return to your world, I will understand. This must all be very confusing to you."

The boots dropped to the floor drawing her eyes to them for only an instant, when he took her hand and drew her closer. "What I didn't know, your father told me. If there is more, then I want to discover you all by myself. I have waited a very long time. Your world is mysterious and strange, but one I will embrace to stay here with you. Your father taught me many things so I could survive. I realize there is still much to learn." His bright eyes erased the moody expression dominating his face most of the time. "You and Jacque can help me. And I will teach you."

Taking a deep breath, Cleo felt herself seduced by a dream. "I'm not sure you'll be up to getting to know me better. I'm pretty hardheaded." He would not be likely to tolerate an independent, twenty-first-century woman.

Wind Dancer kissed her mouth so suddenly, she later wondered if it had happened. "I think we are talking about two different things, Cleopatra." He released her and picked up his boots when the doorbell buzzed.

Her feet became heavy as concrete as the warmth of his mouth faded from her lips. The press of his body paralyzed her with a new kind of longing she both feared and desired. Another annoying buzz of the doorbell jerked her to reality, along with Wind Dancer hopping on one foot toward the door as he tried to wiggle his other into a boot.

"Help me understand your world and I will make it safe for us." He touched the doorknob.

"No. Wait. The front desk didn't call up."

He twisted the knob and the door crashed open.

"Stop," she screamed as Neosho charged into the condo slamming into Wind Dancer with incredible strength.

CHAPTER 8

I don't care if the front doors are locked or not," Jacque yelled into the phone. "Break the damn door down if you have to. There should be someone there to answer. If there isn't then something is wrong. Do. It. Now." He heard gunshots, glass breaking, excited voices, a call for 911, and moaning. He checked his weapon before shoving it into his holster.

"Wait. Where are you going? You can't leave," a dark-haired woman from the CDC shouted as if she had authority over him. "I'm ordering you." She attempted to right her glasses onto her pug nose with her middle finger as she stepped to block him.

"Get out of my way, woman." Jacque grabbed her by both arms to keep from mowing her down. The sudden burst of speed caused her to stumble away into a desk.

Jacque grabbed his faded jacket as he stormed through the outer offices and ordered a couple of patrolmen to follow. Once the two cars pulled out onto the highway, they activated the flashing lights and sirens. Things appeared to be unraveling at Cleo's, so he avoided another call to her. Other information trickled through his radio hinting all hell had broken loose.

"Hang in there, Cleo. I'm on my way," he mumbled through clenched teeth as he hit the accelerator.

~~~~
~~~~

Neosho hit Wind Dancer so hard the Pawnee flew backward onto the floor then slid toward the plate-glass windows, causing a momentary image in Cleo's mind of him crashing through the glass and plummeting to his death. The thought faded as Neosho straightened his body then pivoted toward her. In one fluid moment, he lunged catching her by the arm during an attempted retreat. She tried to peel his fingers from her wrist without success causing him to tighten his grip. Frantic, she landed her free fist into his chest as he dragged her toward the door. From the corner of her eye, Cleo saw a blurred form slam into Neosho, freeing her from his grip.

Wind Dancer jumped onto the Osage's back, but the man flung him off with a piercing howl. The Pawnee fell against the foyer wall as Neosho reached both hands to grab Wind Dancer's neck. The attack continued with each man landing blows to the other, reminding Cleo of two wild animals sparring for the attention of a herd of females. Mixed with their grunts and groans came the crashing against walls. Pictures hit the floor and shattered. The two filled the exit so Cleo couldn't escape for help.

She grabbed her purse and dug through the piles of receipts, mismatched makeup items, and various things she'd delayed in cleaning out, until her fingers touched the tube of pepper spray in the zipper pouch where she usually kept her cell phone. Directing her focus to the two men, she watched Wind Dancer toss Neosho into the living room like a paper airplane. He landed at her feet, where he rolled to a standing position. His musky scent reminded her of the outdoors as he once again snatched at her arm. This time she took control by expelling the toxic spray into Neosho's face.

He rubbed his face as growls spewed from his mouth. Shaking his head, he staggered then tripped over the coffee table before sprawling across the floor. From his speedy recovery, most of the spray may have missed his eyes, but the sting enabled enough time to snatch her cell phone off the kitchen counter, as Wind Dancer moved in to attack once more.

Neosho tilted his head to the side and flexed his arms. Cleo noticed Wind Dancer also cocked his head. She strained to hear, but their heavy breathing kept her a little off-center.

The banging at the front door drew concerned glances for mere seconds then to each other. Wind Dancer lunged forward as

Neosho escaped to the sliding doors onto the balcony. Somewhere in Cleo's mind she could hear loud voices in the hall then a splintering of wood as the door became unhinged.

Jacque rushed into the foyer with his weapon drawn as Neosho crashed through the glass doors and rolled onto the balcony. Wind Dancer jumped onto the same spot only to have the Osage spring to his feet then onto the balcony's six-inch-wide railing. Cleo felt the detective at her side. Together they navigated through a sea of glass shards that caused them to move with unsteady feet.

The Osage moved along the railing like a confident cougar forcing Wind Dancer to scamper onto the same railing. He called out to the Osage, forcing him to pause and stare down at the green space below then at Wind Dancer.

"Get down from there." Jacque lifted his gun with both hands, aiming it at Neosho as he hunched his shoulders like a man ready to run.

Neosho pointed at his eyes then to Cleo before leaping to the next balcony with little effort or concern.

"Stop or I'll shoot!" Jacque rushed forward alongside Wind Dancer who moved down the railing of the balcony with ease. The neighboring tenant opened his sliding glass door and stepped out with concern etched on his face. Jacque lowered his weapon. "Get inside!"

But it was too late. Neosho jumped down then circled the man's neck with a massive arm dragging him to the railing. His screaming and flailing seemed to amuse Neosho as he raised his eyes to the three on the other balcony and smirked. He lifted the man over the railing but let him grab at the edge to keep from falling.

Wind Dancer didn't hear, or maybe ignored, Cleo's scream when he leaped to the next balcony as Neosho escaped through the condo. The man's cry for help faded as Wind Dancer reached over and snatched him up dropping him face first to the balcony floor, before running inside after the Osage.

Cleo jumped aside as Jacque raced through her condo toward the hall door. He leapt over one of his officers who lay on the floor unconscious, a trickle of blood coming from a gash on the side of his head. Wind Dancer joined them as the sound of an exit door swooshed shut.

All three hurried to intercept Neosho. Wind Dancer yanked the door open and let Jacque slip through, with gun drawn. Other officers filled the stairwell.

"The roof." Cleo pointed up. "He'll be trapped. We need him alive, Jacque."

He nodded as both he and Wind Dancer continued with caution toward the top floor. Cleo got pushed aside as other men in uniform followed. What would Neosho do if cornered? She returned to the hallway to help the downed officer and call for an ambulance. She couldn't help but wonder about the staff on the main floor who managed the comings and goings of the tenants. Kneeling down by the officer, the image of Wind Dancer and Neosho scurrying along the balcony railing, without fear of falling, overtook her check on reality. How could they do such a thing? And, now, law enforcement and two warriors would congregate on the roof with no place to go except down. She squeezed her eyes shut to block out the possibility of both Native Americans locked in a struggle that could propel them over the edge.

As the injured officer groaned, the image of Wind Dancer filled her mind. Cleo mumbled, "Be still my heart."

~~~~

The rooftop door stood ajar as both Wind Dancer and Jacque barreled out into the open space. The cold air smacked them with a Lake Michigan wind gust, staggering their progress. Wind Dancer pointed at a figure disappearing behind a heating unit.

"Stay behind me. I got this," Jacque barked.

"No. You don't understand. Neosho is stronger here. Like me."

Jacque could feel his mouth and forehead pinch in a frown. He withheld any comment of disbelief. "He's flesh and blood. He'll bleed like anyone else when I shoot him." Two more officers joined them, guns drawn.

"I hear him, Jacque." Wind Dancer hunkered down while tilting his ear up. "There." He pointed at the corner of some construction, resembling a storage shed. Jerking his chin up as a sign to move, both men raced forward, each diverting to the left or
~~~~

right.

Neosho bolted away, running toward the parapet, stopping to look over at the ground below before he faced his pursuers.

Jerking up his gun to level it at the Osage's chest, Jacque couldn't outmaneuver Wind Dancer who cut off his line of sight and raised his hands to show he carried no weapons.

"Neosho." Wind Dancer took a step forward forcing his enemy to jump onto the rim of the parapet. "Let me help you."

"Like you helped my people?" Neosho spat with a snarl. "I will have my revenge."

"You may be sick. Dr. Cleopatra can help us." He dared take another step, only to encourage the Osage to step backward toward the edge. "Let the doctor—"

"Us? There is no us. You brought sickness to my people, and now they are gone or scarred from the sickness. These people"—he swung out his arms then slammed a fist into his own chest—"will find their way to us, bringing their poison, their disease, and their destruction of the land. Do you see around you, Wind Dancer? Is this the life you want?"

"Step down and we'll figure this out, buddy. There's no need to do this." Jacque returned his gun to his belt holster then showed his hands.

Neosho threw his head back letting loose laughter that echoed off nearby buildings. His eyes moved between the two men before one corner of his mouth turned up as other officers approached with exposed guns. "I am not your buddy and I did not come here to kill myself."

Neosho pivoted in a blur as he darted down the parapet. Wind Dancer pounced onto the rim in hot pursuit with Jacque trying to keep up with little success. The two warriors barreled toward the end, both picking up speed. As Wind Dancer reached out to grab the hem of the Green Bay Packer jacket, Neosho leaped out over the open space toward the building next door. Jacque's momentum faltered. He watched the Osage land safely on the roof next door as Wind Dancer lost his footing and fell forward. Jacque reached out and grabbed his arm, which flew out in his attempt to stop the fall. He fell flat and rolled up to stand, panting. Jerking around, Wind Dancer peered over at the neighboring building in time to see Neosho escape while Jacque shouted orders to the other officers.

Both men watched Neosho run across the building only to leap to yet another rooftop before disappearing from sight.

"Are you alright?" Jacque continued to stare after the Osage in disbelief. "I've never seen anything like it." He turned to Wind Dancer with a little awe escaping from his mouth. "How are you guys able to do these things?"

Wind Dancer straightened to his full height, a gust of wind blowing his hair across his face. "Magic," he said simply and headed toward the exit that would lead him to Cleo.

"Magic," Jacque moaned. "You're pullin' my leg, right?"

~~~~

The lobby staff needed medical attention from the paramedics, but nothing required a lengthy stay at the hospital. They heard the CDC staff had arrived at the hospital to give tetanus shots deciding not to inform the injured about including a smallpox booster. Given a list of possible side effects and strict orders to return to only the emergency room if they appeared, tenants were soon released from the hospital.

Cleo reassured them. Asking her medical questions, sharing aches and pains or, showing her a rash or cut as if it might be the onset of the bubonic plague, was nothing new. Keeping an eye on them would not be as tedious as in the past.

"The police departments throughout the city are scheduled for inoculations with an explanation of a highly contagious Asian flu showing up in three patients at Christian General Hospital overnight after arriving at O'Hare International Airport the evening before from Myanmar," Jacque explained as they entered his precinct building.

Cleo took Wind Dancer's hand to lead him inside since he continued to be amazed at the world around him. She let Jacque know the instructions she'd left for medical personnel. "They needed to be on the lookout for people who complain of fever, overall discomfort, and severe headaches. Crippling back pain and vomiting would also be a telltale sign."

"All passengers on those flights are currently being notified and encouraged to report to their physician immediately. A stern warning about speaking to the press has been issued by the CDC,
~~~~

which caused a great deal of grumbling and complaints from medical personnel and first responders until their superiors were brought into the loop about the true nature of the situation."

Jacque opened his office door and stood aside for them to enter. He grinned at his newfound partners. "Instead of saying a parallel-universe-jumping Osage, who may or may not have smallpox, might be running loose in the city, we created a spin involving an infected worker from a research lab in Indonesia."

Even the CDC didn't believe the true story, but after hearing about the events earlier in the morning, they decided something unprecedented had occurred that needed to be explained away in the event an epidemic was imminent.

Some authority combed her condo in hazmat suits, hoping to find bodily fluids from the fight in order to test for smallpox. Tenants were forced to leave without much of an explanation except a terrorist may have caused the commotion in the lobby. For everyone's safety, a thorough search of their floor made sense in such dangerous times. Cleo realized terrorism had become such a part of everyone's life, people accepted the situation without complaint. They were instructed not to speak to the press until they caught the man. Of course that was going to be almost impossible, and it would only be a matter of time before they showed up in front of her building.

"Dr. Boris Kuzma is here to see you." The officer led a tall gentleman well into his fifties into the conference room where Cleo, Wind Dancer, and Jacque sat around a table talking in whispers.

"Dr. Kuzma." Cleo scooted out of her chair and joined him as he opened his arms, smiling like a patient grandfather. "I'm so glad to see you."

"Moya, printsessa," he spoke in Russian while patting her shoulders as she embraced him.

"It's been a long time since you called me your princess. I've missed you." She led him to the table. "This is Dr. Boris Kuzma. He worked at NASA as a physicist specializing in parallel universes, string theory, and a bunch of other things I will never understand."

Dr. Kuzma chuckled and waved a hand in the air as if to dismiss the importance of her praise. "What is this all about, Cleo?

The police met me at my front door this morning and insisted I come here. I refused until they told me it was at your request. Are you in trouble?"

"No. No, I'm fine. I needed, rather we need your help in discovering more about your theories on a parallel universe."

"Unfortunately, my work went nowhere. I moved on."

"Break it down for us science dummies, Dr. Kuzma. Please." Jacque spoke through gritted teeth and his eyes narrowed, allowing his condescension to show through.

Before the doctor took his seat, he studied Wind Dancer with interest, but didn't try to engage him. Cleo guessed the scowl etched on the Pawnee's face might be the reason, since even she felt a chill. She wondered if it had to do with the near-death experience on the roof or the confusing chaos going on in the police station where they waited.

"Okay, Detective. First I need coffee."

CHAPTER 9

"I find it strange Chicago PD has developed a sudden interest in physics." Dr. Kuzma took a sip of his coffee.

"Dr. Kuzma, we have reason to believe there may be an opening to another dimension or parallel universe." Cleo glanced over at Wind Dancer who observed them with intense scrutiny. "This is Wind Dancer. I believe he crossed over."

"Impossible," he chuckled glancing over the edge of his cup at the Pawnee. "And why would you think such a thing? I worked for years to prove this, and nothing came of it. Your father and I talked about it all the time. I never told you this, but the week before he disappeared, he thought he was on the verge of finding an opening. I waited for him to call me that night."

"Did you tell the police?" Jacque interjected.

"Of course not. It sounded crazy and I feared the investigation of his disappearance would end if I mentioned such a thing. Who would believe an old physicist? Even NASA got fed up with me and put me out to pasture." He offered a contemptuous smirk toward Wind Dancer. "Why should I believe you crossed over, Wind Dancer? What have you been telling these people?"

Wind Dancer turned his head to focus on Cleo but said nothing. His face became a mask, free of emotion and interest in the topic at hand. She wondered if he even understood the turmoil he'd caused. She gave a terse rendition of the last couple of days.

Jacque chimed in from time to time as if he grew impatient.

When the story ended, the physicist eyed Wind Dancer with a little more respect. "And you know Dr. Sommers?"

"I do," the Pawnee spoke with a deep, clear voice. "We waste time. Neosho is out there. He will harm many if we don't find him. Your men are no match for him."

The CDC woman slipped into the room and took a seat. She stole a glance at Wind Dancer. "This ranks right up there with *The Walking Dead*, doesn't it?"

"I'm going to guess you know little about other dimensions, so I will start at the beginning." He touched his fingertips together forming a pyramid. "One thought is if you go far enough, you'll get to return home."

"Remember, Dr. Kuzma. Keep it simple," Cleo warned.

"Yes. Of course. This means it is probable other planets exactly like Earth exist somewhere out there. It's a big space. However, they are so far away we don't even know where to search."

"I don't think this is what we're talking about, Dr. Kuzma," Cleo voiced, a little confused.

"Level 2 is, if you go far enough you'll fall into another wonderful land. The trouble with this is the universe is expanding faster than the speed of light and therefore unreachable."

Jacque ran his hand through graying hair. "Are you getting any of this, Cleo, because I'm lost."

Dr. Kuzma held up his hand. "Hold on. I'm not finished. Level 3 is what most sci-fi fans think of when talking about parallel universes. These parallel universes are different from the others because they take place in the same space in our own universe. You have no way to access them. You have never had and will ever have contact with these. Yet you're telling me this man comes from such a place, except it is from the early nineteenth century." He chuckled. "So why is this so important, and why on earth should I believe this character?"

"I will show you, Doctor." Wind Dancer stood and picked up a pencil from the table by the wall. He stood rigid for a few seconds as if searching for something.

The CDC lady straightened in her chair then crossed her arms over her chest, offering a sour frown at the Pawnee. Dr. Kuzma continued to sip his coffee as he tried to cover his smirk.

"In Native America, we know of these universes. This is why we are more spiritual than the white man. There are many worlds man cannot cross. Yours is not one of them, although until Dr. Sommers came into our world, we did not know this was possible."

"Oh for heaven's sake," moaned the CDC lady with a huff of disbelief.

"There are holes into this world everywhere, even in this room."

"In this room?" Dr. Kuzma chuckled. "And you can see these, I assume."

"Yes. Native Americans, especially the Pawnee, have always lived on a higher plain than you. Our minds are open to the possibilities. We feel life all around us."

"All very poetic, Wind Dancer, but I don't think there is a parallel universe within this room," Dr. Kuzma commented in a scholarly tone.

Wind Dancer held up the pencil. He stood and moved to an interior wall. "Some holes are small, Doctor. Others are large enough for a man. This one." He rested the eraser against the wall and gently pushed until the pencil disappeared halfway up the body. With a gasp, the woman and doctor rose to their feet as he extracted the pencil and held it up for them to see.

"Just a trick," the woman exclaimed.

"Dr. Kuzma, will you trust me to show you into my world?"

"Yes. Of course." The doctor couldn't get to Wind Dancer's side fast enough. "What do you want me to do?"

"This hole is small. Too small for even your finger. These kinds of holes open and close all the time. It won't last long. Do exactly as I did."

The doctor took the pencil and applied a gentle force so it entered the wall. He tried to bring it back, but it broke off in his hand.

"Remarkable. I could feel the emptiness then the sudden clamp broke it." He held it up to his face as if examining a piece of lost treasure. "It is true, then." He looked up at the solemn Indian and laughed. "You have made my life worthwhile, young man. So why is everyone in such a lather about this Neosho who crossed over with you?"

The woman from the CDC lifted a hand to her chest, perhaps realizing for the first time all the nonsense she'd heard from the detective was true. Her voice quivered as she spoke. "Because he may have smallpox and is loose in our city."

~~~~

"We've got to find the Frenchman," Jacque declared as he glanced at his watch. "Will he look the same?" He'd brought Wind Dancer across the street to a small café while Cleo helped vaccinate the other police officers in his precinct. Ordering some pancakes for them both along with glasses of milk didn't keep the Pawnee from getting up from the booth to move around or pace in front of the window to watch the police station.

Wind Dancer nodded as he slid into the booth and patted the seat until it sounded like a drum. "Yes. He still look like you only"— he squeezed his lips together— "except rougher." He motioned to his face to pantomime then to his head. "Hair is longer, a little more frost."

"I remember. And I think you mean gray, not frost. I thought since he was a skinwalker, there would be other changes."

"I believe so. Stronger. Can do things humans cannot, like appear without warning or walk through walls. He will be tortured until he finds his purpose."

"Purpose?"

"He will want Neosho dead, to seek revenge for killing his wife and sons. He wants to destroy his soul so he will be doomed for eternity."

A whistle escaped Jacque's lips. "Wouldn't want a spook creepin' through the streets lookin' for me."

"Spook? I don't understand."

"Another name for skinwalker. Sort of." Jacque felt uncomfortable at the confused glare making the Pawnee's brow furrow.

"If he finds Neosho first, it is good. But then we must make sure my friend returns to the land of Tirawa."

"Who the hell is Tirawa? Is this someone else I need to be concerned about?"
~~~~

"No." Cleo flopped down next to the detective as he slid over to make room for her. She noticed a surprised expression cross Wind Dancer's face for a micro-second. "Tirawa created the world through a series of violent storms then created star gods, who in turn created humanity." She shrugged as she grinned over at Jacque. "What can I say? My dad used to read me this stuff when other kids got Dr. Seuss. Didn't mean to interrupt you guys." A waitress arrived to take her order of coffee and toast. "Anyway, Tirawa is the least of our worries," she sighed as the waitress scurried away.

"Glad to hear it. Wind Dancer said the Frenchman might help us if we can find him, but then we'll have to deal with him since he's a skinwalker. Got any input into how, Miss I-Know-Everything?"

Cleo elbowed him good-naturedly and decided she liked the man in spite of his rough mannerisms and bluntness. "I'm not sure. What do you think, Wind, I mean Joseph?" she self-corrected as the waitress set her breakfast on the table then moved to another table.

"I think you should eat more. This is not how a strong woman lives."

"Trying to make me fat?"

Wind Dancer cocked his head to the side as if trying to understand. "I don't know how to do fat. You are beautiful the way you are, Cleopatra."

Jacque choked on his coffee. "Nice save, Joseph. Women here are obsessed with the way they look and don't like to add on pounds."

He nodded. "Not so different where I'm from."

The three shared a quiet laugh before changing to a more serious topic.

"How'd it go with the CDC, Cleo?" Jacque stretched out his cup when the waitress passed by with the coffee. He waited a second to make sure she'd moved on before continuing. "She's a pill."

"She settled down after Joseph's demonstration. She cracked the whip and her team hopped to it. We got done pretty quickly. Homeland is reaching out to the other necessary agencies like fire departments and hospital staffs. School nurses and superintendents have been called in for a meeting this afternoon at the Field Museum."

"Any idea where Neosho might go, Joseph?" The detective held his cup to his mouth.

"Wherever Cleo goes, he will try to find her. The Osage put a lot of value on family. Because he blames me and the Frenchmen for taking the surveyors to his village, he wants revenge. I believe he plans to take her to the other side to heal those sick, especially the children. Osage don't put much thought into death, but a great deal on the life of a child. They do not understand afterlife."

"Maybe we should use you as bait, Cleo." Jacque's words came out slow as he kept an eye on the Pawnee. "How do you feel about that?"

"Scared. Nervous." She took a deep breath and then let it escape in a puff that moved her bangs.

Wind Dancer reached across the table and took Cleo's hand. "I will protect you. You have nothing to fear."

She laid her free hand on top of his. "What if he kills you? I would never forgive myself." She realized her voice transformed to a soft, almost sensual tone. He somehow brought the vulnerable side of her to the surface.

Jacque cleared his throat. "You two need a room?"

"Don't be flippant, Jacque," Cleo cooed, releasing Wind Dancer's large brown hand.

"If you're going to use big words, Doc, I'm going to have to get a dictionary," he snapped in mock irritation.

"A thesaurus, Detective."

"Sometimes, I think you are speaking another language." Wind Dancer shook his head. "Your father did not teach me these words you speak. I'm sorry."

"She's trying to show us how much smarter than us she is, Joseph. Women are a pain in the neck here. Let's get back on topic. Now that Neosho knows where she lives, she probably isn't safe to stay there. Will he return through another opening into your universe to hide?"

"He will find help. If he goes, he may not find his way across again. I'm sure he knows the earth lodge at the Field Museum will be watched. Remember, he is flesh and blood like me, but stronger than men here. He may know of another place to cross." Wind

Dancer shifted his eyes to Cleo then took her hand again. "He will try and take you through there. You must fight if this happens. I won't be able to get to you on the other side if the opening closes."

"What kind of help, Wind Dancer, I mean Joseph?" She couldn't keep the quiver from her voice.

Jacque rubbed his hand across his face. "Gangs are my guess. If he's walking around acting like a badass they'll find him. Plenty of garbage in Chicago these days. When they find out what he can do, they'll be falling all over themselves to enlist his help in gaining territory." The cell phone Jacque had laid on the table vibrated. "Hello. Okay. On our way."

"Our Osage slept at a homeless shelter last night. Officers are taking a CDC agent and a Homeland guy over to check who stayed there last night."

"They all need to be vaccinated." Cleo eased out and grabbed the check. "My treat. Let's go."

CHAPTER 10

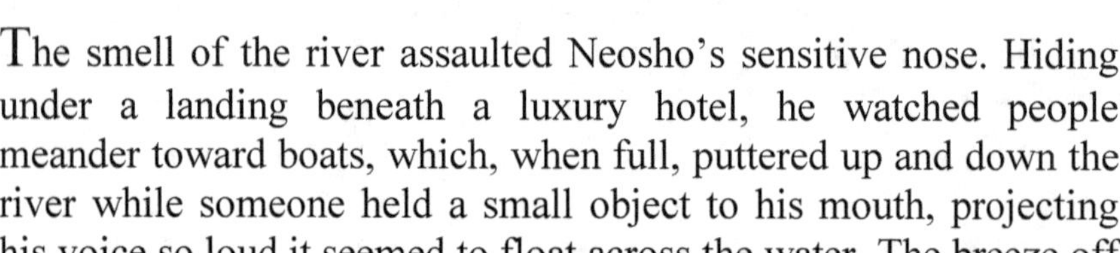

The smell of the river assaulted Neosho's sensitive nose. Hiding under a landing beneath a luxury hotel, he watched people meander toward boats, which, when full, puttered up and down the river while someone held a small object to his mouth, projecting his voice so loud it seemed to float across the water. The breeze off the water forced him to pull his Green Bay Packer jacket tighter.

He observed the path of the boats floating with some kind of noise attached. Experience told him they would spill out into the great body of water he'd seen from the museum. So many people in this place. What had happened to the land of his ancestors? Why could he taste the bitterness of the air as it burned his eyes? Even the sky appeared gray here with buildings touching the clouds.

He remembered the night he'd reached the floor above the city where he'd first found Cleopatra all alone. He'd missed his chance because he'd watched her too long from the shadows, drinking in the softness of her hair, the color of red embers. He hadn't expected her to be so beautiful in person.

In the museum case, he sometimes could only hear her and other times glimpse her through a frosted haze swirled in his protective enclosure. Even so, sometimes her appearance became so vivid, Neosho tried to reach out to her and draw her to him. In those times, she faced Wind Dancer and talked quietly to him as if he could participate in the conversation. Only her profile ever appeared in those moments the glass cleared. Even then, she ignored him, except to tease him once in a while.

When his family died of the white man's sickness, he discovered by accident Cleopatra was a doctor. She'd disappeared for years from the museum. When her father, Dr. Sommers, appeared in his land, he understood the path to this world could be crossed. He would bring Cleopatra to his home and begin life anew. She would protect his people from the sickness. If Dr. Sommers spoke truth about a medicine, then hope remained. To take her from Wind Dancer was a gift he dare not question or examine too intently. When he captured her, he would not wait to make her his willing partner. In the end, Cleopatra would love him, bear him sons and beautiful daughters while keeping them safe with her medicine.

And he would destroy Wind Dancer, his hated enemy.

"What are you doin' here? You some kind of freak?" A young black man stood level with Neosho's shoulder, possessing the swagger of a man much bigger. An unlit cigarette wedged in the corner of his thick lips, squinted weasel-like eyes, and a nose with a broken twist impressed Neosho as being tough. "What are you, like a giant or somethin'?"

Neosho glared down at the young man who invaded his space then growled a response. "You should leave."

"Like hell I will. Do you see this?" He jerked down the flimsy neckline of his hoodie to reveal a five-pointed yellow star on his neck. "I'm a Death Apostle."

Neosho glanced at the star for only a second before he grabbed the young man around the throat and slammed him up against a pillar. He held him there without any trouble as the captive kicked and squirmed until Neosho tossed him aside in a pile of litter. It lifted up at the sudden disturbance.

"Man, are you crazy?" He rubbed his neck with vigorous strokes, concern etched on his face. "You can't be here. This is my walk. My boys will kill you, man."

Neosho reached down and snatched the young man up to wobbly feet then shook him. "Are these boys your tribe?"

"Yeah. Yeah. Sure. Why not?" He jerked free of Neosho then took a step away. "They will whup your ass, no doubt."

"How many in your tribe?"

"Maybe fifteen, twenty. I dunno. Enough to handle you."

"Are all your tribe as small as you?"

"Hell, no. And I ain't small. You're a freak is all."

"Take me to your tribe, Little One." Neosho raised his chin as a sign to leave.

"My name is Ty, so don't be callin' me Little One around my boys. Got it?" He moved up the steps.

"Got it."

~~~~

Returning from the homeless shelter, Cleo rode in the car next to Wind Dancer. He gripped the seat so hard his knuckles turned white until she pried his hands loose and held them in hers.

"Focus on me, Joseph." She talked in the softest voice she could muster, considering the terrifying realization Neosho could be spreading smallpox throughout the city.

Wind Dancer did as she asked, gazing deep into her eyes, smiling at times or touching her face with his free hand. He seemed fascinated with her hair and stroked it, even smelled it once and trailed his fingertips down her shoulder then her arm, giving her goose bumps. If this kept up, they might have to get a room as Jacque had suggested earlier. He bombarded her with sensory overload until she worried her speech might slur. When his hand dropped to her thigh, Cleo glanced at Jacque in the front seat who met her eyes in the rearview mirror. His brows arched and his mouth puckered enough to make Cleo gain some control of her desires.

She removed Wind Dancer's hand while shooting him a nod of warning. He lowered his lips to whisper in her ear. "You are everything I hoped, Cleo. Soon we will be together. I don't want to rush you into our joining. I've waited so long to meet you. All those years I wanted to speak and couldn't. I am searching for words to tell you how I feel."

A shiver traveled up her spine causing her to exhale a pathetic sigh of resignation as to her fate. "This is still a little overwhelming for me, Joseph. I need to concentrate on our current problem. We've got to find Neosho."
~~~~

~~~~

Jacque parked the car in the precinct parking lot and assisted Wind Dancer, who always appeared a little unsteady on his feet when they exited a car. He recovered in short order, whether it was to save face in front of Cleo or him, remained anyone's guess. Either way, the Pawnee would roll his shoulders, raise his chin in some kind of pride then stare down his nose at him as if he might issue a challenge of some kind. He hoped their budding friendship wouldn't come to that.

The three found their way into the detective's office and sat around the desk. He watched Wind Dancer take in the room with a concentrated effort. After watching Jacque break the point off his pencil and then shove it in the electric pencil sharpener, the Pawnee picked it up, examined the hole, held the cord, and traced it to the wall where he jiggled the connection. How funny would it be if the guy got a shock? No sooner had the thought occurred than Wind Dancer shoved his finger into the sharpener hole.

"Hey! Stop it, you idiot." Jacque jumped out of his chair and slapped at his hand. "That will hurt. There's no parallel universe in there. Let me show you." He showed him the pencil shards in the bottom tray.

"This world is very curious to me. So many things I don't understand. Everywhere I see magic. The Morning Star must live here."

"Before you ask," Cleo chimed in, "the Morning Star is one of the important deities of the Pawnee. She lives in the eastern sky. They often sacrificed a captive to her."

"Nice folks, you people." Jacque spoke with a degree of cynicism. "We don't do those things anymore and, for your information, the government put a stop to all kinds of nonsense when it came to the Native Americans."

Wind Dancer turned his head to Cleo for clarification. "What does he mean?"

"The Ghost Dance, sacrifices, multiple wives, hunting buffalo—"

"They took hunting the buffalo away, too?"

"Yes. They moved many native people to small parcels of land because they feared you, discovered gold, or hated you." Cleo
~~~~

cringed. "I'm sorry, Joseph. Your people, all native peoples, did not fare well with the government. You trusted them, and they betrayed you." She reached for his arm, but he stepped away and stepped to the glass windows that created a partial wall to stare into activity of the precinct.

Jacque felt a twinge of regret toward what history did to the Native Americans. He'd never known one until Wind Dancer. He seemed like a straight-up guy. How he could ever survive here without continued assistance needed to be addressed later. He didn't like feeling guilty and didn't want to play nursemaid to a renegade universe jumper.

"Here is a map of the gangs in Chicago, Cleo." He laid a rolled map on the table and smoothed it out.

"So many," she gasped. "I had no idea. What are these symbols?" She pointed at several designs next to the names.

"Usually it's their tattoo or the design you'll find on their clothing. They all have colors, certain words they speak. Some are ethnic in nature, and others are a mix. You'll have neighborhoods where a single gang holds the territory. Doesn't mean other groups don't try to come in. There are always problems. It's gotten almost too big to handle since the mayor cut our forces in these areas. Now he'll have to rethink the mess he's created. Put out the fire while it smolders, or it will burst into flames."

"How are we going to find the right gang? Maybe Neosho won't even try them?"

"From what the homeless shelter guy said about the Osage, he strutted around like a major pain in the ass. If he is still wearing the Green Bay Packer jacket around town, someone will notice. Cops on the beat have the information and are asking questions in the area last seen. Someone from the river cruises called in about an hour ago saying a couple of thugs were spotted near their boarding ramp. Some of the tourists backed out of the cruise. Wanted the cops to do a walk by?"

"And?"

"They mentioned a tall guy with a Mohawk haircut wearing a green jacket. Couldn't say as to his ethnic coloring, but the guy with him was definitely black. Wearing a dark-colored bandana around his head. They left together."

"Neosho is intimidating to others. It is the way of the Osage. I have known braves surprised by their sudden appearance who surrendered without a fight. Their tribe can be menacing. Can I see your paper, Jacque?" Wind Dancer's voice lacked emotion and sounded flat.

Jacque motioned closer. "Do you know what a gang is, Joseph?"

"Is it like a tribe?"

"Yes. Except they do bad things. They frighten people into following their orders, murder and a number of illegal activities. They're bad for the city."

"My people would make them outcasts to live on the fringes of our village. They could not participate as good Pawnee. You should do this."

Jacque chuckled. "You cannot even imagine the outcry of injustice such an order would stir up in this day and time."

"Maybe this is why you have a problem. There is no consequence to be a gang member. Separate him from all the right and good. Give him nothing."

"You may be onto something, Joseph, but, unfortunately, we'll have to explore those options another time. Here are the gang locations."

"What does this mean?" He pointed to a yellow star.

"Death Apostles. Wear DOA on their shirts meaning 'dead on arrival.' Purple bandana." Jacque imitated a wrapping around the forehead. "One pant leg cuffed. Tattoo of a five-pointed yellow star on their body, usually their neck or upper arm. Sometimes they have more than one, depending on the crime or accomplishment. The more stars, the more important."

"Are they Pawnee or another tribe?"

"No, Joseph. There are no indications of gang activity among the few Native Americans in the city. Most live north of here in Wisconsin or Michigan." Jacque straightened.

"Then I think Neosho will go to these Death Apostles."

"Why do you think so?"

Cleo examined the map a second time. "Joseph is right. Their symbol is the yellow star. The Morning Star would be familiar to Neosho. Even though the Osage didn't necessarily follow the Evening and Morning Star deities, he might be superstitious enough to believe in the possibility of their importance. He would want as much power on his side as possible."

"Neosho has lived among the Pawnee from time to time. He would know of the religious powers in belief of the sun and stars. He has seen firsthand the miracles of sacrifice and belief." He tapped the map with his index finger and met Jacque's gaze. "You will find him here."

Jacque dared stare at the Pawnee for a few seconds before going to send several officers into Death Apostle territory. "I'll call the police commissioner so he can pass it along."

~~~~

While Jacque talked on the phone, Cleo led Wind Dancer outside the office. "What about your friend, the Frenchman? Should we be searching for him as well?"

"He will find us soon. Then we will go after Neosho together. You must not tell the detective. He will not understand the power my friend holds. He could easily take Jacque's body and make it his own, and no one would know the difference. Skinwalkers can do much harm if unleashed. My friend wants to destroy Neosho, but I am not sure if he can do it without a human body."

"Will he try and take yours?" Cleo's voice cracked as the words left her lips.

"It would be easier to take Jacque's. I have no way of knowing what a skinwalker thinks, if they do at all. I must remember he is part evil, like Neosho. I am not sure if he will try to get me to help."

"What if he decides to occupy Neosho's body?"

"I do not know if this is possible." Wind Dancer frowned. "I am hoping there is enough of my friend left, he would not want to do that. He hates the Osage for murdering his sons and wife, as do I."

Cleo gripped his hand. "Was his family Pawnee, too?"

"His wife was my oldest sister. I loved the boys like they were my own."

A wave of sadness welled up inside her at the pain he must feel at so much loss. She stepped closer letting Wind Dancer slip his arm around her waist. "We'll find him."

"My fear is he will take you when I can do nothing to stop
~~~~

him. You must never be alone, Cleopatra. Do you understand?"

She smiled up at him then pointed around the bustling precinct. "I think I'm pretty safe here."

Jacque hurried out into the hall. "Let's go. A beat officer spotted Neosho fifteen minutes from here." He eased Cleo out of Wind Dancer's embrace and glared at the Pawnee. "Can you help us or not?"

The Pawnee raised his chin with an expression of determination. "I help you, Jacque."

CHAPTER 11

The Frenchman stepped out of the shadows to discover people on the street ignored him. Dressed in jeans and a dark hoodie he'd secured from a street stand while the owner attended to a tourist, he managed to blend in enough to be like everyone else. The cold sidewalk pressed against his bare feet but did not cause any kind of discomfort for the once trapper and mountain man. After seeing a street maintenance worker slip into an alley to take a leak, the Frenchman followed and relieved him of his work boots, orange vest, and hard hat. He remembered from his recent life how such men moved and imitated the swagger of confidence that came easier since his limp had disappeared.

The steam rising from manhole covers reminded him of clouds as he passed through them toward a rendezvous with retaliation. Without knowing why he chose his direction, he headed to a busy street where police cars roared in and out of traffic. He found a place where uniformed men and women entered a nondescript building bearing the scars of time and years of neglect.

Stopping, he raised his nose to the wind and inhaled. The Frenchman squinted, listening. A satisfied twitch toyed with one corner of his mouth as someone bumped into him and complained he needed to move. The sudden reality check caused him to step away and wait, while he lowered his head and cocked his ear to the building.

A tingling crept up his arms when he spotted three people running down the steps of what must be the police station, the shorter man he'd fought at the museum among them. As a result of that battle, he dwelled between the living and the dead. Except for having a bit more weight around his middle, the detective could pass for his twin. Something inside him whispered of a chance to survive this world if he chose to harvest the soul of the man with a badge.

Then he recognized the daughter of his friend Dr. Daniel Sommers who'd tried to save his wife from her injuries. Although smart, the daughter remained clueless as to what lay ahead for her if Neosho found her.

The Frenchman had crossed over to bring her to her father as a thank-you gift but stayed too long, having been caught up in the ways of this world. Like Wind Dancer, he'd been a student of Dr. Sommers, learning the ways of modern man. He'd been gone from his time for what seemed like years but must be only weeks. When he'd seen her on the water taxi coming from the Field Museum, he knew life would again morph to yet another event he couldn't comprehend. Even then, he could feel in his bones the coming storm that could change everything. He wanted to warn her but managed to frighten her instead. Once he'd picked up her scent and heartbeat, tracing her movements became a rescue mission. Surprisingly, he could feel the flutter of her heart against his eardrums, reminding him of a baby bird.

"Wind Dancer," he breathed. The Pawnee stopped. Had he heard him?

The Frenchman dressed like the other modern men around them, allowing him the freedom to invite trust among these people. The question of whether the two with him had any idea the power the Pawnee possessed toyed at the recesses of a mind oscillating between good and evil.

"Wind Dancer," he sighed again. His friend reached for Cleo's arm and escorted her to a car, his gaze darting around. "I will take her, Wind Dancer. I am sorry. It is the only way I can draw out the Osage. Do not try and stop me." The detective held the door open and the other two climbed inside.

The detective navigated out into traffic, accompanied by the sound of squealing brakes and a horn blast. Lights flashed on the roof of the car and other vehicles ceded right of way to the official vehicle. Wind Dancer pressed his face against the rear window and placed his palm against the glass, connecting to him.

"I understand, old friend, what you must do." Wind Dancer stepped into his friend's mind like a warrior counting coup. "And I will finish what the detective tried to do to you at another time. If harm comes to Cleopatra, however, you will wander among the dead forever."

The Frenchman nodded and touched the brim of his hard hat in salute.

"What is it, Joseph?" Cleo asked and touched his arm. "Is it riding in the car? You don't need to worry."

Wind Dancer faced forward and fastened the seat belt as Cleo demonstrated earlier in the day. "No. I am fine." He took her hand in his. "You must stay close to me at all times. Do you understand? Only then can I protect you."

"I'll be surrounded by police carrying really big guns, Joseph. It will be okay." She patted his hand.

Wind Dancer switched his interest from her to the streets packed with traffic. The Frenchman could follow their trail since he'd picked up their scent. Guns would have no effect on him.

~~~~

"What do you mean you lost them?" Jacque didn't try to hide his irritation as he pushed his face into the young officer's. His focus switched to another, even younger officer. "What good are those long legs of yours if you can't keep up with a couple of misfits?"

"Sir, with all due respect, we were told at command to wait for backup."

Jacque exhaled a grunt of disapproval, knowing he spoke the truth. "Tell me what you saw."

"Some tall dude wearing a green jacket, Mohawk haircut…"

"White? Black?"

"Neither, detective. Brown. Kind of like him." He nodded toward Wind Dancer, who stood a few yards away. "The other guy was definitely black, wearing gang colors."
~~~~

Jacque fished out a picture of another gang member from the Death Apostles from his coat pocket. He glanced at it before shoving it toward the officers. "Like this?"

"Could be. Dark purple or black. Too far away to see any tats. We're not far from Firestorm Park. Gangs meet up there all the time. Ten shootings in the last two months. Two kids playing on the swings got in the way, ended up dead."

"I remember." He motioned for the officers pouring out of their cars to join them. "Joseph, you come with me. Cleo, I'm going to lock you in the car with an officer posted here."

"No. It isn't safe," Wind Dancer protested, positioning himself between Jacque and Cleo.

"Well it sure as hell won't be safe where we're going. You see the officer approaching? He's got a gun that could bring down a stampeding buffalo. Understand? Not even Neosho can stand up to one of those."

"Can it stop a skinwalker?"

"Hell, yes," Jacque lied. He remained unclear as to what a skinwalker was or if they even existed. He could tell Cleo bought into the story. Understandable since her father forced the stories on her as a child. Some kids had the boogeyman and she had a skinwalker.

"I'm not so sure, Jacque."

"Trust me." Jacque put a hand on the Pawnee's shoulder. "My job is to serve and protect people like Cleo. I'm locking her in the car and putting Dirty Harry in charge of her protection."

"Dirty Harry?" Wind Dancer eyed the officer who bore a gray mustache and eyebrows. Jacque caught the officer straightening at the comparison and guessed he'd try to live up to the compliment.

Cleo chuckled as she opened the car door. "Dirty Harry means he is really brave, mean, and protective."

"More words I do not understand?"

"I'm afraid so, Joseph." Cleo slid into the backseat. "Go with Jacque. He needs your help. If Neosho is there, only you can confront him or at least stop him. You have the same strength he does."

Wind Dancer put his hands on top of the car and spoke to the officer. "Dirty Harry, take great care. She is in much danger."

The officer jutted out his lower lip and frowned at Wind

Dancer then cut his eyes to Jacque before speaking. "Sure. Got it. Safe as a baby in its mother's arms." He smirked as he spoke in a gravel-like voice. "This will make my day." Jacque and Cleo chuckled, but Wind Dancer continued to glower at the two men.

The words somehow reassured him enough to shut the car door. "Thank you, Dirty Harry."

Jacque shrugged at the officer as a questioning glance crossed his face. "Stay close to me, Joseph. Maybe you can sense something we can't."

"I understand."

They hurried across the street to join the others already searching for Neosho. Park visitors hustled away, speaking in low voices. A few stopped to talk to the officers, shook their head at whatever answers they received before looking around them.

"Neosho is here, Jacque."

"How do you know?"

"I smell him. I hear his heart. The one with him is afraid."

"How close?"

Wind Dancer shook his head. "I cannot tell. But they are walking or Neosho's breathing would be different. He is not afraid of these police. You must tell them to be careful."

"He's not going to become invisible or something, is he?"

Wind Dancer smirked. "No, Jacque. He is like me. We are men not gods or skinwalkers."

They moved along at a steady pace as Jacque tried to gain understanding. "Then how do you explain the display of strength and agility on the balcony this morning. Scared the hell out of me."

"I do not know. I did not have this gift in my world. But Neosho and I strongest in our village. Maybe we become more so here." He jerked his head up and sniffed. "There." He pointed to a covered shelter where picnics and family reunions gathered. Several trees budded out into soft shades of pink, blocked a clear observation of the area.

Jacque didn't see them at first but spoke quietly into his mic to alert the others to move in when he noticed movement ahead. Drawing his weapon, he hunkered down and displayed the stealth approach ingrained in him since he graduated the police academy way too many years ago. He felt Wind Dancer do the same next to him and wondered if this was some kind of nineteenth-century instinct for the hunt kicking in.

Neosho and the gang member appeared to be in a heated discussion when Jacque stepped out in the open. "Get your hands up, Neosho, or so help me God, I'll shoot you down."

The black man raised his hands instantly. "I didn't do nothin' wrong. This whack job forced me to come with him."

Neosho kept his hands at his sides as he glanced down his nose at the young gang member then at Wind Dancer who stood with his legs slightly apart and hands out from his side as if ready to catch a fly ball at Wrigley Field. The Osage's eyes narrowed as they connected with Wind Dancer's. He moved forward.

"Stop or I'll shoot," Jacque promised. It didn't stop him. Jacque fired once landing a bullet in Neosho's shoulder.

The Osage stumbled back slapping a hand over the bleeding wound. Without warning he let out a warrior bellow. Jacque twitched, giving him a precious second, but Neosho already knocked him to the ground and his gun into the muddy grass. The sound of other uniformed reinforcements filled the air as the two men rolled on the ground.

Wind Dancer jerked Neosho up by the collar of his Green Bay Packer jacket and tossed him away as if he weighed no more than a child's toy. Wobbling to a stand, Jacque gasped for air and listened to the two combatants argue.

"You are sick, Neosho. You can be saved with this new world medicine."

Neosho stood in slow motion and glanced around him as more officers arrived, all with drawn weapons. Jacque noticed how Osage checked the area around him until his eyes landed on the gang member who had been taken aside by another officer.

"Then bring Cleopatra to me with this medicine."

"She waits for us. She will give you what you need. They can take care of your arm, too. Come with me." Wind Dancer extended his hand.

But before he could say more, Neosho slammed into him like a raging bull, knocking him back. Jacque watched as Wind Dancer remained standing, aware once more of the strength he possessed in this place.

As they ran at one another, the police drew closer. Jacque held up his hand so they wouldn't make a dangerous move and stoke an already smoldering fire.

The detective rubbed his chest as he staggered between his men and further danger. He waved them back. Only Wind Dancer could handle this beast. If his Glock couldn't do it, then he didn't have much hope another shot would do the trick. The sound of two grunting warriors bent on revenge reminded him of battling buffalos butting heads.

One blow met with another as each warrior tried to subdue the other. They were evenly matched until Wind Dancer knocked Neosho to the ground and the Osage laughed.

"Why do you cackle like a yipping coyote, Neosho?" Wind Dancer panted, wiping a trickle of blood from his nose.

The Osage rolled to his knees. "Your hatred and jealousy of me prevents you from recognizing the real danger." He pushed to stand, fell then jumped to his feet. Both men raised their chins and sniffed the air. "Your woman is not safe. Go. I need her, too."

Wind Dancer's eyes widened as concern flooded his face.

"You smell him? He comes for her."

Wind Dancer let out a howl and shoved the Osage before racing toward the parked cars. Before Jacque could react, Neosho snatched the gang member away from the officer who held him by the arm, and the two tore down the street away from the police.

"After them!" Jacque yelled, starting after Wind Dancer. "Don't let those two get away." But he could already tell Neosho could outdistance any of his men.

~~~~

Cleo edged closer to the window, but the officer stepped away from the car and spoke into his radio. The locks popped up, and the rear driver's side door swung open. Startled, she saw Jacque bending down to peer inside. He grinned and motioned for her to come out.

"Where is Wind Dancer? Is he okay?" Cleo took Jacque's hand, letting him help her out. "Your hands are like ice, Jacque. What is going on? Did you find Neosho?"

"No." Jacque glanced over his shoulder toward the park. He waved the officer guarding her away. He stood too close to her— unease crept into her bones. His eyes traveled from her hair down
~~~~

her face and rested on her mouth. "Wind Dancer will be here soon."

Cleo tried to move back, but the car blocked her way. "Where did you get those clothes?" He removed his hard hat and stole a glance at his orange vest. At a sudden awareness of the danger lurking in front of her, she sucked in breath to scream but froze as the Frenchman leaned in to inhale her scent.

"You smell wonderful, like the flowers growing on the plains along the Platte River."

"Jacque?" She dared to hope the detective might be making a move on her.

"Cleopatra!" Wind Dancer yelled from across the street. "Run!"

<h1 style="text-align:center">CHAPTER 12</h1>

Cleo shoved at the Frenchman's chest, but he blocked her escape by trapping her with a hand planted on the door frame on either side of her. He continued to grin as his eyes traveled around her face as if mapping a memory. The fear welling up inside paralyzed her so she could only whimper when his hand moved to touch her cheek.

She squeezed her eyes shut against his icy touch, until she felt his hand jerked away. Wind Dancer threw him with incredible strength, but the Frenchman moved only a few feet.

"What are you doing?" he panted, stepping between Cleo and the Frenchman. "You can't be here." He lowered his voice. "Neosho is close. Go to him, but stay away from Cleopatra."

"You finally get to be with her. I am happy for you, my friend. But I need her, too."

Before Wind Dancer could protest, Cleo came alongside him to face the Frenchman. "Why? How can I help you?"

"You will draw Neosho out. He is already gone. The police can't catch him. I can do many things, but so can the Osage. His anger blocks my ability to follow."

"Yet, you found us."

He cocked his head to the side. "I found you." Laying a hand on his chest he addressed Cleo. "Your heart is good. Helping others, like your father, is a way of life for you. Not so for us." He tilted his head toward Wind Dancer. Taking a deep breath then holding it for a few seconds before exhaling with a slowness that seemed to go on forever, he took in his surroundings. "The air is bad here. It smells of garbage and urine. But you"—he paused, a soft smile on his face—"smell like a spring rain and flowers from long ago. Neosho will have no trouble finding you. I will be there to catch him."

Cleo gazed up at Wind Dancer. "Maybe we could work together, Joseph."

"No. Skinwalkers are deceiving. He will take your soul and wander with it forever."

"I could not do such a thing to you." The Frenchman's brow wrinkled. "You who gave me a chance to live a little longer to revenge my wife, your sister's death. Have you forgotten how brutal he was to your nephews?"

"No. I have not forgotten." Wind Dancer's heavy tone drew Cleo closer.

"Hey!" Jacque's voice carried a tone of panic as he barreled across the street, catching sight of the Frenchman. The man should be dead, not walking around like he hadn't taken a bullet to the chest several days earlier.

"Good-bye, Wind Dancer." The Frenchman picked up his hard hat and strolled off toward the nearby barricade.

Jacque tore after the skinwalker, but he disappeared around the corner. He returned to the officer he'd called Dirty Harry. "What the hell were you doing?"

"Sorry?"

Cleo, followed by Wind Dancer, came to stand next to the bewildered officer. "I got out of the car on my own, Jacque."

"I thought he was you, Detective Marquette." The officer wilted under his superior's anger.

"Did you notice how he was dressed? Do I look like someone from the Village People?" The officer opened his mouth as if to respond, when Jacque landed a disgruntled glare at him then addressed his new friends. "Why didn't you stop him?" He pointed a finger so close to Wind Dancer's nose, the Pawnee's eyes crossed. "Then there's Neosho. We had him, rather you had him, and what? You let him escape, knowing we could never catch up?

He took a bullet and barely flinched!" His shout drew no reaction from Wind Dancer.

"Lower your voice, Jacque." Cleo laid a hand on his arm, but he jerked away to stare down the street. "I'm beginning to wonder whose side you're on, Joseph."

Wind Dancer bumped his chest into Jacque, eyes narrowed to slits of fire. "If I hadn't returned, Cleo would be gone. Your man could not protect her. I knew this, but I trusted you anyway. And, if you aren't careful, he will take you as well."

"Me?" he scoffed. "Why?"

"Isn't it obvious? What did he do a few minutes ago? He can impersonate you and go anywhere. If he steps inside you—"

"Wait a minute! Are you saying he's like a body snatcher or something? I'm not buying it."

"Jacque," Cleo whispered. "I think what Joseph is saying is the Frenchman could take over your body without your permission. I don't understand all of this either. He may not want your soul. It seems he wants the chance to kill Neosho."

"Well, that makes two of us."

"I prefer he be alive, Jacque. I want to run some tests on him to see if the strain of smallpox is the same we face in this universe." She reached for his arm, but he stepped away again.

Several uniformed policemen came across the street to join them.

"He got away, Detective Marquette. The guy runs like a gazelle. He practically carried the kid with him. For once, I think a gang member actually wanted to be taken in by the police."

Jacque thanked him then ordered a roadblock to be set up to enclose the park and a few surrounding blocks the Death Apostles frequented. "Maybe we'll catch a break and spot him again." He took a call on his cell phone then clicked off. "Great. More complications. Let's go."

"Why? What happened?" Cleo climbed into the backseat of his car.

When he got behind the wheel, he told them, "The Department of Defense wants to talk to you, Cleo. The FBI is standing by as well. We're to head over there."

"Department of Defense? That can't be good?"

"My feeling exactly. Buckle our boy in. This is going to be a quick ride."

~~~~

Wind Dancer turned in circles as they entered the two-story foyer of the FBI building. Wind Dancer stared upwards through the wall of glass like a little boy searching for his missing kite. He stumbled when someone bumped into him and said, "Excuse me," then continued on. The décor in the center of the foyer held oblong planters of greenery, surrounded by empty benches. Sunlight streamed in through the octagonal panes of glass, making a pattern across the floor.

"Why are these plants hard and brittle, Cleopatra?" Wind Dancer fingered the leaves.

"They're plastic."

"Plastic. I don't understand." He peeled off a leaf and lifted it to his nose then took a bite out of it before spitting it out onto the floor.

"No. Joseph, they're artificial."

"Art. Ti. Ficial." He broke the word down to remember it.

"Not real. These are pretend plants."

"Why are they pretending?" Wind Dancer cocked his head.

Jacque grinned as he halted his quick pace. "Yeah, Cleo? Why?"

"Are they trying to trick people into eating them so they will grow thin?" Wind Dancer removed another leaf to smell. "They would not eat much, I'm sure."

"No—" Cleo began.

Jacque interrupted. "Exactly. Maybe you haven't noticed, but Americans tend to have a weight problem these days. We put these in various places so when they get the munchies they can graze on this crap. No calories, no taste, and won't induce a diabetic coma."

Wind Dancer nodded with seriousness. "I don't know what calories and diabetic coma is but you might want to try this." He handed Jacque a plastic philodendron leaf. "You are getting thick around the middle. It would be bad, I think, if you caught a coma."

Cleo's laughter echoed upwards, and Jacque's sheepish grin thinned as he threw the leaf in the planter. "Thanks. I'm good."

"I'm not sure you are trying hard enough," the Pawnee added.
~~~~

"No. I mean…" Jacque threw up his hands. "Never mind. This is hopeless. Cleo, don't let this guy talk when we meet up with the DOD. Those guys won't be amused about some universe-jumping Indians bent on destroying life as we know it."

Cleo chuckled and he grinned.

~~~

Jacque rolled his eyes upward then noticed two suits and a military man coming around the corner of a nearby hall. He took a deep breath then cast a concerned glance toward Cleo and Wind Dancer.

"Detective Marquette." The older of the two FBI agents extended a hand that he guessed could lift a basketball like a snowball, his thin smile as plastic as the plants behind him. "I'm Agent Farentino, and this is Agent Crosby." Another round of handshakes. The man in uniform didn't appear as ready to make friendly gestures.

Jacque shoved his hand at the colonel. "And you are?"

The African American army officer impressed him as someone who might eat thumbtacks instead of granola for breakfast. He bet smoothies had no place in his regular diet. He wore a no-nonsense scowl on his round face and stood a good three inches taller than him. His wide mouth drooped down at the corners. The colonel eyed the detective in a slow examination.

"Colonel Thaddeus Jefferson." He grabbed the detective's hand in a firm grip as if to measure an opponent. An effective tool in the intimidation department. "Department of Defense."

"Detective Marquette. Chicago PD." He couldn't help but smirk as he squeezed the colonel's hand with his own form of posturing. "What can we do for you?"

The colonel observed Cleo and Wind Dancer with cold disregard as they approached. Cleo immediately extended her hand, but Wind Dancer stiffened.

Jacque noticed how Cleo offered a sweet smile that possessed the ability to disarm the tension between the two men. Even so, the hairs on his neck stood at attention. Just because she melted his resistance, didn't mean two bullheaded Neanderthals would respond the same way.
~~~

"This is Joseph Wind Dancer."

"Yes. We know." The colonel took Cleo's hand but released it almost the moment he touched it. His focus remained on the Pawnee. He motioned in the direction of a long corridor. "This way. We need to clear a few things up before you are allowed to leave."

Jacque bristled, stepping into the colonel's personal space. "Excuse me. We came here to be helpful. We'll leave when we're damn good and ready, Colonel Jefferson. You have no jurisdiction over me or these people. Maybe that's how it works in D.C., but here it ain't going to happen."

"Settle down, Detective." Agent Farentino held up his hand. "We're not detaining you or these people. Right, Colonel?"

The colonel arched a brow and stepped aside. "This way."

The detective took Cleo's elbow and took a step away then stopped when he realized Wind Dancer and the colonel still stared menacingly at each other. "Joseph," he snapped, "let's go."

Wind Dancer raised his chin, glaring down his nose at the colonel who was a little taller than him. "Are you a buffalo soldier?"

Of course, he referred to the 10th Calvary soldiers made up of African Americans during the eighteen hundreds. Their regiment fought the plains Indians on a number of occasions and would be their only reference to African Americans in uniform.

One corner of the colonel's mouth curved up. "No. But my great, great, great-grandfather had that honor. Do you have a problem with that?"

Wind Dancer took a threatening step toward him, but Jacque stepped between the two. "Later, Joseph. Whatever happened in the past has nothing to do with this guy. Keep your head in the game. This isn't the Wild West."

The colonel continued to smirk, but Jacque could do nothing about his attitude.

They followed the FBI agents and the colonel down a long, sterile white corridor to a conference room. The lights automatically flipped on when they entered. Wind Dancer crouched then stood up and looked around, hands fisted at his sides. The FBI agents exchanged glances as if wondering if the man with hair down to the middle of his chest and very much a

Native American might be simple in the head. Cleo's explanation about the environmentally friendly lights must have added to the impression.

"Be seated please."

Cleo sat down first and rolled out a chair on wheels for Wind Dancer, who, once seated, rolled the chair back and forth with a fascinated expression. She whispered something to him and he ceased moving and folded his arms across his chest to resemble a ferocious enemy from a John Wayne movie. His mouth took on a pouting appearance, and Jacque noticed Cleo slipping her hand off the table onto his leg. Jacque decided he'd settle down, too, if she stroked his leg. He sat on the other side of Wind Dancer. Something whispered trouble in his subconscious.

"We've asked you to come to discuss Mr. Wind Dancer's entrance into this world." The colonel crossed his legs and leaned back drumming his fingers on the table, never taking his eyes off Wind Dancer. When they locked glares, the colonel never wavered as if he might be getting ready to do an interrogation. Jacque used the tactic often enough to recognize the beginning of intimidation. However, although he'd known Wind Dancer for only a short time, he doubted it would work on him.

"So you know?" Cleo sounded relieved. "You believe he did this?"

"Yes. We've known for some time there are parallel universes, most of which are beyond our reach. Dr. Kuzma did extensive work in this area for NASA."

"But his research was terminated when funding dried up." Cleo spoke with caution.

"Yes. The funding and research became property of the Defense Department when we suspected the possibility other life forms could access this universe and destroy life as we know it, with bacteria, viruses, even creatures could wreak havoc on our fragile ecosystems."

"How long have you known about this?" Cleo blinked.

"Approximately four years. Your father notified us of a possible opening into another world. His concern fell on deaf ears until we discovered Dr. Kuzma was somehow involved in his research and ultimate discovery. After his disappearance, we investigated with DARPA's assistance."

"What the hell is DARPA?" Jacque scanned the room, hoping others were as clueless as him.

The colonel raised his eyebrows and clicked his tongue. "Defense Advanced Research Projects. They answer to the Defense Department, thanks to President Eisenhower who oversaw their creation in 1958. Their job is to handle, develop, and spot emerging technologies: everything from the neurosciences to bionics, cloaking devices, and parallel universes."

"Those the guys who invented the Internet?" Jacque mocked with a smirk.

"Exactly."

Jacque's flippant disregard for the colonel's authority faded into a thin frown.

"And all the while you let me believe my father was dead?" She addressed Jacque. "Did you know anything about this?"

"I never even heard of the case until a few days ago when the Field Museum reported some missing artifacts. I worked drug enforcement when your father went missing."

Agent Farentino checked some notes he'd been taking when they'd sat down. "Mr. Wind Dancer, where exactly did you come from?"

The Pawnee stared straight ahead, ignoring the agent.

Cleo cleared her throat and spoke in a calm voice. "He's trying to understand, Joseph."

"I come from the land of the Platte."

"As in the Platte River?"

Wind Dancer nodded as he shifted his eyes from Cleo to the colonel.

"Can you tell me if you've been sick?"

"Once. I almost die of smallpox. Very high fever." He lifted his hair to show his neck and the area under his ear. "Left scars."

Another soldier entered the room and whispered something in the colonel's ear. He straightened and caught the eye of Wind Dancer. The Pawnee jumped onto the table then tackled the young lieutenant to the floor, landing multiple blows as the others tried to drag him off the bloodied soldier.

"What the hell, Joseph!" Jacque snapped, trying to free him of the FBI agents. "Are you nuts?"

Wind Dancer struggled and managed to shake his guards off.

"This is the man who brought smallpox to the Osage and to me. Because of him, my sister, her children, and her husband are dead."

CHAPTER 13

Neosho and Ty sprinted through alleys until they reached an abandoned garage behind a boarded-up house. There were charred streaks around several windows adding to the shabby appearance. Ty peeled a section of chain-link fence away for the Osage to slip through while continuing to scan the direction they'd escaped. The fence clinked and moaned as both moved to a side door of the garage. The sturdy steel gave an impression of security and set the stage for a safe meeting place for the Death Apostles.

After trying the door without success, Ty banged on the door then waited and rapped some kind of rhythm with his knuckles. The door jerked open to reveal a young man pointing a gun at the two. Neosho's face continued to be free of emotion or concern over his new situation. After Ty explained they might have a problem, they were allowed inside.

The garage was large for Chicago. With room enough for only one car, at some point the original owners built a second story, probably for a rental or retirement apartment for aging parents. The inside of the lower level needed a good sweeping, and the mismatched furniture on the far end resembled something from the curb of a Goodwill center. The colorful pinball machine sitting in the corner took center stage, considering it sat idle without the access to electricity. A small window at the rear donned a covering of the cartoon section of a newspaper, now faded and ripped in several places, allowing ribbons of light to pierce the darkness. A few boards nailed on the outside gave the impression of danger.

"Who's he?" a man who stood a head taller than Ty asked. He watched the Osage with more curiosity than concern. "Ashanti ain't gonna like you bringin' a stranger here."

"I didn't have a choice, man. Where is he?"

He flicked his eyes to the steps leading upstairs then to the Osage who moved around the room lifting items for examination then dropping them to the floor.

Ty cleared his throat drawing the Osage to his side. He pointed upstairs, but was shoved aside by the gang member dressed in the same sort of drab clothing as Ty.

"You stay here. I'll take him up." He grinned, revealing a mouth full of yellowed and gold capped teeth with a pink tongue that he slid across his dark lips. "This way," he said.

Ty shrugged then pretended to find interest in his feet. "Tell them," he managed to mumble from the corner of his mouth as they moved up creaking steps.

Nothing but silence at first, followed by loud voices until the sound of moving furniture being tossed and thumps against the floor drew Ty to move to the side of the stairs and sneak a peek upwards as a dragging sound drew closer. He jumped away when the man who had taken the Osage upstairs rolled down the steps like a slam-dunk basketball in the last seconds of a game. Ty caught his breath as he glanced from the man to the Osage standing at the top. Ashanti appeared beside him to examine the result of crossing the newest member of the Death Apostles.

He removed a toothpick from his mouth and growled at Ty, "Get up here. We need to talk."

Ty stepped over the man trying to gain traction to stand at the foot of the steps. His grunts of pain encouraged Ty to move quicker and take the steps two at time until he reached the top.

Ashanti's rolling desk chair squeaked when he sat down. "Your friend doesn't have much to say. Maybe you can fill in some gaps for me, Ty."

"Sure, Ashanti. Found this guy down by the riverboat tours. Thought he was claiming some of our territory. He's a boatload of trouble, too."

Ashanti leaned in his chair as he watched the strange man in a Packers jacket continue to sit so still he appeared to be a statue. His robotic gaze seemed as piercing as lasers emitted from some kind of futuristic alien in a science fiction movie. The leader twisted in his chair. Ty expected the worst.

"So what's the story, big guy? You gonna let Ty speak for you?"

The Osage turned his head as if it were atop a wooden neck and nodded to Ty.

"He don't talk much. But he's one hell of a fighter." He offered a slight grin and raised his hand for a high five but only managed to make the Osage's eyes narrow. Dropping his hand, he addressed Ashanti. "You ain't gonna believe this."

Both men watched the Osage grab a knife from a nearby table and dig the bullet from his shoulder.

~~~~

Colonel Jefferson helped the lieutenant to his feet. "Everyone sit down," he demanded through clenched teeth.

"What are you talking about, Joseph?" Cleo placed herself in front of the Pawnee to distract him from further attack. The amount of firepower in the room could fill him with holes like a piece of Swiss cheese. "How is it possible you saw this man?"

"He is the one. This I know for sure. I took him myself to show him the village of the Osage. Neosho came out to meet us because he trusted me, unlike many of the other Osage. We not always friendly, but because Neosho lived among us for a time, he believed I meant them no harm. Because of my actions, he lost his entire family and much of his village."

Cleo whirled on the colonel. "Is this true? Do you know how to cross over into his world?" When he didn't answer, she shifted her gaze to the FBI agents. They shook their heads in confusion.

The colonel waved toward the chairs, but no one obeyed.

"Do you?" Her voice pitched a little higher than she intended.

"The short answer is yes."

"There's a long answer?" Jacque shoved Joseph several times before the Pawnee moved toward the swivel chair he rolled to the back of his knees. He patted the leather, but Joseph refused to sit. "Let me guess. You sent a bunch of your knuckle draggers across with smallpox to see if it changed on the transfer?"
~~~~

"Not so simple." The colonel eased himself into his chair as the lieutenant dragged a handkerchief across his bloody nose.

"Really, Colonel?" Agent Farentino chimed in. "Enlighten us, because you may have succeeded in exposing the entire city, if not the whole country, to smallpox because of your desire to have military might over the enemy. In case you've forgotten, biological warfare has been against the law since 1972. Where the hell did you get the idea this was okay?"

"In a world where terrorism is running rampant, the military decided to explore options that would eliminate the threat of biological agents we feared could go airborne in a short amount of time. Three different labs have mishandled smallpox containment areas in the last six years. We thought we'd manipulated the components that make smallpox so deadly. It was too late to destroy what remained of research smallpox, so our people managed to change the chemical makeup to force it to destroy itself."

"I don't understand why you took it to Joseph's universe. What were you trying to prove?"

The colonel shifted in his chair a bit before nodding to his lieutenant. "Care to elaborate?"

Cleo reached out for Joseph's hand and tugged gently so he would also sit in his chair.

"We knew multicellular organisms which produce their food by photosynthesis have the ability to thrive and spread outside their native range. These plants can be especially invasive when introduced to a new habitat."

"Like the Asian kudzu plant in the south?" Cleo interjected.

"Exactly. Kudzu causes about six million dollars of damage each year in spite of the herbicides to control it."

As silence stretched on, Cleo fidgeted in her chair. "So how does smallpox fit into this?"

The lieutenant continued. "Our primary concern might mean our people would be exposed and ultimately bring it here or possibly even die. Throughout history smallpox has attacked populations. We believed DARPA had finally discovered a way to destroy smallpox once and for all. All of us were vaccinated, but something happened when we crossed over."

"Did you break out in smallpox?" As a doctor, Cleo wanted to sound outraged, but her interest grew with each revelation.

"We didn't believe so. All of us suffered cold and flu-like symptoms."

"Indicating the onset of smallpox."

"Yes. But it lasted only twenty-four hours, and we thought the crossing might be the cause of our fever and distress since it vanished so quickly."

"And you had no contact with the Pawnee or Osage during this time?" Jacque quizzed.

Wind Dancer twisted restlessly in his seat. "When I found them near the Platte River, they were starved and sick. I took them to my campsite, where I had been hunting with two other warriors. We shared food and water."

"Did you cough, sneeze, or expose any of your bodily fluids during this time, Lieutenant?" Cleo already knew the answer.

"Yes. But we still believed it to be an adjustment to the crossover. After all, we were convinced the vaccination would prevent this kind of thing. The new strain of smallpox should have destroyed itself. History showed native tribes exposed to the virus would be decimated. Even though we knew their exposure would be inevitable with westward expansion, we didn't want to be the cause."

Agent Farentino weighed in next. "Explain your mission."

Cleo stood up and pointed a finger at the colonel. "You knew those men were infected." The colonel opened his mouth to speak, but she cut him off. "Yes. You vaccinated after infecting them. You had no clue if it would be safe."

"Our tests showed 90 percent effectiveness."

She shot him an incredulous glare and flopped down in her chair when Agent Farentino slammed his fist on the table.

"The mission," he snapped, his face flushed. "What the hell were you after?"

The colonel's thicker bottom lip protruded. "We went to collect samples of the flora and fauna in hopes of manipulating the DNA. We also wanted to check for indications of change in parallel universes that could be beneficial to us. Believe it or not, we have samples from our 1800s. Comparing those samples could make great strides in environmental stability."

"Since when did the Pentagon care about environmental

stability?" Agent Crosby interjected.

"One of the biggest concerns at the Pentagon is water. With climate change, whole populations find themselves in drought areas that destroy access to successful farming. Even in this country, we've had years of drought out west. The plains provide wheat to the world, but in recent years has fought climate oscillations as well. For the last three years, the corn crop has produced half of its average annual yield."

"So you want to monkey around with the DNA in hopes of creating more genetically modified foods."

"If the world is starving, there's no need for us to join them. Think of the peaceful possibilities."

"I don't follow." Jacque frowned. "How can GMFs affect world peace?"

Cleo fingered loose strands of hair behind her ears. "We hold governments hostage with the promise of food, technology, and agricultural advancement with a price of allegiance and natural resources."

"We don't actually need natural resources for the most part. The reason OPEC keeps lowering their price on a barrel of oil is due to our increased independence. We'll buy theirs until it's gone then start selling to them. We want to rein in countries hostile to our government and those who support terrorism. Such hostility jeopardizes our way of life; from the movies we watch to the fast food restaurants we frequent."

Jacque whispered, "That doesn't sound like a bad thing, Cleo."

"And the smallpox?" she quizzed, ignoring Jacque.

"An unfortunate discovery."

"Unfortunate?" Wind Dancer growled. "Many people died. The Osage, Neosho, was exposed to smallpox and he is here. What will happen?"

"He's right, Colonel Jefferson." Agent Farentino locked his fingers together on top of the table. "What did you discover when your team returned with samples? Did you test the men as well?"

"We did. The virus mutated when they crossed back. Even though the team had been inoculated against the virus, they suffered a mild form which didn't manifest completely."

"I don't understand," Agent Farentino said.

Cleo began to put it all together. "The men were inoculated against the disease so even though they exhibited symptoms, they didn't completely break out. It's like when an older patient who exhibits symptoms of shingles. We can give a ten-day dose of medicine to keep it from ever breaking through the skin into the blisters that lead to excruciating pain. Older patients often already have compromised immune systems, so this is a real breakthrough for them if they come in for treatment right away. Except, in this case, those men remained contagious."

Wind Dancer crossed his arms on his chest, an expression of a gathering storm covering his face. "And when these men returned to this time, this universe, did the smallpox change again?"

"Yes." The lieutenant hesitated. "The virus in all three of us remained alive and more dangerous than before. We went into quarantine for several months, undergoing tests and therapy until we found a new anti-virus that could protect the population. We believed only our team managed to cross over and survive the return trip. It seemed too preposterous to think the indigenous population could follow. There was no indication of anyone else following."

"Why? Because we are ignorant savages who believe in evil spirits and worship things you do not understand?" Wind Dancer's voice sounded amused. "We have known of these portals into your world for generations. Dr. Sommers, Cleopatra's father was the first white man to survive the crossing. Many of our people have tried, but the openings…" He flexed his fist in some kind of motion then waited for Cleo for help.

"The portals fluctuated shut?" Cleo slapped her hands together. "Kind of like this."

He nodded, his eyes wide. "Yes. They also moved. Some lasted only for a blink of the eye and could be large. The smaller ones stayed open longer, but dark inside, and we thought they held evil which could be brought into our world." He shifted his gaze to the colonel. "I guess we were right."

"But the good news," Cleo interjected, "is you have a way to inoculate against the disease."

"Not exactly."

"Excuse me?" came the quick response offered by most in the room.

The colonel twisted his shoulders as if a kink manipulated his comfort level. "We have labs working 24/7 on the antivirus. The vaccine you gave your people today will protect them from any breakout occurring in Chicago." He leveled a scowl at Cleo. "You'll need a booster, Dr. Sommers. Although our records indicate you have been vaccinated, we aren't sure it will be enough to protect you. Better safe than sorry."

"Maybe the time to think about this scenario should have come before sending your people into new lands, Colonel Jefferson," Jacque mumbled as his phone vibrated. He glanced at the screen then stood and headed for the door. "Sorry. Need to take this."

"So the seven million doses in stock for emergencies are worthless?" Cleo continued.

"Tests indicate they are only partially effective. The elderly and children are the most vulnerable. The older populations vaccinated in the fifties and sixties are no longer protected. But, having been vaccinated in the last few years, you already have some degree of immunity."

"The Osage may have exposed her when he broke in this morning." Wind Dancer's brow pinched tight over his nose as he laid a hand on her arm.

"Most likely." Colonel Jefferson raised his chin toward the FBI agents. "You are exposed as well by being in the same room. We've called the CDC to bring the vaccine here to immunize you who haven't been already. A hazmat crew is cleaning the foyer and corridors even as we speak." He stood and tugged at the front of his uniform. "We'll keep you informed of any changes. The FBI needs to take this out of the hands of the Chicago PD, ASAP."

Cleo moved to cut the colonel off as he approached the door. "What happens if Neosho refuses to come out of the neighborhood where he was last spotted?"

The colonel took a deep breath then held it longer than she thought possible before he exhaled slowly. He chose to speak to the FBI instead of her. "Extreme decontamination."

<h1 align="center">CHAPTER 14</h1>

"I did not understand the words of the buffalo soldier, Cleopatra." Wind Dancer had refused to let her return to the condo without him. Jacque waited downstairs to catch up with the detail posted at the front doors.

They found her condo in disarray from the morning skirmish. The smell of some chemical cleaner remained in the air. She'd been informed a hazmat team had also taken bed sheets, towels, even the dirty dishes in the sink. Even the trash cans had disappeared. Her broken door to the balcony displayed a plywood covering. The front door now resembled a flimsy dressing room door which probably was supposed to create protection against curious neighbors; in spite of the fact everyone on her floor had been moved to a fancy hotel for a few days.

Even her clothes had vanished. Not being a clothes hound like her friends Julie and Erica, the thought of having to replace them filled her with dread. The need to pick up a few things to spend the next couple of days at a hotel complicated her ability to think straight.

"Okay. Guess I won't need to pack anything. Nothing to take. Maybe Jacque can drop me at Macy's for an hour or so to restock my wardrobe… Oh. Sorry. You were saying?" She regarded Wind Dancer, who followed her into the bedroom.

"I don't understand 'extreme decontamination.' Is this better medicine?"

Cleo stared at the Pawnee standing in the last rays of light seeping through the window. He appeared both stoic and bewildered. His high cheekbones and oval eyes, which seemed almost out of place above such a narrow nose, reminded her of how his hard, angular face had always drawn her to him in the museum case. Not quite handsome, but oh so mesmerizing. She knew before speaking she would need to slow the rapid heartbeat and the rising flush of heat on her neck and face.

He stood straight as a statue, calm as a cucumber, and more patient than she'd ever known a man to be. "Extreme decontamination means they would burn the neighborhood down, maybe bomb it."

"Wouldn't it be hard to get everyone out?" He cocked his head suddenly.

"They would not get them out, Joseph. They would all die."

"And they call us savages." He shook his head and moved away. "This is my fault."

Cleo stepped toward him and laid a hand on his shoulder as he stared out the window toward another building. "You had no way of knowing those men had smallpox. If you had, you'd never have taken him to the Osage or brought sickness to his people."

"This holds no comfort for me, Cleopatra. Your father isolated me from the others when he heard about the Osage. It was two weeks before I showed symptoms, so my people remained safe. My sister and her boys waited for the Frenchman to return from the buffalo hunt. He took my place so we could eat." His voice cracked. "Neosho took his revenge because of me. Left alive, I must suffer her death many times." He pulled her around to face him and touched her strawberry-colored hair. "Now he wants to steal you from me. He will carry you across to his land."

"I'm more afraid of your friend who has become a skinwalker than Neosho." Her arms circled his body. He lowered his mouth to hers as Jacque stomped into the condo making enough noise to give them warning, she guessed. She stepped away and hurried out into the main living area to meet him.

"What a mess." Jacque tried to act nonchalant until Wind Dancer joined them with a sour expression. The detective smirked. "Where's your stuff, Cleo?"

Cleo gave a matter-of-fact explanation and requested a stop at Macys. "I can do everything in less than an hour."

"And who says miracles don't happen anymore?" He flashed a boyish grin. "Trust me, Joseph, when I say this will take a lot longer. Women."

"Women," he repeated in a serious tone.

"Then you can drop me off and call it a day…or not." She'd left her purse behind and it was also gone. "I don't even have a credit card."

"Not taking you to Macys. Still don't know how contagious you guys might be or if at all." Jacque retrieved an envelope from his pocket and handed it to her. "Your new card came in the mail today. You see? Another miracle."

"You went through my mail?" She found it difficult to sound enraged when he chuckled. "You're lucky I'm homeless tonight or I'd be up in your face."

"Maybe we'll put you up with the CDC at the Sheraton on Water Street. Like?"

She let out a whistle. "Not too shabby. And what about Joseph?"

The Pawnee stepped closer. "I stay with Cleopatra, to protect."

The detective glanced at Cleo and shrugged. "Yeah. That ain't gonna happen, buddy."

"Buddy?"

"Friend."

Wind Dancer slapped the detective on the arm causing him to stagger a few steps aside. "Friend." Outstretched arms pulled them both into his embrace. "I protect both of you."

Jacque shoved off Wind Dancer's arm. "I booked an adjoining room for us, Joseph. The doc has been through a lot today. We're going to let her rest. Okay?"

Even though Cleo caught the drift of what *rest* meant, dropping her eyes couldn't keep a rush of heat from creeping up her neck and face. Wind Dancer laid a hand on her cheek before pointing to her face.

"She is very warm, Jacque. She has the smallpox."

Jacque arched an eyebrow at the doctor as she tried to clear her throat and remove his hand from her face. "I think maybe she's got something else, Joseph. I wouldn't worry about it."

They moved toward the door as Wind Dancer began his own line of questioning. "What else could she have, Jacque? Can we catch this?"

"I think you already caught it, Joseph."

"Enough, Detective," Cleo snapped as she punched the elevator button. "It's complicated."

Wind Dancer nodded as if he knew what they were talking about before repeating, "Yeah, Jacque, it's complicated."

~~~

Morning light slipped into the hotel room as Cleo fell into a deep sleep. She'd rolled and tossed all night with dreams of her father running from Neosho and skinwalkers. Then there remained the matter of Wind Dancer. What of him?

She didn't want to have feelings for him. But she did.

She didn't want another failed relationship. But she wanted to try.

She didn't want to do a lot of unhealthy things with him, but the possibilities kept consuming her common sense as he strode about like some romantic hero from the past. If he rode in on a wild black stallion, the story would be complete. Opening her eyes, she remembered him riding the policeman's horse their first night together. His ebony hair whipping against her face, and his muscular torso flexing beneath her fingertips kept her imagination swirling into a vortex of insane longing.

It would never work. Wind Dancer knew very little of this world and the danger lurking around every corner. Disease. Crime. Environmental hazards. Geopolitical conflict. He reminded her of an innocent child set loose in a room where someone dropped hundreds of knives and then told to go play.

"He wouldn't last two weeks here," she mumbled, hands over her eyes.

"Who?" came the voice of Wind Dancer from near the desk.

Cleo gasped and sat up, letting the sheet fall down around her waist. When he eyed her like she might be on the breakfast menu, she snatched up the comforter to cover her thin nightgown. The hotel boasted a nice boutique, although she'd spent more than she usually did in six months on the few items she'd purchased. The
~~~

nightgown had been an impulse buy, or maybe a what-if buy.

"What are you doing in here, and how long have you been watching me?" She tried to sound outraged, but his bewildered expression nearly made her laugh.

"Jacque snores very loud. I came in before the sky turned pink. You snore, too."

"I don't snore." This did make her angry. "I never snore."

"You do now." He imitated how her short bursts of blowing through her lips then a little nasal breathing. "Like that." He stood and approached the bed as if he tracked prey. "I wanted to comfort you when you cried out, but Jacque says I should not touch you because I could give you sickness of some kind."

"Good ole Jacque," she moaned with a little relief mixed with regret.

"Good ole Jacque." His face held such warmth she almost threw off the covers and invited him in. "You are beautiful, Cleopatra." He sat down on the end of the bed and touched her leg on top of the covers.

"What? Ah, my hair is a mess and..." She fumbled with unruly strands around her face then moved the pretend cobwebs from her tired eyes when he reached out and took her hand.

"Beautiful." His smile widened. "The morning agrees with you." He stood and pointed to the sky. "Even the Morning Star shines less next to you."

If she'd been standing, her knees would have felt like Jell-O. Thankfully, Jacque came to the doorway. "Oh, for crying out loud, Joseph. You've got to stop saying things like that. It makes the rest of us look bad."

Cleo waved them both away. "I'm pretty sure you manage that on your own, Jacque. You're single, right?"

"Nobody likes a know-it-all, Cleo," he said, lifting his chin toward their room. "Get dressed. We've got someplace to be."

~~~

The Frenchman strolled along the riverfront below the Sheraton Hotel, enjoying the first signs of morning light. The scent of the detective had led him here. This alone would not have been enough if not for Cleopatra and Wind Dancer. Their heartbeats
~~~

pounded a path for him. The Pawnee would be able to trace his movements as long as the woman didn't distract him, which she seemed to be doing at a steady pace. He didn't understand how she blocked his ability to follow him. Could one woman divert such a focused warrior? Then he remembered his wife and how he'd done many crazy things to make her happy. He missed her.

The detective had killed him and Wind Dancer gave him another chance; a chance to destroy the man who took the only reason he lived and breathed. He'd tracked the Osage to the cliffs, a year earlier, along the Platte where he'd hidden outside a cave. He'd never trusted the warrior, even before he'd killed his family. Seeing Cleo's father and his friend emerge from the opening, he'd alerted them, thus giving Neosho an opportunity to escape before he could confront him. They had tangled several times and suspected the Osage of plotting against his friends.

His two friends seemed more concerned about their discovery than the fact Neosho may try to kill them. The conversation came in bursts of nonsense, but he remained quiet with an occasional glance over his shoulder to search for Neosho who'd disappeared as quickly as he'd appeared on the cliff edge.

Words he didn't understand kept spilling into the conversation, words like parallel universe, time jump, hypothetical, and coexist.

"What does this mean, Dr. Sommers?" the Frenchman remembered asking.

Wind Dancer answered instead of the doctor. "It means the land from which he came can be reached through this hole." Wind Dancer acted so proud of himself. "It means I can find Cleopatra and bring her here."

The Frenchman remembered thinking they both may have gotten into the special brew they used for a captive about to be sacrificed to the Morning Star. Even though he thought the practice a kind of barbaric nonsense serving no purpose whatsoever, the practice continued to bring harmony among the Pawnee. He wondered how long before the government of Thomas Jefferson or whoever was in charge in the east would impose their view of a higher power. From his talks with Dr. Sommers, it wouldn't be long. He knew the history of this land and often told stories from the future. His warnings both entertained and frightened him.

"So what is the problem? Go get her." The Frenchman pivoted to leave so he could search for the Osage and finish what he'd set out to do. "This is not helping us." He frowned at the doctor. "Your stories are no longer amusing."

The elder Dr. Sommers grabbed the Frenchman and pulled him around before forcing him into the cave. That's when he discovered the truth.

Now here he wandered in another time, dead and alive. He moved among the living in a final attempt to kill the Osage who murdered his family. It wasn't supposed to end like this. Cross over. Find Cleopatra. He would convince her to return with him.

Only it had worked out differently than planned. After the sickness and the murder of his family, he wanted to relieve his pain and hoped retrieving the good doctor's daughter would give him something worthwhile to ponder. Then he could devote his time to hunting down the animal who butchered his family.

With the education given to him and Wind Dancer, they planned to come across together. They had no way of knowing the lightning storm might close the opening so rapidly. The Frenchman had jumped through first, but Wind Dancer didn't make it. From what the doctor surmised, the hole would open again. He'd waited in the dark until he feared the opening into the museum might close entirely. Then all would be lost. Once he'd stumbled into the earth lodge in the Field Museum, a whole new world opened up to him. He became drunk with the possibilities in this world.

Months of exploration and wonder educated him more than the few lessons from the good doctor. Although he tried to find Cleopatra, the amazing distractions clotted his focus so the objective died. Then he saw her a few days ago on the water taxi. Her father carried a picture of her and, in the end, gave it to him. Wind Dancer watched her for years through the museum cases and spoke of her as if they'd shared personal moments for decades.

Discovering her scent, his enhanced senses and old-fashioned tracking abilities found her easy enough. Then the news broke of the museum theft. Somehow, he knew Wind Dancer and Neosho had crossed over.

The old rage surfaced like a tsunami, reminding him he could be robbed of his chance at revenge.

Why would Neosho come here? Then he understood, after

seeing Cleopatra. The Osage wanted his own revenge against Wind Dancer. The Frenchman refused to allow this to happen.

He stared up at the windows, searching for a sign of his friend. He could hear many heartbeats but searched for the beat to a different drum. Wind Dancer was so focused on the Morning Star, he failed to sense his presence. Being so near to water helped hide his smell of death.

"Soon, my friend, we will meet once more. I won't take the soul of your woman, but I cannot promise the same for the man who killed me."

A wave of hatred washed over him, knowing the detective ended his life too soon to finish the job set before him.

CHAPTER 15

"Why are we at the museum, Jacque?" A gusty breeze whipped Cleo's hair into her face. Tourists grumbled to the officers at the foot of the steps who prohibited them entering the museum. They suggested trying the Shedd Aquarium a few feet from the Field Museum.

"I want Wind Dancer to meet some people." Jacque moved toward the front doors then stopped, as he watched Wind Dancer staring out at Lake Michigan. His body stood rigid and made the detective think he waited for something to appear. A chill creeped up his back as he observed the Pawnee shift his sight to survey the entire area. Did he sense the skinwalker nearby? He dropped his hand nonchalantly to his weapon and took a long, slow visual scan to survey the area. When he let his gaze land on Cleo, he realized she had already moved up the steps. A whistle to Wind Dancer got him to follow.

"Everything okay, Joseph?" he asked as he joined Cleo who chatted with one of the local officers. She even laughed softly as if she wasn't burdened with the possibility of danger.

Wind Dancer tensed and straightened for a mere second, but Jacque caught the movement and flipped off the strap securing his weapon. He continued to face the lake as he walked up the remaining stairs. Jacque wondered in that moment if the Pawnee might be afraid to look away from the lake and Shedd Aquarium.

With sloth-like movements, Wind Dancer climbed the steps to join Jacque. "He is here. I can't see him, but I smell the stench of death."

Jacque inhaled then shook his head. "All I smell is the wind off the lake. Fishy. Maybe that's what you smell."

"No," Wind Dancer mumbled, scanning the surrounding area once more. "We should go inside," he said, speeding up to catch up with Cleo.

Jacque stood frozen in place for a few more seconds then motioned for a couple of uniformed officers. "Keep your eyes open. If you see someone who looks like me—it ain't. Call me on your radio." They agreed with confusion etched across their pinched foreheads. Jacque continued up the steps to join his new weird friends entering the museum.

He entered the main foyer, surprised at both the quiet and activity. Although the public remained expelled from the joys of natural history, the scientists, archeologists, and numerous other people it took to keep such a place in prime condition and relevant, continued about their daily tasks. The ones who worked with the Native American exhibits received inoculations against smallpox as did other scientists who processed the crime scene from the night Wind Dancer and Neosho crossed over. The CDC continued their due diligence, taking blood samples of everyone present the night everything went to Hell. For now, it appeared they'd dodged a bullet. The good news had come on their way to the museum; both Cleo and Wind Dancer tested negative for smallpox.

When asked why they needed shots, the CDC explained they'd found strains of a rare form of flu virus from some jungle in Southeast Asia. They planted the suggestion it may have found its way to the Field Museum through whoever stole the priceless artifacts from the Native American Exhibits. Since this remained a hub for out-of-town tourists, it seemed prudent to shut down the museum for a few days. The story made a ninety-second blurb on the evening news then it no longer mattered. The gang problem took center stage again.

Seeing Susie, the large T. rex in the foyer, always caused one corner of Jacque's mouth to curve up. As a kid, he'd loved dinosaurs. Watching Wind Dancer see it for the first time amused him even more. The night he'd crossed over he hadn't come through here. Jacque watched as the Pawnee jerked Cleo behind him and fanned out his arms in a show of protection, terror marring his face.

"It's a dinosaur, Joseph," Cleo tried to explain as she pushed down his stiff arms. She slipped her hand into his. "It's okay. These are bones."

"What kind of monsters live here?"

"These lived millions of years ago. This would be a good place for you to learn about the world. My father loved this museum. It gave me a very unique education growing up. Maybe we can explore it together when this mess is cleared up, Joseph. There is nothing alive here to be afraid of."

He stared down at her in concern. "Yet, here I am."

Cleo's eyes widened. "A very good point. I suppose if you can cross over"—she stared up at Susie, the T. rex, with new awareness—"so can something like a dinosaur."

"Well let's get the bogeyman talk over with so we can move on, shall we?" Jacque said shoving past them toward the Native American section. His voice edged with contempt, but Cleo guessed if a skinwalker who looked like her was traipsing around the city infected with smallpox, she might be a little unnerved, too. Probably didn't relish the thought of his double gobbling up souls right and left either. She understood the detective didn't really believe the Indian lore, but, to be proactive, he went along with the possibility of all the madness unfolding around them. After all, he saw the Frenchman himself and how he tried to lure her away and would have if not for Wind Dancer.

"You two are creepin' the hell out of me." Jacque stomped past them.

Cleo offered a patronizing chuckle then tugged Wind Dancer along after her as he kept a watchful eye on the T. rex. When they started to enter the wing of Native America, she noticed he'd spotted two large African elephants at the other end of the grand foyer. Cleo jerked him inside the Native American exhibit before he could begin another litany of questions.

"I know this a strange new world for you, Joseph, but we need you to focus on how we can best track down Neosho. Don't let all this stuff…" Jacque waved his arms toward the main foyer.

"Distract you from our job. Understand?"

He nodded. "Yes. Understand." This section appeared to bring comfort to him as they walked around the exhibits. Sometimes he would touch an artifact or gaze longingly at display cases with mannequins dressed in traditional native costumes. He found the empty case and pointed as Cleo came alongside him. "Free now."

"Free." She took a deep breath and locked onto his warm gaze. "I'm glad, Wind Dancer."

Jacque let out an exasperated sigh then rolled his close-set eyes. "I feel like I'm in some romantic comedy when I'm with you two. This way." He motioned with an impatient wave of his hand.

He led them to the Pawnee earth lodge where a number of people waited. Cleo could see them even before they entered, sitting around the walls of the structure on the crude beds covered in buffalo hides. As Wind Dancer passed through the opening, he stopped abruptly, as they met his curiosity with apathy. A quick head count revealed ten men between the ages of mid-thirties to maybe late sixties. Their features and skin tone, although not as dark, reminded her of Wind Dancer. Modern life had added a few extra pounds on the older ones, and the younger men also bore expressions of boredom.

Dr. Kuzma stood at the rear as if he'd been lecturing to a group of disinterested junior high students. He moved toward the detective in short, jerky movements, rubbing his hands up and down the outside of his pant legs as if he'd eaten buttery popcorn.

"Detective." The physicist spoke with enthusiasm as he extended his hand. "I finished catching the Pawnee delegation up on our discovery."

The absence of expression on their faces reminded Cleo of Wind Dancer when he evaluated his surroundings. The younger ones, even sitting down, were taller than their elders and most likely taller than Wind Dancer. She noticed Jacque shiver as a cool breeze swept through the lodge. She'd experienced the same sensation many times throughout her life. As a child, she'd thought it magical. Now she knew forces other than magic dictated the world. Stepping closer to Jacque, she made room for Wind Dancer to fully enter the earth lodge.

The other Pawnee got to their feet in slow motion and stared in disbelief at Wind Dancer who met their curious stares with his own. Cleo could imagine him on the plains staring down his enemy as he plotted his next move.

"They must look strange to him but somehow familiar." Jacque took a deep breath, speaking out of the side of his mouth.

"He's watching, but his nostrils are flaring like he's smelling them. With all the deodorant, body wash, and shampoos on the market, you think he can detect the real men standing before him?" Cleo wondered out loud.

He appeared formidable as he approached them and sized them up as if they were about to receive his hatchet in the head.

They stood still, letting him evaluate each of them. "I think somehow they know this is no ordinary man." Jacque cocked his head as if fascinated by the encounter.

To the oldest one, Wind Dancer spoke in his native tongue and received only a small nod of recognition. He laid a hand on the senior's shoulder and squeezed. The younger men watched with suspicion and distrust in the way they shifted their weight from one hip to another.

"Jacque, can you sense there may be a wave of intimidation and testosterone flooding the room?"

"Yeah, but they remain respectful even in their silence," he whispered in her ear.

The physicist tried to explain. "Wind Dancer, these men have come here to celebrate the Morning Star ceremony. It is a program set up by Cleo's father." Dr. Kuzma motioned for Cleo to stand next to the Pawnee who appeared to not be impressed with their presence. "This is a Pawnee earth lodge."

Wind Dancer frowned. "I know what it is," he said offhandedly as he moved away and inspected the entire area. He moved to the rear wall and laid his hand on the very area where Cleo had seen someone peek in and motion for her days earlier.

"This is all very confusing for Wind Dancer." Cleo tried to explain his aloofness.

"We wish to speak to him." The older Pawnee shifted his attention to Wind Dancer. "Alone. Leave us."

"Yeah. I don't think that's such a good idea," Jacque quipped as his phone vibrated. He took it out and read the text. "Maybe another time."

"The time is now, Detective. You"—the old Pawnee pointed

to the physicist "must go as well."

"You don't have to tell me twice," Dr. Kuzma said, hurrying out of the earth lodge.

Cleo stood her ground, nudging Jacque. "Go. Take your call. I'll stay with Joseph." A dubious expression flooded his eyes. "I mean it. Go. I know more about this culture than you anyway. You'll probably put your foot in your big mouth if you stay."

"Hey! I resemble that remark." Jacque twisted his bottom lip as if insulted.

"You certainly do, Detective. Go." Cleo laid a hand on his forearm and whispered, "If I haven't already told you, thanks for everything."

He rolled his eyes in impatience and sighed to cover up what she knew to be soft feelings he fought to embrace for his two new friends. "Watch yourself. You guys are a migraine waiting to happen." With his exit, she patted his shoulder.

~~~~

All this feeling of friendship and giving a rip about more than the big picture toyed with Jacque's tough-guy image. He was too old to be taking care of grown people with the reasoning power of two teenagers with raging hormones.

He walked out into the grand foyer and found the café and ordered a black coffee. Pulling out a nearby chair from a bistro table, he could see all the comings and goings of the few people who meandered inside the museum. He set the cup down then took out his phone to check in at the office. While the phone buzzed, he took two sips of the dark brew and wished he'd added cream and sugar to dissipate the crude oil thickness.

"Detective Marquette here. What's up?" He listened, eyes drifting to each person who came too close. "Excuse me. What did you say? Are you freakin' kiddin' me?" he snapped. "On whose authority?"

~~~~

"I am Thomas Two Feathers. They say you crossed over from another time," the older Pawnee said, moving to the center of the room. He motioned for the others to sit down. "Is this true?"

Wind Dancer evaluated the group as he faced the men. "It is true. You seem to be surprised."

"Yes. My father and his father talked about the holes to another place and time when our people roamed free with the buffalo and made war with our enemies, the Sioux and Osage. These holes were forgotten. We do not know how to find them anymore."

Cleo took a seat to stay out of the way and stared at the unfolding story before her. She wanted to drink in the beauty of the past meeting the future.

"It is hard on the other side to find them as well."

"Dr. Kuzma told us how you showed him the openings. How do you see them?"

"I could not so much on the other side. But my friend Dr. Sommers, Cleopatra's father, could see them clearly. On this side, they are visible to me and not to others. We knew sometimes the buffalo disappeared into these holes to hide from us."

"It makes sense," the older man voiced as he nodded in agreement.

"But they always returned. We watched them emerge many times. Those holes do not stay open long and open only after a storm. There are more of them in the spring and summer than times of great cold."

"I want to go there, to see the land of my people."

"It is a hard life, wise one. The jump is hard on the heart." He lifted his fist to pound on his chest.

"I would like to try, Wind Dancer. I could teach my people." He grinned with mischief twinkling in his eyes. "I could warn them to tell the generations to come to buy much land in Oklahoma where the oil is plentiful and then build many casinos." The others laughed, too, and elbowed each other as the warrior cocked his head and furrowed his brow.

The old one held up his hand when Wind Dancer's next words tumbled out quickly in their native language. "You speak our tongue, but most Pawnee no longer understand the words. The modern world has made our children forget and think of other things as important. I am ashamed to tell you this. Even my sons"—he indicated two men in their thirties— "can barely say a few sentences. Please. We must speak English."

"An Osage crossed over to this world. He carries smallpox." The bluntness affected the tribal members as Cleo expected. They exchanged concerned glances with one another. She wondered as they pulled back their shoulders and straightened if it was a century's old instinct when facing an enemy. "I must find him before he infects the city. We may already be too late."

"How can we help?"

"I do not know. Why do you come each year to do this ceremony?"

"To educate the children of our ways. To show them our culture was once strong and full of hope and beauty."

"I am afraid there will be a battle here." He glanced at the others. "She will be the center in the end. All this talk of smallpox puts fear into those who would try and stop the spread of disease. This is in the Osage's plan. While these white men search for answers, he will find a way to return to the past and take Cleopatra with him. It is possible he will have other diseases to carry to our land and could destroy many people. I can't let this happen. He must not be allowed to return or we will be no more. You will be no more."

The older man stood straighter and focused on his delegation as if to evaluate their interest. "How many do you need?"

"The detective speaks of gangs. They are involved and exposed to this smallpox. You could be, too."

"We have been idle too long. It is time we stood up to fight the evil of the world." The elder once again took in the entire lodge then the men who rose to their feet. "You will have what you need, my friend." Cleo stood with the realization something amazing was happening before her eyes. "Our children will know how their fathers, uncles, and brothers fought to save our way of life."

Cleo could imagine them standing on the Nebraska plain, wind blowing through their hair, getting ready to raid their enemy. Their appearance morphed from apathetic men to anxious warriors. The fierce façade and rigid stance created a glimpse into the past when the Pawnee knew no fear of their enemies. A prickle of dread crept into her common sense, hoping Wind Dancer hadn't persuaded these good men to sacrifice themselves for nothing. Would they be up for the task?

CHAPTER 16

"You can't seal off part of my city." Jacque stormed at Colonel Jefferson when he entered the precinct. The man stood waiting in his office, staring out the window as if consumed by thoughts he kept hidden. "And you sure as hell can't order my men around like they work for you, because they don't. This is America not Afghanistan. So get out of my office."

"The FBI called your men in to help secure a six-block perimeter. No in or out."

"You can't keep people from going and coming. People need food, medical supplies, and they have jobs."

"My men are distributing what is needed. Businesses in the area have been closed for the time being. The CDC continues a door to door along with the FBI to see if there has been any contact with members of the Death Apostles. Then they can receive treatment or be confined."

Jacque placed his hands on his hips and separated his legs to form an angry stance then laughed. "You think they're going to talk to you? They're suspicious enough of the police, much less the FBI and other Feds poking their noses into their lives asking questions they think is none of your business. You'll leave soon enough and then they'll have to pay for talking to the wrong people about what they did and didn't say to you." He snorted then rubbed his eyes. "They see the military passing out food and water and they'll panic. Do you want a riot on your hands?"

"Of course not, Detective. But I don't see we have a choice."

"No. You had a choice when you sent those men across some parallel universe with smallpox in their system. Are you proud of the mess you created?"

"Our intentions were honorable, Detective."

"Gee whiz," he mocked. "I feel a lot better, Colonel."

"There's no need to be sarcastic."

The detective rushed around the desk and got in the colonel's face then jammed a finger in his chest. "I'm way past sarcastic, you pompous ass. Get those officers off the street or I'm going to the press to tell them what is really going on."

"In such a move, I'll have you arrested and locked up until this thing settles down. Do you really want to sit in a jail cell with some of Chicago's more colorful residents?"

"Sure as hell beats the company I'm keeping in this office."

The colonel moved toward the door then sniffed as he peered down his nose at Jacque. "Stay out of my way, Detective Marquette. It would be most unfortunate for you to get caught in the crosshairs, if you catch my drift."

He strolled out into the chaos and disappeared into the crowd of other officials Jacque didn't immediately recognize.

"Hey, Detective." A young officer who more resembled a high school band major than part of Chicago PD, poked his head into the office. "Better flip on your TV. Looks like the Apostle neighborhood is up in arms about being detained. Might get ugly by nightfall."

"Thanks, Pete," Jacque said lifting the remote and hitting power.

He listened to a pretty reporter speculate on the situation then interview a spokesman for the mayor's office. From the story being spun, the area went on lockdown due to a terrorist threat. Federal agencies could be spotted going door to door in order to bring the situation to a peaceful conclusion that would ensure residents an opportunity to continue with their daily routines.

Listening to the lines of drivel spewing out of the spokesman's mouth managed to irritate Jacque even more than talking to the colonel. When did hunting a terrorist become commonplace? He had no doubt this would appease the listener as well as the news outlets. They continued to salivate anytime a disaster, negative crime statistics, or mistakes made by his department became a blip on the evening news radar. He hated those guys. Going to them might possibly make it worse.

His phone vibrated a text message waited for him. Thank goodness Cleo had her head screwed on tight.

Where are you? Burgers are here. Joseph is trying to figure out how to kill it.

For some reason the silver lining in all of this was his newfound friendship with two of the most unlikely people he never wanted anything to do with. Strange how things worked out. Although he couldn't be more than a couple of years older than them, he felt much older. This fatherly sense of responsibility toward them annoyed him. Wind Dancer continued to be an accident waiting to happen, and Cleo struck him as a bleeding-heart liberal who wanted to save the world. Not a good combination. His stomach growled as he headed out to meet them at the Chicago style pizzeria and burger joint down the street.

Entering the building with the peeling paint and too much information written on the scrubbed windows, he noticed the silence and the frozen glares of everyone at their table. Normally the place buzzed with loud patrons and calls to fill a new order. The smell of pizza always made him feel at home, but this time he detected trouble. Out of habit, he put his hand on his gun as he scanned the small dining room until his eyes fell on Wind Dancer standing nose to nose with a man a bit taller than himself. He could see the gang colors of the Fifth Street Marauders in the bandana he wore under his Chicago Cubs ball cap. Cleo sat paralyzed, in what he could imagine was fear, as things unfolded into ugly.

Both men glared at each other as if by doing so would somehow make the other back down.

"What seems to be the problem, gentlemen?" Jacque fished out his badge with one hand, careful not to take his hand from his weapon.

They remained mute.

He tried to get Cleo's attention for the sake of clarification. She continued to stare at Wind Dancer.

Jacque noticed a waitress picking herself up off the floor and stumbling toward the counter separating them from the kitchen.

The owner and cook moved to assist her.

"Get out of my way, chief," the tattooed man growled as he jammed a fist against Wind Dancer's shoulder.

With lightning speed, Wind Dancer threw the larger man on the floor then grabbed him by the collar and dragged him toward the door. A patron rushed to open it as the Pawnee threw him out onto the pavement, where he rolled to the curb. Jacque hurried to stand beside him as the man lumbered, dazed and shocked, to his feet only to level a warning glare at his attacker. He took a step forward but stopped, when Jacque exposed the inside of his jacket so he could see his holstered weapon.

"You're lucky today," he fumed as he stormed down the street, bumping into several passersby.

When Jacque shut the door, the room erupted into applause. Wind Dancer, as usual, tilted his head and surveyed the room filled with the sudden noise. When he shifted his gaze to Jacque then Cleo, who beamed a look of hero worship his way, he relaxed his rigid stance and nodded to the others in the restaurant.

"I can't leave you two alone for ten minutes without trouble finding you." Jacque sat down then swiped a French fry.

"I ordered for you, Jacque," Cleo said as the waitress set a plate before him.

"On the house," she announced.

The room filled with chatter as Wind Dancer watched Jacque and Cleo eat their burgers. With caution, he took a sniff then chomped down on his and chewed slowly.

"Good." A drip of ketchup escaped to his lips, and he immediately retrieved it with his tongue.

The three continued to eat as Jacque informed them of the confrontation with the colonel.

"It will not stop Neosho. You saw how strong and quick he can be." He reached for a few more fries. "Then there is the skinwalker."

"What about him?" Jacque took a gulp of diet soda. "He's a spook. No big deal."

Cleo locked eyes with Wind Dancer before nodding to the detective. "You should think differently about that. It is a big deal if he takes over your body."

Jacque shrugged. "Not goin' to happen. I googled it and all I have to do is say his name then shoot him in the head. Easy. Peezy."

"Google? I do not understand. Is this some kind of magic?" Wind Dancer lowered his voice.

The detective choked on his drink then wiped his mouth with several napkins. "You're killing me with this stuff. I keep forgetting you're a babe in the woods here in the twenty-first century."

He frowned. "I am not a baby," he insisted.

"What he means, Joseph, is you have a lot to learn in this world." The corners of Cleo's mouth curved up. "He didn't insult you. Google is how we search for answers on a computer."

"Is this like praying to God?"

Before Cleo could answer, Jacque entered the conversation. "You don't know how close to the truth you've come, buddy." He didn't try to hold in his chuckle.

"Don't pay any attention to him, Joseph." She explained Google and computers in a simple fashion. Jacque hoped to drag out the line of questioning which gave him more enjoyment than he imagined possible.

Wind Dancer directed his warning to Jacque. "You can use the Google magic all you want, but it will not protect you. He can be invisible until it is too late for you to know he is upon you. He means to destroy Neosho. Taking your body will get him there faster."

"Whatever. I'm not going to be looking over my shoulder for this guy. I thought I killed him. I didn't. By some miracle he's strolling about Chicago, scaring the dickens out of everyone, mostly you guys, and is hunting the same bad guy as us. The way I see it, we can use all the help we can get."

"You shouldn't underestimate the Frenchman, Jacque. He is evil and can hurt you."

"I'm more afraid of the stray dog that followed me here." He drained his drink then held it up so the waitress would refill it. "Kept growling at me. I was worried it would bite somebody before I got here. Called animal control."

"A dog?" Wind Dancer snapped. "Jacque, skinwalkers hide in animals. If you see this dog again you must shoot him in the head."

"And have the animal activists down my throat. No thanks.

Those guys really are scary. I'll take my chances with a skinwalker, thank you very much."

"You're taking this too lightly," Cleo moaned.

"How can you, a woman of science, believe in this stuff?"

"There are a lot of unexplained things in this world, Jacque."

"This is pointless to discuss. Our focus should be on catching Neosho and stopping him from spreading a super virus throughout the city," he whispered as he surveyed the room for listeners. "I figure he's probably infected a number of gang members who have taken it to their families. I hate to admit it, but the colonel has a point in setting up a quarantine area. It won't catch him, but at least we'll be able to assess the exposure to others. I hope."

"In two days, it will be time for the sacrifice to the Morning Star. Even though he is not Pawnee, Neosho knows of its power and will try to take Cleopatra."

"Why me?" She covered her mouth in a gasp. "Will he try to sacrifice me?"

"I think he would rather take you with him and force you to be Osage. If he cannot cross, then he may use you another way to hurt me. He knows"—he stole a glance at Jacque before directing his comments to Cleo—"you are very special to me."

Jacque scrolled on his smart phone. "Says here we're in for storms again in a couple of days. These look like doozies, too."

"Doozies?"

"Big. Terrible," he explained. "These kind make grown men shake in their boots."

"Then maybe we can stop him. I'm thinking he will not want to stay here."

"And you, Joseph," Cleo said in an even voice. "Will you stay?"

He took a deep breath, letting a serious expression mask any emotion. "That depends."

"On what?"

Jacque moaned as he ran his hand through his premature gray hair. "For someone so smart, Cleo, you are the dumbest doctor I know." He stood up and grabbed the check to figure the tip even though there was no cost. "He's waiting on you." He headed toward the register to pay the bill as he mumbled a final observation. "You two make me want to throw up." When he returned, he smacked Wind Dancer on the arm. "You and me are going to have to have a little birds and bees talk tonight, buddy."

"I know all about these creatures." He nodded as he stood and helped Cleo to her feet.

"Not these creatures, you don't." He choked through gritted teeth then laughed. "Maybe I should take him down to the red-light district."

"Don't you dare," Cleo fussed as she joined the two men as they headed toward the door. "If anyone is going to teach him about birds and bees a doctor should do it."

Jacque laughed so loud other customers in the restaurant took notice. "That is one lecture I want to be a part of because I have a feeling neither one of you has a clue."

CHAPTER 17

Neosho observed the Death Apostles as they gathered in the dingy garage. Darkness would soon blanket their movements through the streets. The soldiers and police surrounding nearby neighborhoods dominated the conversations, mixed with threats of retribution if anything happened to their families. This he understood.

What the authorities failed to realize was this gang met in another location some five blocks from the quarantined area. Their secure location allowed them to plan without concern for interference. Since such a concentration of law enforcement appeared to be focusing on some terrorist threat, the Death Apostles wanted to make a move on their rivalries for new territory in the drug market. Neosho didn't understand this but agreed to help them make it happen. The fever inside needed an outlet. Maybe a fight would relieve the gnawing sensation something was wrong inside him.

Wind Dancer had said he might be sick. Could it be smallpox? He remembered his beautiful wife and how the sickness ravaged her body, transforming her into a hideous creature before she died. Seeing his children and the others in his village die from this terrible menace haunted him. Why had he not suffered, too? Did he possess some strong magic that protected him?

Then he remembered the visitors to his village—the white men with Wind Dancer. They brought the sickness to his people.

His friend became his enemy. Even the Pawnee suffered the sickness, but it meant nothing. Tracking the white men to the cliffs above the river, he'd realized they disappeared forever. He remembered the few times he'd followed Wind Dancer to a special place where he watched a magical world through a clear wall. For many years, he thought he only dreamed of such a place. When he found his way again to the museum case and stood once again to watch, he saw them, the white men who destroyed his village.

He'd tried to break through, but his body would not move. How had they returned to this land? Could he be dreaming? Why come to such a place? Now they dressed like soldiers and seemed curious about the museum as they searched for something. Neosho wondered if they had been searching for another way into his world. Would they return to finish what they started?

These things about his crossing over still confused him. He did not like this new world where everything smelled of garbage, smoke, and the air burned his eyes. The intense sounds made his head hurt, and the fast things on wheels frightened him. Either this place possessed magic or so much evil that only a sacrifice to the Morning Star would save him. This place was the reason he felt sick.

As the voices around him grew louder, his thoughts returned to Cleopatra Sommers. Like Wind Dancer, he had watched her for a number of years, watching her blossom from a skinny, pale kid into a woman. After his wife died, she sometimes haunted him in the middle of the night.

His friend talked of her whenever they slipped away from their villages. For some reason when she stopped coming to the museum, Wind Dancer concentrated on other matters as well. Only later did he realize Cleopatra's father had crossed over and taught Wind Dancer how to survive this land. He became obsessed with searching for a way to cross so he could take the woman for himself. It compared to counting coup on the enemy. He longed to see this land without the periodically fuzzy film that covered his case.

"You in, Neosho?" Ashanti shouted from across the room as he lifted a beer.

"In," he said, matter of fact, not really understanding what he'd committed to. Talk continued about something called heroin and crystal. Why these things meant money escaped his ability to reason. But if it got him closer to Cleopatra and Wind Dancer, then he would take a chance.

"That's my boy," Ashanti boasted as he moved toward the fierce Osage. "We will take our streets from the Red Tigers and make them pay for stealing our women."

This Neosho understood. "Where are these women?"

Ashanti and the others laughed. He meandered over and slipped an arm around Neosho's shoulders. "Don't worry about it. They'll come crawlin' to us when we take our means of makin' a livin'. Am I right?" He lifted his half-empty bottle into the air, drawing cheers from the twenty or so young men. "Neosho, do you have a piece?"

Neosho had learned not to fully answer questions he didn't understand. Leveling a disgusted glare or show of irritation got him a lot more traction. He removed Ashanti's hand from his shoulder. "No" answered most of their questions. Whatever a "piece" might be would be revealed soon enough.

"Get my boy one, Ty."

Ty brought him a beat-up pistol and eyed Neosho with caution then mumbled from the corner of his mouth. "Do you know how to use one of these?" The hard expression on the man's face revealed nothing. "I bet you don't. You ain't like my brothers. No problem, though. Better let me show you."

He took the gun from Ty and pointed it toward the window where several other gang members stood. They yelled then scattered when Neosho pulled the trigger until it emptied. Ty grabbed the Osage's wrist and squeezed until the weapon fell into his waiting hand. The smell of gunpowder permeated the room. Some of the men lying on the floor to avoid being shot jumped up and barreled toward Neosho, screaming threats and obscenities.

"Man, what you doin'?" Ty snapped as he put himself between the Osage and the angry gang. "Are you crazy?"

Several men bigger than Ty slammed their bodies into him, trying to grab Neosho who stood rigid and unafraid of their intimidation tactics. "He didn't mean nothin'. He's not right in the head is all. Give him some slack."

One chubby man shoved Ty so hard, he staggered then tripped to land on the floor. He tried to bounce up as several of the others ringed him, shouting insults and a call for revenge.

Neosho lowered his head toward Ty who struggled to his feet. Understanding the much smaller man had placed himself in harm's way to protect him caused an unexpected urge to return the favor to flash inside him. When Ty got to his feet, another man knocked him down adding a kick to his side before facing Neosho.

As Ty groaned on the floor, Neosho stepped to his aid. He picked his entire body up in his arms then carried him to a table where he sat him down as gently as if he might break. Ty's eyes grew wide and shoved the Osage's hands off him, but the warrior patted him on the head anyway. Another man jumped Neosho from behind, but the Osage slammed the attacker onto the table next to Ty with no more effort than slapping a pesky fly from his neck.

Ty scooted away from the body, moaning. Neosho stepped in a circular fashion in slow motion to confront several others lining up to charge.

"Who do you think you are?" a muscled man growled before nodding over at Ashanti. "You let this thing in here? What's wrong with you?"

Ashanti folded his arms across his chest, a kind of wickedness toying with the corners of his grin. "I stand by my choice. If you want to throw him out, then you try. I chose Neosho to be my warrior, not you."

The man sized Neosho up and down then walked a circle around him. The Osage stood like a statue, not at all prepared to fight. The man stepped so close their noses almost touched. When the Osage didn't blink, he stepped away, but Neosho grabbed him around the neck and squeezed so hard it immobilized any aggressive behavior. Even when his eyes bulged, no one made a move to rescue him. Finally, Ty slid off the table and laid a hand on the Osage's arm.

"Let him go." Neosho shifted his cold stare to his smaller friend. "Let him go," he repeated, tugging at his wrist.

Neosho dropped his hands so suddenly the man staggered and fell against the table, choking and rubbing his neck.

Ashanti lowered his arms to straighten his shoulders. "Anyone else want to second-guess my judgment?" He waited. In spite of a few grumbles, no further complaint came forth. "I didn't think so. So let's hit the streets and take what's ours."

This Neosho understood. The white man gobbled up land, slaughtered buffalo for no reason, and brought disease to innocent people who trusted them. These ruthless men must have experienced something similar to be so willing to fight. He would fight with them because of Ty and Ashanti who took him in. Later, he would use them to fight his battle as he completed his mission.

~~~~

"I'm not sure about you returning to your place, Cleo." Jacque weaved in and out of traffic like he competed for first place at the Indie 500. "I know you were told everything has been put in order, but from what I've seen of Neosho, he isn't beyond trying to break in again. Even if I posted an officer, which I'm not authorized to do, there'd be no guarantee you'd be safe."

Cleo sat in the backseat with Wind Dancer who for the first time sat relaxed as if he found the ride more interesting than terrifying. "Oh, Jacque," she mused.

Had it really only been a few days since they'd met? Their first meeting had been a turbulent combination of accusations and revelations. He discovered her watching him when he adjusted the mirror. "Don't 'oh, Jacque' me, Cleo. I'd have you stay with me but my place is barely big enough for me."

"Sweet," she sighed.

Wind Dancer joined in the conversation. "I will protect her. I am the only one who is a match for Neosho. Besides, if he is getting sick, then I will have an advantage over him."

"Cleo?" Jacque glanced up at the mirror again to see her reaction. "I mean, I can take you to another hotel if you want. Too many ways in and out of there, though. Too many people."

"I want to go home, Jacque." Cleo laid her head against the seat and closed her eyes. "Joseph can stay. I can make a pallet on the couch for you, too, if you're still concerned. Plenty of room." The weariness hung heavy in her voice as darkness closed in around them.

"What about the skinwalker? He going to be a problem for you, Joseph?"

For the first time, he appeared to take interest in the conversation. "He was my friend."
~~~~

Cleo took his hand. "Yes, but he is not the same person. He may no longer consider you or even recognize you as a friend. I don't know how much my father taught you about these creatures, but they are very dangerous. They can change from animal to human. They want a soul to feed on, and nothing will get in their way until they are destroyed. Why did you bring him to life? I guess a better question is, what did you do to make it happen?"

Jacque whipped into the parking area for Cleo's building then switched off the engine. Turning around in his seat, he addressed the two. "I wondered about that myself."

"Your father told me some of the history and practices of the Navajo. We talked much about the afterlife of many cultures, not just Native Americans. What I know, what I said, belongs to me and no one else. It was not his time to leave. I helped him stay to take revenge if I could. I would not want those words to fall into the wrong hands."

Jacque chuckled and waved a hand in the air. "I can see it now—new TV drama called *Night of the Skinwalker*."

"Do not make light of this, Jacque. You are in danger because he is a mirror image of you. If he takes your body, I might have to kill you." Wind Dancer's voice held no emotion.

This news sobered the detective. "Thanks for the warning. I'll be fine. You two are real downers. You know that?"

"Downers?" Wind Dancer shifted his gaze to his feet on the floor then to Jacque who couldn't suppress a smirk. "Is this another word meaning something different in this time?"

"Yes." Cleo laughed as she patted his arm. "Don't worry about it. Jacque is trying to make us be careful. I'll explain later." She continued with the detective. "You coming in or heading home? The offer is still open. Having two men stay at my apartment will most certainly destroy my good girl reputation. I'm pretty pumped about that."

Jacque opened the car door, shaking his head. "I'm beat. Let's get an early start tomorrow. I'll give you a call in the morning if I know anything. But if you need help, hit number one on your phone. I programmed it in earlier. Then two for 911. Got it?"

They both answered, "Got it," although he doubted either one of them would have time to make a call if trouble came knocking.

"I'm going in to check things out, give the desk attendant

some instructions, and take a final walk through to make sure the building is locked up tight."

Although early evening, it felt much later. The day had consisted of a lot of interviews, fact checking, and the whole FBI-Pentagon thing sucked the stamina right out of a rational person. He could only imagine what his two friends felt. Even the Pawnee who was strong as an ox and possessed some kind of freaky ability to leap-tall-buildings-at-a-single-bound mentality appeared wilted; a good thing since the Pawnee planned to be the pretty doctor's protector for another evening.

Obviously, something brewed between those two, but, so far, it seemed innocent enough. Wind Dancer admitted he'd not "mated" with Cleo the night they spent together and he'd heeded Jacque's warning. But he'd noticed how the Pawnee watched her throughout the day, focused on the way she moved, invading her personal space to inhale her fragrance, letting his eyes caress every inch of her as if imagining something more.

After checking Cleo's condo for any safety issues, he asked the Pawnee to follow him to the elevator. "Buddy, do you remember what we talked about the other night concerning Cleo?"

"Yes. No touching." He glanced over his shoulder as he shifted his weight to one hip. "I think—"

"No thinking, Joseph," he interrupted. "Women here don't like for men to force themselves on them."

"What do they want?" He continued to look like he might break into laughter.

"Romance."

"Like in my time."

"I guess some things don't change, huh?"

Wind Dancer nodded. "Some things don't change. But what is romance here?"

"Geez, Joseph." The elevator doors opened. "I'm not sure Cleo is into you. She finds you interesting. You know her father. You saved her life. She's got this unrealistic idea of who you are. Give it some time." He stopped the elevator doors from closing. "I can't believe I'm saying this, but it's not only about sex."

Wind Dancer gave the detective a gentle shove into the elevator. "You are making more jokes." He laughed at Jacque when he tried to warn him again as the doors closed.

He stared at the elevator doors then down the hall to Cleopatra's place. The joking mood faded as his hand came to rest upon his chest. Even here, he could inhale her scent, the faint smell of sweet grass and rain, and felt the flutter of her heartbeat. He heard her twist on the magical thing called a shower. Imagining her standing beneath the spray forced him to admit to himself he had no intention of heeding Jacque's words. She reminded him of glowing embers that could quickly burst into a fire with the right kind of attention.

The future held too many questions, and the past called his name louder in a land he didn't belong. Those who dwelled in this land of strange machines and powerful enemies could endanger his people with their knowledge on how to cross into his world.

The white man had never been a friend to the people of the Great Plains. They could easily destroy his way of life as well as his people once and for all. The men of his time had tried to destroy them many times with little success. But, like the wind and rain that swept across the plains, the white man's government continued to erode relationships between the tribes and their way of life. He could see where it would end.

Taking a woman like Cleopatra, against her will, to a place and time that could offer her nothing but hardship and disaster, sounded impossible. If he made her his wife, she could die in childbirth, of starvation, or disease in his world. He would sacrifice sharing his life with her if he could have but one night of her surrender.

He moved toward the condo with the stealth of a wolf. "I am sorry, Jacque," he whispered as his hand wrapped around the lever, opening a door to yet another life.

CHAPTER 18

Cleo took longer than her normal routine in the shower. She needed to think—about Neosho infecting hundreds of people, her father and his new life on the other side, the skinwalker, and, of course, Wind Dancer who she called Joseph. The hot water continued to pound her skin even after the creamy soap swirled down the drain and the shampoo squeezed through her fingers for a final rinse. She braced her hands against the tile to keep the heat hitting tight muscles along her shoulders.

How much time before the first infected person showed up at the hospital? Doctors sworn to secrecy by both hospital and federal officials waited for an avalanche of patients with flu-like symptoms. Children posed the highest risk of fatalities then the elderly who thought their vaccinations from the middle of the twentieth century could still protect them. With their already-compromised immune systems, the disease would seek them out like attracting magnets. The dominoes would begin to fall with everyone coming into contact with them: family, health care professionals, grocery stores, and other services.

Then there remained the fact her father remained alive and well in a parallel universe, with a new family. How could he abandon her so thoughtlessly without giving her some hint of what he planned to do four years earlier? He'd left her to grieve alone. She'd even held a memorial for him after a year of no evidence to explain his disappearance. Did she mean nothing to him? Or was it all a mistake he couldn't undo?

Part of her wanted to be angry at the time wasted in distress all those years, wondering if he'd died or suffered. The other part experienced great relief and optimism their paths would intersect again, someday, when she could wrap her arms around him and tell him how much she'd missed him.

The skinwalker scenario left her more concerned. Her father had told her stories about skinwalkers her whole life. She attributed most of it to Navajo bogeyman folktales told to scare the dickens out of young children. Now she knew, after seeing one herself, they were manifestations of real evil spirits moving among the living. At some point, it would have to be destroyed if her father's stories held an ounce of truth. She feared for her new friend Jacque Marquette. If the skinwalker managed to take over his body, what kind of danger would she and Wind Dancer be in? If they destroyed the skinwalker, could Jacque survive the transition back to human?

Stepping out of the shower, Cleo reached for a towel to wrap around her body and hair. Steam covered the mirror as she toweled off then slipped on a white terrycloth robe. She could hear the shower in the other bathroom running and enjoyed the thought of Wind Dancer figuring out the process. Then her thoughts slipped into a more carnal frame of mind.

This attraction for the Pawnee needed to be redirected. Too many things could go wrong with a man like Wind Dancer. Living in another time and place, where women held social status based on how many babies they could produce or how fast they could scrape a buffalo hide, didn't exactly appeal to her. Though she understood Native Americans loved their mates and even honored them, goals and values for women differed vastly from the twenty-first century.

His sideways glances at her during the day, the way he touched her leg with his knee, and the moments he invaded her personal space indicated his attraction to her continued to grow. His smile created creases at the corners of his eyes as they narrowed. Even the faded scars on the side of his neck and jawline brought a desire to touch his face and lips. She hadn't meant to encourage him, but she hadn't dissuaded him either. Seeing him in person drove home how lonely she'd been for intimacy.

After taking over an hour and a half to freshen up, Cleo decided she better think about dinner. She ate most meals at the hospital, so she didn't stock much in the way of the basic food groups. Maybe she could slip downstairs to the adjoining deli. As long as she loaded his plate with meat, maybe Wind Dancer would be impressed. She remembered some condensed vegetable soup in the cabinet and maybe a bag of snack carrots for a side dish. Did she still have some butter-pecan ice cream in the freezer? She thought about the sensory overload when Wind Dancer spooned it into his mouth. Maybe ice cream would be a fun experiment.

With a last glance in the mirror at her faded jeans and long-sleeved T-shirt, she fluffed her straight hair and decided to apply some pink lip gloss. She'd always understood her appearance bordered on earthy rather than beautiful, wholesome instead of memorable, but the way Wind Dancer eyed her almost convinced her otherwise. She'd even caught Jacque taking sideways glances when she'd passed a plate-glass window earlier in the day.

In her line of work, she didn't meet many nice men who weren't covered in tattoos or suffering from a gunshot wound. Then there was her profession. Apparently, her being a doctor intimidated the male ego. So she pretended to be a rock, weathering the storm of isolation and service, to attend to the sick and injured. Relationships never worked out for her anyway. Something always seemed to be missing.

Taking a deep breath, Cleo swung open the door to a darkened room lit only by candlelight. Lights from other buildings added a kind of ambience to the dappled light. The cold May wind off Lake Michigan poured through the open window at the far end of the room. The fireplace flickered, dispelling the cool of nightfall. Soon, the warmth would bathe the room in a kind of coziness needed in such a windy city.

"I grew worried about you. You must show me how to contact Jacque on your talking machine in case I need his help." Wind Dancer emerged from the kitchen, wearing his jeans and a white undershirt. His feet remained bare and his long black hair appeared a little damp.

Cleo envisioned him in a commercial for the military as he rescued puppies from a flooded town to damsels in distress. She tore her eyes away from him as he approached, wiping his hands on one of the antique embroidery towels she kept only for show. "Where did you find all of these candles?"

"I found them in your closet, in a box. I searched for matches like the ones your father brought to my side. You have many of these in this container."

"It's called a drawer."

"Yes. A drawer. I thought you would like this since you had so many candles."

"Thank you, Joseph. I do. Very much."

"I am hungry so I tried to find food. There isn't much."

"Sorry. I'll go downstairs to get us some sandwiches. I won't be long." When she picked up her purse off the counter and moved toward the door, he moved in front of her.

"No. I promised Jacque I would protect you. Neosho can smell you and I think even the skinwalker, since he has touched you, can as well. You will be easy to find."

Cleo noticed he had blocked the door with a small chest of drawers that had belonged to her mother. The door lock still needed some repair, but the furniture blockade should be enough. Earlier in the day the homeowners' association had notified her repairs to the sliding glass doors had been completed, but even those now had her couch as a line of defense.

"Let me see if there is something I can fix for us to eat. I'm warning you, I don't cook much because I don't have a lot of time." She sidestepped him, the warmth of his body radiating against her. "It's easier to eat meals at the hospital."

Wind Dancer followed her into the kitchen and rested against the counter. "Your father says the men today help with the cooking and other chores women do. Is this because they have forgotten how to hunt and fish?"

A chuckle escaped her mouth. "Something like that. We have stores where everything is provided for us as long as we have the money to pay for it."

"These men work hard to pay others for things they could grow or hunt themselves?"

Cleo arranged some cheese and crackers on two small plates with the carrots. "Sounds pretty silly, hearing you say it. My father used to take me to the upper peninsula of Michigan for summer vacations. I never tired of how wonderful it felt to live outdoors, catch our fish for dinner, and cook over an open fire. When we went out west and camped on the reservation, I loved sleeping outdoors and staring at the stars at night. Everything smelled so good and clean."

She brought the plates to the counter and moved out two stools for them. After retrieving two bottles of cold water from the refrigerator, Cleo sat down.

He took several bites before speaking. "This is good. What crunches?"

"Crackers. The white stuff is pepper cheese."

"A little hot to my tongue."

Cleo wanted to say something clever and sexy, but she jammed the last of her cheese and crackers into her mouth and stared out into the living room fire instead.

After moving their plates to the dishwasher, she surprised Wind Dancer with a bowl of ice cream. "Try this. It will take the hot out of your tongue." She handed him a spoon and then demonstrated how to eat the sweet delight by digging into his bowl and shoveling it into her mouth. "Hmm," she moaned. "Try it. It's called ice cream."

He nodded like a little boy and scooped up a big bite then imitated her. Watching him for the first time savor the treat made her laugh. His eyes widened as he gobbled three more bites. "This is better than pizza," he proclaimed, licking the last bite off the spoon. "I like the food in this time."

"If you're not careful, you'll get a belly bulge like a lot of folks around here. This food is pretty fattening." She removed the bowl and spoons to the sink.

"I am not fat." He patted his stomach, drawing Cleo's eyes to the muscles beneath the stretched T-shirt.

"No. You. Are. Not," she mumbled through clenched teeth as he cocked his head, brow furrowed. She pivoted on her heels and escaped into the living room. "The smells of vanilla and jasmine are getting a little thick in here." She waved her hand in front of her nose as she surveyed the candlelit room.

"I will put them out." Before she could stop him, Wind Dancer blew out the candles, leaving only the firelight to illuminate the space. "What is the man doing across the way?" He pointed at the apartment building on the other side of the green space.

"He is dancing," she said, joining him. "He must have music on."

"You can turn music on? I don't understand. This is how we dance." He used his foot to shove the ottoman to the side of the room then chanted and danced in a circle.

Cleo had seen these steps many times at powwows, cultural celebrations at the museum, movies, and celebrations of Native Americans throughout the country. But seeing someone from the past dance without inhibition touched her so deeply she began to imitate the steps. He stopped, straightened to his full height, and smiled.

"Okay you are going to learn how I dance." She selected some soft jazz for the CD player. When the music drifted out, Wind Dancer once again appeared both interested and confused. "This is the way I like to dance."

She stepped up to him and placed his hand on her waist to make it easier to draw him near. "Like this. Slow. Move your feet this way." Her hand slid up his arm onto his shoulder. She chuckled at him, watching his feet. "It will go better if you don't think about it. Just move with me, Joseph." He stepped on her foot, and she grimaced as he jumped away. "It's okay. Let's try again."

"Like this?" He slipped his hand to the middle of her back and drew her closer to his chest, causing her to exhale suddenly. She was aware of his thick, black hair that fell down his chest, pressed between their two bodies. His warm gaze continued as he released her hand. He lifted her arms to circle his neck, locking her into his embrace. "You smell like rain again."

Cleo opened her mouth to speak but the search for words failed as her eyes landed on his wide mouth. "Thanks. I guess." She decided if an award existed for best lame response given in a romantic situation, she'd be given something equivalent to an Academy Award.

"Pizza. Ice Cream. Dancing with you. This is a good place to die." He nodded, his lips pooched together.

"If you say so. Although I'd like to postpone the last item on your list as long as possible."

For the first time since he'd crossed over, Wind Dancer laughed. He squeezed her tighter to his body. "I meant this is a good place. I like explaining to you for a change."

"This must seem all very strange and frightening to you. Do you miss your village?"

"Not at this moment." He continued to smile down at her.

His warm gaze filled her with a sense of belonging. "What did my father tell you about me?"

"Nothing I didn't already know. I probably could have told him a few things."

Cleo remembered spilling her guts a number of times to the Pawnee in the case. The heat of embarrassment flushed across her face. "Hopefully, you didn't share any of my secrets with him."

"No. I kept them to myself." He took a deep breath and transferred his gaze to the city lights outside the open window. "The white man has created a new world I do not understand."

"When you return"—she realized how painful the image made her feel— "you can warn your people and prepare them for the future. They must be educated to hold on to their past so they can share in this world, good and bad."

"Cleopatra?" Wind Dancer stopped moving and lifted her chin so she couldn't avoid staring up at him. "I am not going back, at least not without you."

He lowered his mouth to hers and kissed her, gently at first, as if he feared rejection. Withdrawing, he placed his hands on each side of her face then buried them in her hair.

Cleo jerked him forward so she could kiss him harder, her heart filling with desire. He needed no further encouragement as he caressed and pressed her against the wall. Then he slid from her arms to crumple onto the floor.

Neosho stood over his body holding a baseball bat with a faded Chicago Cubs insignia, in his hand. His eyes lifted from the body to Cleo who stood frozen in fear, calling out Wind Dancer's name. When she tried to kneel, the Osage grabbed her by the arm and yanked her up then slung her onto the couch.

Jumping to her feet, she rushed to the kitchen where she'd left her phone on the counter, only to be cut off by the man who meant to destroy her. As she grabbed the phone, he squeezed her wrist so hard it fell to the floor. He picked it up and threw it into the fireplace.

"No." She tried to escape only to be stopped by his large hand wrapping around her neck. He glanced to the fireplace where smoke poured from the firebox.

Neosho released her long enough to offer a warning. "If you try and fight me, Cleopatra, I will kill him right here. Come with me, and he lives. You decide. Either way, I will have you."

She could see Wind Dancer trying to move as he grunted her name.

"If he wakens, then I will finish him while you watch."

"Okay. I'll go with you. Let me get my—"

"No. We go now." He took her arm and dragged her toward the front door.

The chest had been shoved aside like a toy, and the door stood ajar. The music, dancing, and rising passion must have crowded out any sounds to tip them off of him pushing inside. The thought of Jacque lecturing her about safety concerns came to mind too late to help Wind Dancer. Would he die of smoke inhalation?

"Where are you taking me?" She struggled to free herself from his grip, but he tightened his hold with an added shake.

"Home."

CHAPTER 19

A prickle went up Detective Marquette's spine as he slid into his car after grabbing a sub sandwich at a deli near his apartment. The wind tunneling down his street left him chilled. Squinting, he took in his surroundings, observing the many people who meandered on the sidewalk or sat at window tables of the restaurants lining the streets. Horns honked and the squeak of brakes pierced the darkness, mixed with the occasional burst of laughter or sound of shock, all normal for the city and for this time of night. Still, he experienced uneasiness as he reached up and adjusted his rearview mirror then turned on the ignition.

"Wind Dancer and the woman need you," came a whispered warning at the nape of his neck.

Jacque flinched and stole a glance up into the mirror. Red glowing eyes met his then faded away. He fumbled to find his gun as he turned around in his seat, proving to be an awkward task. A new kind of fear swelled inside him at realizing the skinwalker had touched him.

With nothing visible in the backseat, he released the seat belt and scrambled out of the car, finally able to draw his weapon. He surveyed the area around the car, only to discover a skinny dog, which looked a lot like the same one he'd seen earlier in the day about a mile away. Something about the way the animal stared at him made him reconsider not shooting him. The dog stared down the street, followed by a howl.

Jacque glanced in the same direction to discover what had drawn the animal's attention. Distracted for only seconds, he discovered the dog had vanished. The detective walked around the car then peered behind a couple of trash cans to see whether the mutt was hiding.

He rushed to get in his car, and as he turned the key, called the station. "Need a well-check on Dr. Cleo Sommers, if you have a unit nearby." He offered the address. "I'm on my way there, but I think something might be wrong." After flipping on the flashing red lights, the detective merged into traffic then stomped the accelerator.

Even before he reached the corner to Cleo's building, Jacque heard familiar sirens. Other cars slowed his progress as he laid on the horn only to inch forward until he could see several fire engines coming to a halt outside her building. Leaving the vehicle double-parked, the detective sprinted to the front doors only to find them locked as he'd instructed the desk clerk to do earlier in the evening. No amount of rattling or banging on the glass got anyone to appear. Desperate, he leveled his weapon and fired several times, shattering the glass. The fire captain pushed him aside and reached inside, unlocking and opening the door so they could all move inside.

"Got a call from the tenth floor," a burly firefighter called over his shoulder as he squeezed past the detective.

The desk clerk staggered from the rear of the corridor as the lobby filled with firefighters and a couple of uniformed policemen.

"What the hell happened?" Jacque grabbed the clerk to steady him from falling.

"Dr. Sommers," he moaned rubbing the side of his head where blood trickled from a split ear. "Some big guy dragged her out of here. I tried to help her."

"Was it the man we brought in earlier?"

He shook his head as a paramedic joined them. "No. He looked like him, a little. And he wore a Packer's jacket. I mean, who does that in Chicago?"

"Was she hurt?"

"I couldn't tell, but really scared."

"So you didn't see her friend, the one I brought in this

evening?"

He shrugged. "Not sure about him. I had other things to worry about. Several people said smoke was coming from her floor, and the fire alarm sounded. Everyone tried to evacuate. Didn't see him. I tried to help people out the rear doors. I never made it to unlock the front."

Even before the last words left his mouth, Jacque raced away to the stairwell.

"You can't go up there, Detective," yelled one of the firemen.

"Watch me," he snapped as he flung the door open and took the stairs two at a time.

By the time he'd reached the fifth floor, he had to stop and pant until he caught his breath. Grasping the railing, he pulled himself along for a few steps then tried to make his legs work faster, no longer two steps at a time, promising himself he'd take up jogging again when his life made more sense. Even though he liked to think of himself as fit and trim, too many pizzas, free doughnuts, and beer took a toll on his body, especially around his middle.

When he opened the tenth-floor exit door, the smell of smoke hit him hard. Raising his arm up against his mouth and nose, he raced down the hall to Cleo's condo, where he found the door ajar. Smoke was much thicker in here. "Joseph."

"Here." A figure rose from the floor, coughing and staggering forward.

Jacque caught him and dragged him into the hall as several firemen burst through the exit doors. "This way," he called, lifting his chin toward Cleo's place. "Let's get out of here, Joseph."

Except for the blood trickling down his neck, by the time the two men made it to the fourth floor, Wind Dancer walked and talked as if he hadn't been exposed to heavy smoke. The Pawnee even picked up more speed as they emerged into the foyer, but Jacque forced him to an ambulance where paramedics could administer first aid.

"How did you know I was in trouble?" Wind Dancer sat in the rear of the ambulance and frowned in confusion up at his friend as the paramedic moved on to someone else.

"I think your skinwalker friend paid me a visit." He shivered from the memory but shook it off for Wind Dancer's sake. "I'm going to shoot the damn dog next time I see him."

"You must wait because Neosho has Cleo."

"How did he get the drop on you anyway?"

Wind Dancer diverted his eyes to take in the unfolding scene around him with a certain degree of interest. "I had other things on my mind at the time."

Jacque laid a hand on his shoulder, drawing the Pawnee's attention to him. "I'll bet. See where it got you? Cleo is in real danger. Couldn't you smell him or something weird?"

"I could smell only Cleopatra."

The detective rolled his eyes in disgust. "Really? You decide to get all romantic at the most inopportune times."

Wind Dancer's frown deepened.

"This is your fault. If you'd listened to me and been on your guard, then Cleo would be with us instead of some gangbangers and Neosho. If anything happens to her I'm holding you responsible." He jammed a finger in the Pawnee's chest. He strode away to talk to an approaching fireman then several uniformed officers before pivoting to deal with Wind Dancer.

To his horror, the Pawnee had disappeared.

~~~~

Neosho managed to maneuver Cleo outside the building, but not without having to stop a number of times to try and subdue her attempt at escape. She fought him at every opportunity, knowing this might not end well for her if he somehow crossed over to the other universe. The chances she'd ever find her way home would leave her to be his captive forever. A black paneled van waited for them, complete with sketchy characters who reached out to drag her inside and dump her on the floor.

The smell of cigarette smoke and body odor assaulted her senses, making her already-watery eyes burn. Neosho climbed in beside her body then reached over to slam the door shut at the same time tires squealed and the vehicle lurched forward.

"Ain't you a pretty thing," one man said as he touched Cleo's face and neck.

Neosho grabbed him by the throat and shoved him then reached over to slam his fist into his nose. "No touch." For
~~~~

whatever reason, the Osage helped her to a sitting position next to him. He lowered his lips to her ear and whispered, "I take care of you." He nodded toward the others who returned a murderous glare. "If any of you touch her again I will kill you. Understand?" No response. "Understand?" His growl garnered a reluctant nod.

"This your lady?" A young man in the front passenger seat peeked around to stare at her and let out a whistle. "Woo-wee, Neosho. She's the prettiest doctor I ever seen. How she gonna help us?"

Neosho opened and closed his fist as the van sped out into the night. Considering how speed affected Wind Dancer, the possibility existed the Osage suffered from the same confused fear at all the technology. She hoped hitting him on his softer side would make the next few hours easier on her. With a timid movement of her hand she laid it on top of his and squeezed. Immediately, the gesture drew his eyes downward.

"It's okay," she sniffed softly. Moving closer, she hooked her arm through his to help steady him against the swerving in and out of traffic. Her lips nearly touched his ear to explain until he faced her so she was nose to nose. "It helps," she stammered, "to hold on to something so you aren't thrown around."

He nodded then released her grasp and slipped his arm around her shoulders to hold on tight.

She felt torn between pity and an urge to capitalize on the newfound weakness. In some ways, he was no different than Wind Dancer, a stranger in a strange land, confronted with monstrous inventions no one in his time could have imagined. Perhaps Jules Verne had crossed over and gathered information to create his books. If she lived through this, maybe a little research would explore those possibilities. But, for now, she was trapped with several gang members, dressed to rumble, with an open crate full of weapons pushed near the rear.

"Neosho. Let me go. Better yet, come with me." She dared touch his cheek with her hand. "You're running a fever," she whispered into his ear. "You're sick with the same disease that killed your people."

He frowned down at her.

"I can help you. Save you. But I need medicine to do it." He jerked his head around to snarl at the others who appeared to be trying to listen to the conversation. "I won't hurt you."

Cleo felt his muscles flex as his jaw tightened then released, over and over. Even in the dim light of passing streetlights, she recognized the stubbornness in his eyes.

"No." Something about his voice reminded her of a hungry pit bull.

"You guys are in danger," she pleaded with the other four men in the van.

The fat one chuckled. "Yeah? How ya figure? Seems to me we got all the guns, the chief here, and you."

"He's sick. You've been exposed to the same thing."

"A little cold. No big deal." They all laughed at the absurdity.

"No. It isn't a cold. It's smallpox."

"Had it when I was a kid. Can't get it again," the second man said out of the side of his mouth as he chewed on a matchstick.

From the front, Ty seemed to stretch his neck around. "No. You idiot. You're talking about chickenpox. Smallpox is way badass. Kill you freakin' bad. Somethin' a terrorist would use."

The other three men laughed.

"That's us," Ashanti said as he stopped the van. "So, Miss Doctor, you best keep your mouth shut and not be scarin' my boys about getting sick. Hear? The chief isn't used to this Chicago wind is all. Don't you got some aspirin or somethin' to give him?"

They pulled the van into a dark alley behind a garage. Ty offered Cleo a gentle hand while his friends were piling out. Neosho's focus went to his surroundings and the others while his young friend took care of his captive.

"Are you freakin' kidding me? Smallpox?" Ty mumbled under his breath.

"Yes. He has smallpox. And if you don't get vaccinated soon, you'll have it as will all of your friends. You've got to let me go or better yet, take me yourself to get help. I don't know how to get out of here. Where are we?"

Before he could answer, Neosho grabbed her arm and yanked her after him. "We go inside." She tried to jerk free but he squeezed her arm so hard a whimper escaped her mouth. "We have work to do tonight. You wait here."

"Neosho, you don't want to do this. You know Wind Dancer will find me, and when he does, he will kill you. The police are searching for you, too. It's only a matter of time before they're here."

"What's she talkin' about, Chief?" Ashanti stopped and eyed her then Neosho. "You in some kind of trouble? We don't need the police down our necks any more than they already are." Then he nodded for them to follow as he held open the garage door for them. Neosho continued to grip her arm until they entered then gave her a slight shove of release. Ashanti smirked at his newest recruit. "Then again, maybe we'll do a little payback with Chicago's finest if they come snooping 'round here."

Ty arched an eyebrow as he stroked his chin. Cleo wondered if she could manipulate the young man's concern to her advantage, even if the risk of making a pact with the devil could hurt her down the road. Could she trust him and what would be the price?

She believed Neosho would indeed protect her up to a point; the point being when he either had no more use for her or took her to his universe. Neither option thrilled her. His goal involved making Wind Dancer suffer, and her death might accomplish that, but there remained the chance his primary objective would be to kill the Pawnee. She didn't want the love of her life to die in a rescue attempt. He had risked everything to cross over and find her. The least she could do was come up with a plan to save herself.

"Want somethin', Doctor Lady?" Ty stepped in front of her, and she took a step back and bumped against a table that felt greasy as her fingers braced her for steadiness.

"Some water?" Cleo whimpered. When a devilish smirk toyed at the corner of his young face, she adjusted, straightened her shoulders, and stood erect. "Please. Water." She tried to inject bravery into her tone.

"I'll see what we got." He nodded then moved away toward a dimly lit area of the room.

"What's the plan, Chief?" The man named Ashanti headed up the stairs.

Neosho once more invaded Cleo's space. It was all she could do to keep from falling against the table again, but she stood her ground. "You give us medicine. Where is it?"

"I don't know." As the last word came out of her mouth, Neosho grabbed her around the neck with his large calloused hand

and squeezed. She dug at it, squirming to be free, even as the lights around her dimmed and her strength fled to yet another universe she wasn't ready to explore.

CHAPTER 20

The warm winds of the Gulf of Mexico barreled up the Mississippi River Valley then headed toward Chicago and Lake Michigan. For late May in Chicago, the eighty-degree weather felt remarkable. People jogging along the lake commented they loved global warming and thanked El Nino for the much-improved weather.

News outlets recited their litany of preparedness speeches, which they knew not many would heed. Chicago was more likely to be hit by a blizzard than a series of tornadoes. Even if one did head their way, it generally struck outside the city in some cornfield. With sharp blue skies and warm breezes, the temptation of shorts, flip-flops, and sunscreen lured citizens into a state of complacent disregard for what headed their way. Memories grew short concerning the severe thunderstorms that hit the city a few days earlier.

With the warmer weather, authorities feared people exposed to smallpox strolled among shoppers on Michigan Avenue or along Navy Pier where thousands of tourists gathered every day. City officials discussed casting caution to the notorious winds of Chicago and reopening the Field Museum the following day. The mayor refused in spite of dozens of tourists' complaints concerning their ruined vacation plans. When the bottom line threatened to override common sense, the CDC advised the mayor to stay the course or else.

Short of shutting down the city and making a plea for calm by

Homeland Security and the CDC, they discussed the possibility of pandemonium erupting in the streets if the truth were leaked. Fear and ignorance bred the likelihood of the disease spreading beyond the perimeters of the city; best to keep people in town.

Cleo's friends had been escorted to a safe medical facility and given a battery of tests. They appeared to be disease-free, which meant smallpox had not yet spread to other parts of the country. Even though they were misdirected from the truth, her friends remained in a secure facility in their home cities for their own protection. They received the booster to protect them, as did everyone else on their respective planes. Keeping them sequestered in a medical facility with little or no contact with the outside world guaranteed other populations remained safe.

Jacque rose from the lopsided leather couch against the office wall he'd collapsed onto a few hours earlier after searching all night for the Pawnee and Cleo. They remained in the front of his mind even while he slept. He could smell coffee, sour and strong, and wondered then how it would come across if he had the added sensitivity of Wind Dancer.

"Probably puke," he mumbled as a uniformed officer carried in a Styrofoam cup.

"What? You calling me a puke, Detective?" The officer paused and took a step back. Jacque had a reputation for being a grouch with the young officers.

"Not if that is for me." He wobbled to his feet and grabbed the cup. A few drips sloshed over the rim onto his hand. A swear word exploded out of his mouth as he switched the cup to the other hand. "Any news about Joseph or our doctor?"

"No, sir. Sorry. Some activity about five miles from here with gangs. Not the area with the Death Angels, but thought to be involved."

"Explain." He tried to sip the brew then frowned down at the black contents as if doing so would make it taste better. He set it down on the corner of his desk.

"Confrontation with a rival gang. Something about getting their territory back. Two dead and about seven needed medical attention. A few others treated and released."

"So they ratted the DOAs out? Hard to believe."

"Not exactly. They weren't outnumbered according to one of

the nurses who overheard them talking at the ER. Said some badass Indian busted heads faster than they could make contact. They seemed pretty freaked out about the whole thing. Kept calling him a Packer's Indian so probably our guy. Even street thugs have a little loyalty to the home team."

"None of the DOAs hurt?"

The officer shook his head.

"Interesting."

"Maybe they didn't show up at the ER because they've got your doctor friend to patch them up. There was a break in at a mom-and-pop pharmacy near the area. Took drugs, of course, but the owners say they also took first aid supplies like antibiotic creams, bandages…well, you get the picture."

His phone vibrated on the floor where it had fallen out of his pocket. Chasing it down, he snatched it up and stared for a second at the caller ID. Taking a deep breath then releasing it in a gush, he took the call as he waved the young officer away.

"Detective Marquette." He picked up the coffee again and gulped it like a shot of Jack Daniels then shook his head to free himself of brain cobwebs.

"You sound like hell." It was FBI Agent Farentino. "No luck finding your friends?" The word of their disappearance had traveled to other law enforcement agencies at the speed of light.

"Thanks for your perceptive observation." He let the sarcasm sink in before continuing. "And nothing on Joseph or Cleo. Anything on your end?"

"Maybe. CDC went to the storage facility this morning and found their vaccines compromised. Headed there now. Want to ride along? From what I hear, there is someone on the security tape you might know. They're waiting."

"Meet you out front." Jacque twisted around looking for his wallet.

"You better get those gangbangers vaccinated."

"On it."

The storage facility, located only a few blocks from the precinct, was locked down and crawling with Homeland Security and CDC agents. The nondescript brick building gave no evidence of the contents. When the detective exited the car, he paused and admired the blue sky. The wind seemed a little too calm for

Chicago and gave him an uneasy feeling, a sense of storms headed their way, not to mention the growing ache in his leg.

Would these approaching storms open up more holes to a parallel universe, letting Neosho escape with Cleo? He had to find her before the weather grew ugly.

Several low-level Homeland agents raised their chins in a "what's up" gesture as Jacque and Agent Farentino passed them. Once inside the facility, the CDC woman scurried toward them, winded as if she'd taken a quick run around the block. Her gray-streaked hair still showed the wind-blown Chicago style. Jacque couldn't get past her small rat-like eyes of some undetermined color, so unlike Cleo's pale-green eyes with flecks of gray. He shook it off.

"What you got for us?" Agent Farentino addressed the CDC woman in a cool, polite manner.

Jacque strolled past the CDC woman as if he didn't care about her answer. She jabbed her glasses higher on her pointed nose with a frustrated huff.

"I'll tell you," she said, leading the two men to a computer monitor, "what we got." She offered a snarl toward the detective. "Dr. Sommers broke in here last night and stole some of the smallpox vaccine." Her voice reminded Jacque of a rusty knife scratching on a piece of metal.

He watched the video loop several times before commenting. It was Cleo, all right, with some young black man who appeared to be in his early twenties. He dressed like one of the Death Apostles and seemed a bit more careful around the security cameras than Cleo. It was the man seen with Neosho in the park.

"Didn't the alarm go off?" Jacque glanced toward the woman who had folded her arms across her chest and shifted her weight to one hip.

"No. Dr. Sommers got us this place and knew the code. Guess we know why." The words seem to vomit out of her pinched mouth. "Guess you can't trust anyone these days."

The detective didn't believe in harming women, but for the first time in his life he had the overpowering urge to smack one. Cleo had become a friend. The doctor would not purposely steal lifesaving vaccine. She'd impressed him the moment he'd first interviewed her as both determined and innocent of any crime. It didn't hurt she was smart and easy on the eyes.

Reviewing the security loop, the detective watched the video feed again. Cleo moved at a determined clip, seeking out the camera several times as if she wanted to be recognized. The black guy put his hand between her shoulder blades to keep her momentum on track.

"What are you trying to find, Detective?" The CDC woman snapped then exhaled in disgust.

Both the detective and the FBI agent ignored her.

"No gun, but look here," the agent said, pointing to the man's shirt.

Jacque nodded. "Shirt is too big, and there is a pistol bump. Probably carrying it in his waistband since his drawers aren't falling down around his butt. And here"—he pointed to the bottom of his pant leg—"too fat, probably another weapon, maybe a knife or small caliber gun. Kind of the DOA's signature. They wear boots, and usually there's a sheath sewn around the top or attached with Velcro."

"Is there audio?" the agent asked the CDC woman.

She shook her head no.

"Watch when she faces the camera."

"I see it. She's saying 'help me.' And when she puts in the combination, she's holding up fingers against the door, four, then two then…"

They watched her step sideways and do something else with her hands as the man fumed at her then said something to someone they couldn't see.

"Seems like this guy on screen is a bit protective when he whispers in her ear. Maybe a warning. She doesn't seem worried about him." Agent Farentino touched the spot with his index finger.

"Hmm," Jacque continued. "But he didn't touch her in any threatening way. She nods and tries the combination one more time then puts her fingers like earlier."

"What the hell is she doing?" the FBI agent said, peering closer.

"She's telling us where she is." Jacque couldn't contain his excitement over the discovery. "I think it's sign language. Her old man probably made her learn it somewhere along the way or maybe she had to, working in the ER dealing with every Tom, Dick, and Harry she treated."

The FBI motioned to another agent. "Get Maddox in here. Isn't his sister deaf?" The agent nodded and went outside to make the call.

Jacque continued to watch the loop. It took the doctor three times to get the code right. He wondered if she was scared out of her wits or the stress of the situation made her fumble with the security code, but, either way, the fourth time, the door opened. They disappeared inside and returned in only a few minutes.

"Here. See the shadows here? I'd say there are a couple more of those guys staying out of camera range. The one with Cleo must be the sacrifice." The agent straightened. "He'll get caught and won't give them up. Must be a newbie."

"Okay. They leave the refrigerated room with several boxes that Cleo knows contain the vaccine. The man now decides to protect his face then turns around, lifting the box high enough where only his eyes show. Dumb kid."

Cleo glanced up at the monitor again and made another casual hand motion he hoped would be another clue as to where she might be located.

"Here's Maddox. Let's see what he has to say." Agent Farentino made introductions then played the loop again.

He watched with the same intensity as other FBI agents Jacque knew. Even though they sometimes stepped on his toes and stole cases they didn't deserve, he admired them. They could be serious as a heart attack on most issues and counted on when you needed them. It was the times he didn't need or want them which rubbed him the wrong way.

"Yeah. She's signing, all right. The movements aren't perfect but close. From what I can tell, the message is 421 South across playground. Maybe South Cross playground. The last sign says fish."

"Thanks." Jacque took out his phone and dialed about the time Agent Farentino made the same gesture. He gave some information to the dispatcher and hung up. "Maybe we'll get a call with the location. I told them to put all the parks on the grid where a playground and fish pond are located."

"Ditto." Agent slipped his phone inside of his suit coat. "Our computers might be faster."

Yet another thing to rub Jacque the wrong way about the FBI; their toys of mass communication. He bent over the computer monitor and played the loop again as the CDC woman mumbled her displeasure.

"You can watch it all you want. It's not going to change the outcome, Detective."

Normally he would hurl an inconsiderate and possibly belligerent response to someone who got on his nerves, followed with a reference to questionable heritage. She stepped up her retreat when he leveled a sideways glance, hinting he may not be the one to second guess.

"Detective, we've got nothing." The agent returned with a cup of coffee in each hand and extended one to him.

Jacque accepted the cup as he drew out his phone to check for a text. "Me, either." He took a swallow of the black brew and raised his eyebrows before checking the side of the cup. "Fancy. You FBI jerks know how to live. Guess your pay is higher than mine. What this set you back?"

The agent shrugged but flashed a taunting smirk. "So let's take another crack at the video loop. I'm thinking we missed something."

Setting his cup down, the detective watched with crossed arms then rubbed the stubble on his chin. "Maybe the numbers are something else, like adding them together. Instead of 421, maybe it is 61 or 43. It isn't a playground but a name of a place. Maybe it's fish play or cross fish."

"Oh, I've been there," chimed in one of the security maintenance crew who had set up the system.

"What?" asked both men at the same time.

"Fish Play over on South Cross. Best catfish dinner in the city." He patted his stomach, which spilled over his belt. "A little dive, easy to miss, with a psychedelic fish on the window. My wife doesn't like going there. Says it looks buggy." He added a deep laugh and moved to the other side of the room.

Almost at the same time both men used their phones to call for reinforcements. They instructed the men to stay back until Jacque and Agent Farentino checked out the restaurant. But, after slipping inside during a busy lunch hour and talking to the owner, who was also the cook, nothing appeared out of the ordinary. The owner calmly encouraged them to have a look around so he could continue to work.

"Time is money," he reminded them, and then offered to pack them a lunch to go, on the house. After passing along the rave reviews they'd heard earlier, they meandered up the open staircase, stepping aside only once when a waitress rushed past them with an order of fish and chips.

"Thinking I'm going to take the sack lunch," the agent mumbled as they topped the stairs.

This part of the dining area had fewer customers. Several stood to leave when the officers didn't seem to be going to sit down and order. Jacque stood at a window overlooking the back of the property, admiring a series of row houses, all with nondescript one and two-car garages. This time of day things were quiet, with little or no activity. A workday, even in this neighborhood, housed hardworking folks who probably had a tough time making ends meet.

Some reports had the Death Apostles in and out of this area, even though it was on the fringes of their known territory. Most of the gangs he'd come in contact with liked to leave some kind of signature of their domain. The detective likened it to a dog marking its territory. He didn't shy away from expressing his opinion concerning shiftless gang members who preyed upon neighborhoods with their street justice, drugs, and intimidation of good people who needed a break. They became the mangy dogs of society.

"Anything?" Agent Farentino came alongside the detective.

"Maybe." He pointed at a rundown garage with an upstairs. "Other side of the alley. Single-car garage, peeling paint, only one with no usable rear window."

"What about it? Looks like every other crap hole on the block. Guess the street hasn't been part of the urban renewal you see out front."

"Except it appears to be a little worse at a glance. The back window has been covered up with paper from the inside. The gate leading to the yard is iron not wood. Probably creaks when anyone comes through. You can see the side door pretty clearly, and it isn't wood like you should find. More like steel or some other kind of reinforced material, a gray or metallic color. My mother had one put in her basement, thinking it would be hard to break in. Pretty much the same kind of door."

"I don't think I can get a warrant on your train of thought." Agent Farentino sighed.

Jacque kept staring out the window but let a lopsided grin take over his mouth. "You FBI boys always this law abiding?" The agent remained passive. "I'm pretty sure I saw an Indian wearing a Packers jacket goin there."

The agent took out his phone. "You're talking my language. Let me see what I can do."

"In the meantime, I think I'll stroll over there. Need to stretch my legs." The detective ignored the agent, holding up a wait-for-me finger and followed Jacque like an obedient puppy.

CHAPTER 21

"Wind Dancer?" Two Feathers sounded surprised as the Pawnee emerged from out of some bushes behind the Field Museum.

It was apparent he'd slept on the ground with dead grass clinging to his long hair. With his movements, slow and unhurried, he dusted off his body, head to toe while closing the gap between him and the tribal representatives.

"How long have you been waiting here?" Two Feathers nodded toward one of his sons who fished out a bottle of water from his backpack and handed it to the yawning Pawnee. Two Feathers stood with a kind of stoic resolve as did the others. Two Feathers knew they envied the man from the past; their past, they would never know except through books written by anthropologists, historians, and screenwriters. "Are you hungry?"

"Yes. Do you want to hunt with me?" Wind Dancer surveyed his surroundings then narrowed his eyes against the sun. "There is not much to make a cooking fire."

All the men but Two Feathers snickered until their leader leveled a threatening glare. "We can't cook here. There is a place inside we can get something."

"Yesterday I ate hamburger and before that I had pizza. Do they have pizza?"

The older man smiled like a patient father. "Maybe we will find something healthier."

"Okay, Two Feathers. We are brothers so I trust you." They climbed the wide stairs leading to the doors. "I need your help, too."

"How can I help?"

As they passed through the rear-facing doors of the Field Museum, the old Pawnee listened to Wind Dancer explain what happened the night before when he'd lost Cleo. He showed little emotion other than the flat threatening sound of his voice when he spoke.

"I can feel a great storm coming. The opening to my world will return. Neosho must feel this, too, as I do. Now he has Cleopatra and will try to leave here. She could not survive such a land. Our ways, as you know"—he nodded to the entire group as if they were one with him, as if nothing had changed in one hundred fifty years among the native people of North America—"are for strong men and women. Cleopatra is like a flower, beautiful, but without tender care she will fade and die. Even her father struggled at first, but had prepared for the possibility of parallel universes his entire life."

Two Feathers pondered on this information, struggling with the realization they, too, may not be up to such a transition. The night before, they'd discussed with excitement of crossing over if the opportunity presented itself. They all agreed; they would jump at the chance to be on the front lines of their history in hopes of changing the winds of time.

The coffee shop opened right as they stood with some other museum employees. Two Feathers ordered two fruit parfaits, muffins, juice, and two coffees. After arranging the selections on a tray, he took out money and paid.

"I have no money." Wind Dancer felt his pockets and withdrew a few dead leaves from the bush he'd been sleeping behind.

"My treat." Two Feathers nodded toward a table big enough to seat his entire group and set the tray down.

When his new friend made no attempt at taking any food, he opened the parfait and demonstrated how to eat it then lifted the paper from the muffins. Opening the juice box gave Wind Dancer the most trouble, but he drank it down in one gulp followed by a loud, "Ahh."

"Sweet. The food in this time is good. Is this why everyone is so fat?"

The men laughed and Two Feathers couldn't resist joining in this time. "Yes, I believe this is part of the reason. Men do not work hard with their hands like long ago. The land is full of concrete where buffalo, elk, and white-tailed deer fed our people. Today, we hunt bargains at grocery stores. We need permission to hunt and even then, it can only be certain days of the year. Men of all colors will soon forget how to work the land in order to feed their families."

"This is very bad news for Pawnee." He popped half a muffin in his mouth then held up the other half for closer examination before finishing it off. "But these are good." He grinned at his new friends. "I will have to tell Cleopatra to buy these." He stared thoughtfully into the cup of coffee. When he lifted his eyes, they no longer hid his concern and heavy sadness. "I must find her before Neosho… She is in danger."

"Tomorrow is the day of the sacrifice to the Morning Star. We have planned this for people to come experience the blessings and the spiritual awakening given to us from long ago."

"Do you have a human sacrifice?" Wind Dancer sounded surprised.

"No. Such things are against the law, and was even in your time. I am surprised you don't know this."

"Yes. The government of the white man tried to stop us. I did not like the sacrifice and insisted my village stop the practice. Some did not approve, but I believed it to be a serious waste of life. We continued the ceremony each year without the human sacrifice in my village. But even we used a captive for this purpose. Neosho witnessed this ceremony on several occasions. In my opinion, he enjoyed it too much, in the wrong spirit of the ceremony. He thinks it holds magic and gave him new strength. I never did. I believed it holds a closer walk with the spirits who guide us."

Two Feathers chewed his bottom lip as he turned this information over in his mind. "Does he know we are here and what we are planning?"

"We have watched your programs many times"—he pointed to the Native American Exhibition hall—"through the glass cases.

We were not close enough to see your faces."

"I have led this ceremony for years. My sons come with me each time."

Wind Dancer shifted his observation to the sons, eyeing them head to toe. "Neosho will know the time of year has come. Both of us are different here: stronger, more sensitive to the world around us. If he comes here with Cleopatra, you could be exposed to smallpox."

The delegation of Pawnees began a rapid disjointed conversation of concern.

"There is a vaccine." He rolled up his sleeve to show the slight swelling on his upper arm. "The CDC has this. Detective Marquette can get this for you. If you take it today, I'm told you will be protected." He told the story of how Neosho, and the military had been affected with the disease.

"I still don't understand how we can help you. Shouldn't the police handle this?" Two Feathers held up his hand for the others to be silent.

"They cannot stop Neosho. There may be others with him from gangs of this city. With them at his side, there will be much trouble. Detective Marquette says they are dangerous. If this is true, then we will fight."

The group shifted in their seats to stare at their leader, Two Feathers, to see what his reaction might be. The older man laid his weathered hands upon the table, sitting as if he'd become stone. Wind Dancer did not break his senior's concentration.

Two Feathers finally shook his head. "Thank you for waiting with respect. You of all people know that time means little to people of the earth lodge. I cannot speak for them, but I will fight if needed."

One by one, the other men voiced support.

"But I want something from you, Wind Dancer." The words flowed like warm honey.

"I stand willing to help my brothers."

Two Feathers cocked his head at his delegation with some unspoken question. When his oldest son nodded then his youngest, he closed his eyes and tilted his face toward the ceiling. "We want you to take us to the other side. Let us warn the people of the earth lodge what is coming."

"You might never return home."

"We are going home."

Wind Dancer sat silently as his Pawnee brothers talked among themselves about the possibilities that lay before them. He listened to their enthusiasm and longed to tell them of the dangers in the land of their ancestors. Yet he missed the wind songs rushing across the plains and the sound of thundering buffalo as they brought life to his people. The smell of a cooking fire and the taste of meat he'd hunted made him homesick. Would these men love the land they claimed was part of their heritage?

The warrior stood to his full height and raised his chin, his dark eyes narrowed.

"What is the plan?" asked Two Feathers.

"Tomorrow, on the dark side of morning, we sacrifice Cleopatra Sommers to the Morning Star, to save this land and preserve the land of our fathers." He knew in his heart the price of saving Cleopatra would also mean losing her.

Two Feathers stood, followed by the rest of his delegation. "Tomorrow, we paint our faces for the first time."

"You must be ready to cross."

"I have been ready my entire life, Wind Dancer." The senior somehow stood taller than usual, proud to be a Pawnee.

~~~~

"Where are we going?" Cleo found herself in the van again, surrounded by several thugs who had decided to ignore her after Neosho's threatening posturing toward them earlier. Only the one called Ty dared speak to her. Neosho sat on the floor next to her like he stared into a campfire on the plains one hundred fifty years ago.

"Ashanti thought our place might draw attention if anyone saw you. You don't exactly fit the description of the ladies who come and go there." Ty chuckled and elbowed one of his friends without getting a response. "So, another place. We're going to make a couple of stops first to pick up supplies."

Cleo eyed two of the men she'd bandaged up the night before
~~~~

when they'd returned from some kind of altercation. A great deal of excitement and bragging about how they'd taken back their street and taught their rivals a lesson had continued through the night. What she did know was a number of other people had been exposed to smallpox since Neosho participated in the rumble. They spread the possibility of infection to a hospital full of compromised immune systems. She hoped Jacque figured out the seriousness of the situation and had the CDC heading off yet another disaster.

It had been a terrifying night, locked in what felt like a closet, tied, with duct tape over her mouth. Forced to break into the CDC storage facility, she'd set up for the lifesaving vaccine, she stole only one small box, convincing Ty the other boxes needed to cure another two days before they would be ready. He bought the lie, she guessed, because he worried about his own health and the possibility the police would swoop down on them any second. Because of the heavy security system in place, no guards patrolled the area. Thanks to her knowledge of the system, passwords, and codes, she slipped in without setting off any alarms or getting herself killed.

She'd begged Ty to release her, but Neosho stood nearby whenever anyone came too close. The others continued to be intimidated by him. He may have suspected they plotted against him, but showed little concern. Even after they'd returned from the street fight and she'd patched them up, no one dared linger. If they killed Neosho, her prospects of a safe return grew slim. She'd seen too much.

The van lurched to a stop, and in seconds everyone climbed out into a grungy alley at the rear of an apartment complex smelling of sewage. They hurried inside a storage area where some of the men she'd given first aid waited. This area of the city seemed more familiar to her. In spite of landing in a spot needing a fresh coat of paint and a good scrubbing, she knew the Field Museum couldn't be too far, maybe a few miles as the crow flies. If she could escape, then maybe she could reach help before something else went wrong.

"What do you plan to do with me, Neosho?" She couldn't keep from shuddering at the images plaguing her.

He stood still next to her, observing the inside of the building as others moved about, claiming a spot to rest. When his eyes landed on her, he seemed to remember her presence.

"I will take you to my time." He grabbed her elbow and led her into a shadowy corner. "You will be my wife." He stared at her face then her body as his hands came up to touch her hair and face. "Very soft."

She tried to step away from his touch, but her actions only managed to bring him closer. "You don't even know where or when you can cross to your time."

"Soon. I can feel it." A twisted smile spread across his mouth, chilling Cleo. "I will make Wind Dancer pay for his mistakes. He brought the sickness to my family. I will take what he wants most. You." He stole a glance behind him and frowned. Cleo noticed Ty watching him. "I will want sons. You will give them to me."

"I will never be your wife, Neosho. I can never love you."

"You don't have to love me, Cleopatra, and you will be my wife."

"Wind Dancer will never let you take me."

This made him chuckle. "He has two choices: I take you to be my wife or, by my own hand, I sacrifice you to the Morning Star."

Cleo cowered against the splinter-ridden wall, feeling the flood of fear wash over her. The choices left her with little hope of surviving. She tried to put on a brave face and took a deep breath. "I won't go. I'll fight you with every ounce of strength in me."

With the slowness of a boa constrictor, Neosho wrapped his hand around her neck and squeezed tight enough to make her paw at his hands. "I like a fighter, Cleopatra. It will give me pleasure to break you." He loosened his grip only enough to pull her to his body where he crushed his mouth against hers. She could barely move, but her breath came in gulps when he released her. "Hmm." He moaned as he pressed his thumb across her bruised lips. "I do not want to kill such a fine woman." Another evil expression widened his mouth. "I think, before we cross, I will make Wind Dancer watch what he will never have." He shoved her against the wall, causing her to grunt.

"Hey, man. You don't want to hurt the lady doctor. She patched us up." Ty glanced over his shoulder at the others who had perked up at the commotion in the shadows. "They might not help you if you start messin' 'round with her."

"She belongs to me, not you or the others. I will do as I

please."

Ty moved a little closer and peered around the large Osage at Cleo who rubbed her neck, tears trailing down her cheeks. "Maybe so. I'm just sayin' you better be careful. These guys think they owe her for last night. Okay?"

Neosho evaluated Cleo with one swift glance. "Okay. You watch her. I will rest."

"Sure thing, bro. You rest. I'll make sure the lady doctor stays put. Go on." He nodded toward the others who had either slouched down on a couple of worn-out sofas or stretched out between chairs.

When he moved away, Ty approached Cleo and held his finger to his lips. "Shhh. Don't cry," he whispered. He knew the Osage's senses were more acute than any other human. He mouthed the words, "I'll help you."

CHAPTER 22

Jacque gave the okay to kick in the door, with backup spread out to cut off any retreat of the Death Apostles, but they came up empty. The one thing they managed to accomplish was to stir up dust and mold spores. Agent Farentino had a sneezing fit.

"Nothing," the FBI agent said, holstering his weapon.

"Yeah. But this is the place." Jacque pointed to trash, beer bottles, and fast-food wrappers. "But here is the best evidence." He pointed to an empty five-gallon paint bucket with bloody bandages and empty vaccine vials. "I guess Cleo administered first aid after all. Must have taken it on the chin a little more than we first thought."

"I'll get my forensics team over here to collect evidence." Jacque arched an eyebrow of discontent forcing Farentino to add, "Bring your guys in, too, if you want. Make sure they stay out of our way."

"Screw you," he barked. "If it weren't for me, you'd be eating fish instead of getting a new lead. Stay out of our way."

"This isn't a pissing contest, Marquette," the agent growled after being put in his place.

"Just get it done." He ordered everyone to tread lightly so as not to compromise the crime scene and shooed unnecessary officers outside. After moving around the downstairs, he took the stairs to the second level. Agent Farentino joined him.

"My team is headed this way." Agent Farentino moved to a window overlooking the yard between the house and garage. They waited for a second warrant to search the house. "I didn't see the dog when we came in. Think someone let him out of the house. Nobody answered when Agent Crosby went to the door."

Jacque came alongside him and spotted the same pathetic mutt that had been stalking him. He tapped on the window until the dog spotted him. He jumped around, like a puppy, barking his head off.

"No. He's not from the house," he mumbled in a low voice, afraid for the first time of what the beast might be and wondering whether to put a bullet in its head like Wind Dancer instructed. Too many people around to put the beast out of his misery, he reasoned.

"How do you know?"

"Saw him over at the fish place," he lied. "Probably followed us. Geez, we smell like fried hush puppies. I'm surprised the entire canine unit hasn't taken off our legs." They continued to stare down at the prancing animal.

"Speaking of the canine unit, look at those two German shepherds cowering behind their handlers." He snickered. "Some police dogs you got there, Marquette."

The skinwalker hiding inside the dog wouldn't be going anywhere anytime soon. The detective noticed some discarded duct tape by a chair tipped over on its side. Careful not to compromise evidence, he removed a disposable glove from his jacket and picked it up.

"Find something?"

"Duct tape. There are a few strands of hair attached, same color as Cleo's."

"Then she's alive." The agent could have been reading from the phone book.

"We need to find Wind Dancer. Maybe he'll know what Neosho might do next."

"Well, I'm all ears on finding him. So far there's been no sign of him. Even put a call in to the Field Museum."

"And?"

"Got put on hold after listening to 'our menu options have changed' ten times."

"I've got a few ideas. Can you finish up here?" Jacque figured the Feds could handle this end. No use sticking around when he could be doing other things.

"Don't leave me out of the loop, Marquette."

The detective handed off the evidence before heading down the stairs. "Wouldn't think of it," he mused with a smirk, even as the agent trailed after him. "You Fed boys are certainly paranoid."

"That's why we get things done," Farentino quipped. He slipped the duct tape into an evidence bag once downstairs. He gave some instructions to Agent Crosby as he continued to trail the detective.

"You keep saying silly things like that but it doesn't make it true, Farentino." Jacque called for someone to drive his car around to the front of the property then slipped the phone in his pocket.

"Agent Farentino. Would it hurt you to show a little respect?" The agent halted when the scruffy dog trotted up to Jacque and pranced around like he expected a treat. "Are you sure you don't know that mutt?" The animal sat down and growled at the agent.

"Positive." He glanced down at the dog but continued toward the street where a uniformed officer stopped his car and got out.

"Where are you going?" Farentino sidestepped the dog and followed.

Jacque braced one hand on the car and opened the back passenger-side door. The dog barked again as he looked in the direction of Michigan Avenue. For a split second he wondered if the skinwalker tried to tell him something. Even though he planned to head to the museum, Jacque preferred the FBI not know his every move. "Gotta see a man about a dog, Mr. FBI. Do you mind?"

"Way too much information." He frowned.

The detective opened the door and watched the dog trot up only to sit down quietly as he focused his red eyes on him. "Are you comin'?" He raised his chin while cutting his eyes to the inside. The dog jumped into the backseat. Shutting the car door, Jacque hurried around the front to get in before he changed his mind.

"So you're a softy for animals," the agent mocked as he bent down to peer inside the car.

Jacque powered down the passenger window in the front seat and leaned over to speak to the agent. "Let me know if you learn anything." A gust of wind shook the car as the agent bowed his head. "News says we're in for a rock-and-roll night in the weather department. I'll keep in touch."

"Same here." When the dog pressed his face against the glass and bared his teeth, the agent laughed. "That is the ugliest dog I've ever seen."

Jacque adjusted his rearview mirror to check on the dog. In the same instant the animal met his eyes.

He turned the car key on and felt it come alive then eased away from the curb. After finding a place to make a U-turn, he headed out onto another side street. Traffic was always more manageable in a small neighborhood comprised of shops and duplexes under various stages of rehab.

When a sigh came from behind, he checked the rearview mirror to discover his twin staring at him. The skinwalker dog had transformed into the Frenchman.

<p style="text-align:center">~~~~</p>

"I think Neosho is kind of crazy in the head, Cleo," Ty whispered as the Osage sat on the floor in a vacant corner of the room. "All these guys are crazy, Doc."

"What's going on? And why are they taking orders from Neosho?" She rubbed her hand across her bruised lips, an attempt to wipe the still-rough touch of the Osage away.

"Because they're scared of him and envious at the same time. Ashanti, the guy snoozing on the table, thinks Neosho is some kind of enforcer for him. We gained a lot of territory by putting those guys in the hospital last night. They won't be messin' with us for some time. Neosho over there would have killed all of them if he'd had time, but they ran off like a bunch of scared little girls." He let loose a nervous snicker. "Truth is, he scared me, too. That guy is crazy strong."

"Why are we here?"

"Neosho says if we go to the Field Museum there will be money, maybe even some gold."

"That's ridiculous. They keep only enough money to do business, nothing more. I grew up in there. I should know."

"So why would he try and trick us to go?" Ty's gaze darted to

Neosho.

"The police want him. He's sick and infecting everyone he comes in contact with."

"But you gave him the vaccine, too."

"It won't work on him. He's already infected and running a fever. I felt it when he kissed me," she said touching her neck and face. "This is a mission of revenge. He wants to kill my friend because he blames him for the death of his family."

"I can't believe I'm saying this, but why didn't he go to the police?" The bewildered expression on Ty's face forced Cleo to pause before answering.

"He's not from around here. He doesn't trust the police and I believe he wants to return home." A radio playing hip-hop music switched to giving a weather report of storms moving in later in the evening. Cleo imagined with Neosho's heightened senses he could already feel the pressure changes and knew this would be his chance to cross over to his home.

"You've got to get me out of here," Cleo begged.

"And let the police haul me off to jail? No thanks. These guys have a long memory and that's all I'd be if I let you go or betrayed them."

"Come with me. I have friends at the FBI and Chicago PD. You don't want to be with these guys when they come for me."

The young gang member chewed on his bottom lip as if mulling over the idea for the first time.

"Please. I can help you. Do you really want to be a part of this? Neosho is a killer, and he doesn't care who gets in his way."

"How does a fine lady like yourself get mixed up with a guy like him anyway?" He stole a glance over at Neosho as if in awe of the man with abnormal strength.

"Shh. Keep your voice to a whisper. He can hear us if our voices are much louder. Come closer," she coaxed with a nod. "He's not like us."

He stepped closer, a grin toying with his mouth as his eyes widened in interest. "You one of those women who like the bad boys?"

Cleo hesitated at his accusation but decided to use it to her advantage. "I used to be but not anymore." She didn't want to give Ty any false hopes of hooking up with her. "He used to be different. If I tell you the truth, will you help me?"

"No. I have a feeling the words comin' out of such a pretty mouth are going to confuse me." Ty stole a glance over his shoulder at the others snoring. "Neosho wants to head to the museum during the night. Says there will be some kind of magic that will help us get the gold."

"And this makes sense to you?" Cleo frowned. "He's talking about the sacrifice to the Morning Star. And who do you think the sacrifice is going to be? Me, that's who. It's always a female who gets the bad side of a deal."

"Nah. He likes you."

"Doesn't matter. The ceremony has great power for Native Americans. If he doesn't use me, then he'll use someone else, maybe someone at the museum. Do you really want to see somebody get sacrificed to some Morning Star deity?"

"Hell no. My grandma is a Baptist. She'd whip me with a belt."

"Please. I'm begging you. Get me out of here before it's too late." She stepped closer so her breath touched his face. "You aren't like them." For a split second, he appeared to get lost in the close proximity of her body and the penetrating gaze of her green eyes.

"I dunno—"

Before he could finish the sentence, Cleo grabbed his gun from his waistband and jammed it under his chin.

"Careful there." He spoke through gritted teeth with bulging eyes.

"Get us out of here."

"All I have to do is call to my bros."

"And all I have to do is scream for Neosho. What do you think he'll do to you if he thinks you've put your grubby hands on me?"

Ty remained silent, so Cleo continued. "He may want me dead in the end, but he will protect me until the time is right. Heaven help you if he decides to make an example of you or anyone else here tonight." She jabbed the gun up, making Ty catch his breath. "What's it going to be?"

He nodded and dared to slowly lay his index finger on the gun to reposition her hand. "Careful, Doc," he mumbled as she stepped sideways with the weapon pointed at his chest. "Okay. You owe me."

Cleo chose to force her brow to crease in hopes it displayed a kind of toughness.

~~~~

Two Feathers expected the press to converge on the Field Museum to take pictures of the recent crime scene. The Ceremony of the Morning Star also got a sixty-second sound bite with an interview with him showing them preparing sacred bundles at the earth lodge. An invitation to the public to come enjoy the ceremony over the next couple of days wasn't near as interesting as when the reporter focused more on the recent stolen artifacts than the actual ceremony. At this point, the old Pawnee focused his attention on the possible journey ahead of him.

Fortunately, the bigger story remained the weather; storms that rumbled across the plains like an out-of-control locomotive. From Nebraska to the Great Lakes, dire warnings of destructive tornadoes popping up led to charts on how to stay safe. The warm, moist air from the Gulf of Mexico continued some kind of terrifying dance with the cold air of the north as it moved across the map. All of this kept tourists and locals away. The Cubs game canceled in hopes of protecting people who didn't have enough sense to come in out of the rain. Then, one by one, other attractions announced they, too, were closing in hopes of keeping folks home or safely tucked into a hotel.

"Two Feathers, everyone is going home to wait for Stormageddon." The Native American Curator examined the work the Pawnees had accomplished before catching a glimpse of Wind Dancer standing near the platform built outside the earth lodge. "I don't remember him, although he is vaguely familiar." He moved toward the Pawnee but stopped when the warrior disappeared into the earth lodge.

Two Feathers stepped in front of the curator to block his line of sight. "Our work is not done. Can we stay longer?"

The curator tilted his neck to see Wind Dancer, but shrugged with the inquiry. "I thought you might ask. Sure. The two security guards patrol every thirty minutes. Most of the place will be locked down." He nodded toward some cameras. "You'll be watched the
~~~~

whole time and recorded so if you need anything, give them a sign. Hopefully they won't fail like they did during the last storm. Lucky for us the place was full of police."

"Lucky."

After checking his watch, the curator shook Two Feathers' hand. "See you tomorrow. With any luck, we won't get blown away."

"With any luck, we'll have already gone home," he mumbled under his breath as he watched the man leave. He laid his fist on his heart and closed his eyes until he felt a hand on his shoulder.

"Are you well, Two Feathers?" Wind Dancer joined him.

A thin smile spread across his lips. "Never better. My heart and soul can hardly wait for the moment when I see the land of my fathers."

Wind Dancer spoke with a kind of sadness. "It is not an easy life. But you will be free of this world's trappings. I'm counting on you to teach our people the ways of the future. When the senior Dr. Sommers speaks of this, they do not always listen. They think he is a storyteller. But with you, I hope they will believe."

Two Feathers nodded as his eyes moved toward the earth lodge. "We will do what we can." He noticed the warrior lift his chin as his hands went to his ears. "What is it?"

"I'm not sure. Pressure."

"Storms are coming. I don't feel anything. You are very sensitive to change here."

"We are running out of time. I must find Cleopatra. I also need to reach Detective Jacque Marquette. Can you help me with this?"

He carried his cell phone in a shirt pocket. "Let me show you how it's done. I won't be needing this much longer. If you ever return here, then you'll know how to use it." He punched in some numbers. "Yes. I need to speak to Detective Marquette."

CHAPTER 23

Darkness fell enough to make streetlights flicker to life even though the time indicated early evening. The weather hinted at the things to come. A quick thunderstorm blew in, lasting only ten minutes before the setting sun peeked out. Black clouds appeared to swim across the surface for seconds at a time.

Jacque kept one eye on the congested street and the other on the rearview mirror to keep track of the skinwalker's movements. He sat like a statue staring at him, eyes glowing from red to opaque then to a shade of blue that matched his own. The detective wondered if he remained quiet because his former life knew driving in rush hour traffic required a great deal of concentration. When his cell phone vibrated in his pocket, he flinched but managed to answer.

He listened to dispatch inform him someone at the museum wanted to speak to him as he initiated his flashing light and whipped his vehicle into a lane where he could make better progress.

"Patch him in," he instructed as he glanced at the skinwalker who smiled at him. A chill crept up his spine. "Yeah. What can I do for you?"

"Jacque, is this your voice?"

"Wind Dancer." He shouted his friend's name in relief. "Are you at the museum?"

"Yes. I couldn't find Cleopatra. Have you found her?"

"No. But Neosho has her and is hiding among some gang members of the Death Apostles. I'm heading your way." He glanced in the mirror at the skinwalker again. "I'm bringing a friend of yours."

"I do not understand. I have no friends but you and Cleopatra."

Someone pulled in front of his car, causing him to slam on the brakes then the horn as the phone dropped to the floor. A few colorful words escaped his mouth as he zipped ahead of the car, the man inside flipped him off as he passed. His first instinct was to cut him off, followed by jerking him out of the car for a little come to Jesus talk. No time for nonsense, so he let it go. Besides, the skinwalker might decide to do a little damage of his own if he stopped. At least he knew Wind Dancer was alive and well; one less thing to worry about.

"Where in the hell are you, Cleo?" he said as he pulled into the circle drive of the Field Museum.

"We will find her," the skinwalker spoke, breaking the detective's concentration.

"I hope you're right." The detective twisted his body around to give the skinwalker a once-over with a narrowed glare. "Get out. We're going in to talk to Wind Dancer."

The skinwalker remained so still, the only way Jacque knew he might be alive came with an evil grin forming on his pale blue lips of death.

Jacque jumped out the car and circled the front to open the door for the skinwalker. The last few days had opened up a whole new world of possibilities to him. He'd never believed in parallel universes, or even cared. Native Americans came with John Wayne when he watched his favorite Western movies. Stories about skinwalkers or other hobgoblins reminded him of people who had too much time on their hands or smoked too much weed.

Here he'd spent his day babysitting a skinwalker, trying to rescue a doctor from a time-jumping Osage, and feeling a bond of friendship with a guy who probably would end up dead before the end of the week, considering his lack of twenty-first-century survival skills. Throw in the FBI and Colonel Jefferson from the Pentagon, who thought he could just close down the city to stop smallpox, and his life had gotten a great deal more interesting.

When the skinwalker didn't get out, he bent down to release a combination of threats and colorful language when he found the seat empty. "What the hell," he groaned.

He pivoted in a complete circle in search of the creature only to spot a mangy dog about halfway up the steps to the front door of the museum. With a sigh of exasperation, the detective hustled up the steps, pausing when he caught up with the dog. The dog stared out at Lake Michigan, and the detective followed his haunting gaze.

When the dog moved a little closer, he drew his gun and touched the barrel to the animal's forehead. "Stay. I don't want you anywhere near me."

The dog gave a couple of barks then continued the rest of the way up the stairs.

A gust of wind tousled his hair and moved his sport coat enough to make it feel like a parachute fighting flight. Although the worst of the weather wouldn't move in until way after dark, he knew his city could face a blizzard better than tornadoes and super-celled thunderstorms. Those things didn't make any sense and their indiscriminate path of destruction unnerved him. This would be a long night.

He took hold of the door only to find it locked. Banging his fist brought a security guard who stared at him with the obstinate glare of a man too tired and too bored with his job to put up with much nonsense. After Jacque held his badge against the glass, the guard unlocked the door and stood aside for him to pass through. To Jacque's surprise, the guard failed to mention the dog trotting alongside him. Either he really didn't care or he couldn't see the skinwalker—which disturbed him more than he wanted to admit.

As the sound of securing the door echoed throughout the grand foyer, the detective heard a familiar voice.

"Jacque." Wind Dancer hustled out of the Native American wing toward him with a raised hand in greeting, until his eyes fell on the dog, which made him stop abruptly. The dog halted, too, and cocked his head. He wagged his tail as if recognizing the Pawnee from his former life. "You are playing a dangerous game, my friend."

Jacque didn't know if the Pawnee spoke to the dog or to him.

"Yeah, well it is what it is. I don't know about all this skinwalker crap, but I don't see we have much choice in the matter. He keeps showing up and I'd rather have him where I can put a bullet in him instead of his sneaking up on me when I least expect it."

The dog bared his canines as a stream of saliva oozed out of one side of his mouth. There was no growl, but the gesture impressed the detective enough to tread lightly with his threats.

Wind Dancer kneeled down to face the animal. This time a growl did escape from deep in the dog's throat. "I gave you time to do what you must do. But I have to save Cleopatra. You must let me do this first." The dog moved away until it stood beside Jacque where it sat down on its haunches and continued to stare at Wind Dancer.

"You know I don't believe in any of this. Right?" But then again, Jacque couldn't explain how the Frenchman appeared in his car either. When this ended, he planned on taking a long vacation somewhere he could fish and drink as much beer as he wanted without answering to anyone.

Wind Dancer stood, his eyes meeting the detective's. "If you didn't believe, you would not have your hand on your weapon."

He hadn't even realized he'd rested his hand on the butt of the gun. "Being cautious is totally different."

"We are making preparations. Come meet my new brothers." Wind Dancer fanned his hand out in the direction of the ceremony room.

"These are normal people, right? I'm not sure how many more of your weirdo friends I can handle."

Wind Dancer's forehead creased slightly as if he might be processing the question as they moved inside the Native American wing where a major transformation had taken place.

He introduced the group, saving Two Feathers, who extended his hand to the detective, for last. "Jacque is concerned you might be weirdos," the Pawnee offered.

Two Feathers grinned.

"Sorry. We weren't properly introduced the other day." The detective felt embarrassed as the older Pawnee withdrew his hand. "It's just— "

"No need to apologize, Detective Marquette. I understand. I assure you we are of this universe. The vote is still out on the weirdo part, however." He chuckled, dispelling Jacque's feeling of awkwardness.

"Glad to hear it, Mr. Two Feathers."

"Call me Two Feathers. Keep it simple."

Jacque nodded as he took in the transformation of the room. He lost track of the dog he imagined searched for a good hiding place or a tasty security guard to gnaw on. Probably should be more vigilant at where the beast lurked in case he tried to jump in his body or some other absurd nonsense. Maybe he'd be safe until the skinwalker chose a more appropriate time when he could finish his vendetta.

Two Feathers took great pains to explain the history of the Pawnee until Jacque felt a yawn coming on which he covered just as a couple of men his own age ask for his help in carrying what appeared to be movie props. He sure hoped they belonged to them and not the museum. Arresting the Pawnee delegation for theft could get embarrassing for everyone. He didn't need any more complications. He realized too late they kept him busy to avoid the elephant in the room, which was the scaffolding.

"So what do we have here, Joseph?" Jacque moved around the platform rising about four feet off the floor. He didn't know anything about Native American culture, but this place had taken on some kind of Plains Indian extravaganza about to happen. The thought occurred to him the decorations might be a little over the top.

"We will celebrate our deity of the Morning Star by offering a sacrifice."

"I'd like to offer one mangy dog," he mumbled as he looked over the platform.

"We come each year to share with the people of your city. Our ceremony has become very popular." Two Feathers checked out some tie-downs on the platform.

"Morbid curiosity." The detective frowned. "Go figure."

"Yes. I suspect in some cases this is true," Two Feathers agreed. "It is more for us than anything. There are still people among you who believe in the old ways, though. They will be here soon, to assist in our transformation."

Jacque's radar went up. "Whoa. Wait a minute. Transformation? What the hell are you talking about?" He stepped in front of the old Pawnee and Wind Dancer, noticing the others taking a defensive stand.

"I am taking these men to where they belong, with my people, their people, to prepare them for the future."

Jacque leveled a disgruntled glare at the Pawnee delegation. "Okay. I was wrong. You are a bunch of weirdos. Do you realize this could kill you? Who knows if it is even possible? You'll never survive."

"We will take our chances." Two Feathers pointed to the earth lodge. "Wind Dancer has agreed to be our guide."

Jacque eyed his friend. "What about Cleo? You came to this world because of her. You're just going to abandon her?"

Wind Dancer motioned for Two Feathers to leave them alone. "I promised to take them if they helped me rescue her."

"How is an old man and"—he pointed to the other men— "whatever they are, going to help rescue Cleo? She's with gangbangers. These guys might think they're a bunch of badass Indians, but I'm here to tell you they are no match for those guys."

Wind Dancer folded his arms across his chest, reminding Jacque of many a stereotyped Indian he'd seen in movies over the years. The Pawnee squinted. "They are untested but have prepared their whole lives for such a challenge."

Jacque couldn't help letting an exasperated chuckle escape through clenched teeth. "And what are you going to sacrifice?"

"One will be provided. It always is."

"Spoken like a true bogeyman slash crazy person."

"I don't understand your words, but it sounds like you doubt mine."

"Listen to me, Joseph. You need to stop screwin' around and get your head in the game."

Wind Dancer's brow pinched over his nose, and Jacque hurried to clarify.

"What I mean is we need to get serious about finding Cleo. She's in real danger."

"Neosho will protect her until he can bring her before me to see him crossover or kill her. Until then she will be protected." He spoke so matter-of-factly, Jacque almost believed him.

"He is only one man. The guys he's running with are seriously crazy in the head," he said pointing to his own skull. "What if they take Cleo from him? Did you consider that?"

Wind Dancer stared at him a few seconds before speaking. "No." The Pawnee dropped his hands to his side. "I believe he is in charge."

"You don't know squat. There's no way the Death Apostles would go for an outsider to take over."

"He is Osage. There could be ten different tribal elders present, and the Osage would believe themselves to be in charge. If they weren't, they would be when they got through making a point. These gangs you speak of could not take Neosho on their best day before he crossed over. Now it would be impossible."

"I hope you're right." He glanced at his watch. Time seemed to be getting away from him with all this education on Indian hocus pocus. "Almost eleven thirty. I'm going to check in to see if there is any word on the situation."

"Jacque?" Wind Dancer stepped closer. "What would happen to Cleo if she escaped the gang?"

The detective reached for his vibrating phone. "A woman like her, alone on the streets of Chicago in Gangland?" He shook his head. "Not good." Lifting the phone, he hit answer. "Detective Marquette. Talk to me."

A desk jockey at the precinct filled him in. "A call came in ten minutes ago. Two people, one black male and one white female, spotted crossing the street near a warehouse district, not far from here. They disappeared down an alley. The caller had a scanner and thought they heard the person of interest call."

"Text me the location. I'll head that direction." Jacque hurried toward the exit as Wind Dancer followed.

"What is it, Jacque?"

"I think Cleo is on the run. Going to check it out."

Wind Dancer jerked the door open with the kind of brute strength he'd also seen in Neosho. "I'm coming with you."

Jacque glanced at the dog that rejoined them. "Guess you're coming, too."

CHAPTER 24

Cleo squealed in fear when something ran over her feet as Ty pulled her deeper into the shadows of the alley, his tobacco-stained hand covering her mouth.

He whispered, "Just a rat." His chest rose and fell rapidly. "If I move my hand, will you keep quiet?"

She gave a jerky nod of acceptance.

Cleo shivered. Lightning flashes exposed cockroaches scurrying up a dumpster next to them as thunder rumbled across the sky. A drop of rain hit her cheek, followed by several more. They'd escaped around an hour earlier but hidden after someone spotted them and tried to get them to come inside. Ty feared a trap and kept her running until he located a safe place in an abandoned storefront. It provided some protection from the downpour, the downside being it also masked the footfalls of any approaching Death Apostles.

"We gotta find a ride. When they wake up and find us gone, they'll come after us. I don't want to be anywhere around here when that happens, especially with your crazy Indian. Understand?"

Cleo nodded like a scared child, understanding the violence these men were capable of after having treated many wounds over the last few years in the ER.

"Maybe we should split up," she whispered as they peeked

around a corner to see most of the streetlights flickering like strobes.

"No way. You're goin' save my skin with the Feds or whoever you're tied to. I'm not takin' the fall for any of this. You're tellin' them I saved you. Right?" He scowled into her face.

"Right. Let's get out of here."

Rain poured from the sky in torrents as they escaped into the darkness, neglected streetlights flickering like lightning flashes. With such tumultuous weather, it felt unlikely they would come in contact with the shadier side of Chicago. Even criminals had better sense than to come out in this, Cleo reasoned. She took solace knowing the only one who could track them would be Neosho. From what she'd seen of him, a little thing like a severe thunderstorm would be a walk in the park.

"Do you have a phone?" Cleo followed Ty under an awning flapping in the wind. She heard it rip and figured by morning it would be in Lake Michigan or Indianapolis, depending on the strength of the storm.

Ty fumbled with his prepaid phone inside his jacket and promptly dropped it in a puddle. Cleo rescued it with a quick grab, hoping she had been quick enough. There wasn't a dry thread on her, so wiping it off seemed a waste of time. Her fingers trembled from the cold seeping through her body as she tried to punch in Jacque's cell number she'd memorized the day before. The habit of memorizing had gotten her through medical school. Taking notes in her head saved her on many occasions when computers crashed, ER chaos prevailed, or details slipped past others.

"Give me the phone," Ty groaned. "Tell me the number. You're shaking like a leaf."

When the phone rang, he passed it to her.

"Jacque, please, please answer the phone."

~~~~

A clap of thunder startled Neosho awake. He took a moment to make sense of the unfamiliarity of his situation. Nothing made sense in this land. Noises vibrated against his brain with such intensity, it caused a throbbing over one eye. It subsided only if he slept. Soon the pounding would return. Food tasted saltier than the
~~~~

purslane he sometimes ate on the plains in his world. It made him thirsty. These men drank something they called beer that made them act with strange behaviors. He'd seen this even with the white men who visited the plains in his world. It never ended well, so he drank only water, but even this tasted unclean.

But his enhanced sense of smell surprised him the most, even more than the strength, because now he possessed the ability to track without following signs left by sloppy people. This made all the difference since he didn't understand many of the physical signs anyway. All of this must be true for Wind Dancer as well. In the other world, they were evenly matched, so it seemed reasonable to expect the Pawnee to have many of these same gifts.

The sound of rain pelted against the dirty windows he'd noticed earlier. The moan of wind tunneling through the narrow canyons of Chicago kept him in a state of disorientation for a few minutes. Darkness had fallen hours ago. He sat staring out into a room with dim light cascading from the ceiling.

The sound of snores, snorts, and blubbering lips alerted him to the condition of the men who had followed him to the Field Museum. The mindless music emitted from a black box sitting on the floor attached to a cord leading to a wall. How could a box make music, he wondered? Even from where he sat, he could smell their breath and the meal they'd eaten, consisting of round meat on bread with something they called fries. In spite of not eating for hours, he felt little hunger and decided the smells suppressed the urge.

One thing that remained satisfying to him was the fresh smell of sweetgrass on the skin of Cleopatra. She reminded him of home and how the wind carried the scent of cleansing after a spring rain. He closed his eyes to inhale her scent, holding his breath longer than he thought possible, when he jumped to his feet. Her scent no longer existed. In a few strides, he crossed the room to where he'd left her in Ty's care. With an abundance of pent-up anger to fuel his impatience, he tossed tables, chairs, and boxes aside in search for Cleo, even though he had no doubt she was gone.

"Neosho. What the hell?" Ashanti rubbed his belly and stretched like a waking bear.

"Ty took Cleo away. They run."

"I knew I couldn't trust the little weasel." Ashanti stood and moved about the room, kicking the bottoms of feet on the floor or shoving at exposed shoulders of his men. He checked the time on his cell phone. The boom of thunder shook the windows. "It's almost one o'clock. Wonder when they left."

"I got up to take a leak around midnight, but I figured everyone was sleeping," a man with a shaved head commented. "This storm sounds bad. I'm checking the weather," he said playing with the radio dial.

Neosho slipped his Packers jacket over his bare chest, having taken it off earlier in the evening because of the rising temperatures. "I find her." He jerked the door open and let the onslaught of wind and rain slam into his body. "You coming?"

Dissension lifted over having to go out in such weather, but fell flat when Ashanti held his hand up. He jerked his chin toward the Osage. "We're coming." He issued orders and they moved out, leaving Neosho standing in the open door, who stared out into the darkness with the howling wind slamming against his body.

~~~~

"Where is she?" Wind Dancer strained to see through the windshield as fans of water sprayed like fountains on each side of the car when Jacque hit the puddles at a speed considered reckless in this kind of weather.

"Not far from here. Almost there. She's been on the run for several hours to avoid being captured by the Death Apostles. Sounds like she hid for a while, considering how late it is. Said the phone she's using keeps dropping calls."

"Dropping calls is bad. Are they hard to hold?"

Jacque normally would laugh at this kind of conversation, but for the moment all he wanted to do was find Cleo, not explain the English language.

The storm intensified with each hour it moved toward dawn. Jacque couldn't remember this kind of weather ever rampaging through his city. Maybe all the talk about climate change had some merit after all, but he'd leave the questions for the geeks to decide. He needed to find Cleo and get her to a safe place.

After searching several side streets, making three wrong turns, and one backup, Jacque found a parking lot. The surface resembled
~~~~

a shallow pool where bouncing raindrops resembled wet ballerinas dancing to thunderous applause, and escape might be possible. With each gust of wind, they appeared to change direction in some frantic routine.

With a flip of a switch, the red lights on Jacque's vehicle flashed then pulsed like a strobe. With the release of seat belts, Jacque checked his weapon then reached for a couple of flashlights. A flash of lighting followed by a boom of thunder shook the car, creating a moment's hesitation between the two men.

A text to the number Cleo used earlier let her know help had arrived. "Let's go. She should be around here somewhere. Probably hunkered down to stay out of sight in case Neosho is tracking her."

"It will be hard for him to track in this storm but not impossible. I know because I'm struggling." Wind Dancer opened the door and stepped out into water that came up over the instep of his cowboy boots. As he slammed the door shut, Jacque came around the front and tossed him a flashlight.

They moved out, letting the flashes of lightning open up spaces the flashlight couldn't reach. Neither called out to Cleo in case others searched for her as well. The rain soaked them to the skin almost instantly but neither appeared to notice as they moved together toward a dark alley. In a moment where lightning mixed with the strobe of bouncing light from the police car, a shadowy figure stood ahead of them like a statue with his arms slightly out from his sides, carrying a hatchet in one hand and a club in the other.

~~~~

"They're here, Ty." Cleo breathed a sigh of relief as she slipped the cell phone he'd given her into her pants pocket. Even though he'd secured jackets for them before they had escaped into the night, the rain still managed to soak through the exposed parts of their bodies the flimsy jackets failed to cover. In spite of the warm temperature, the icy rain would take its toll soon enough. "How far is the Jamison parking lot?"

"Should be able to see it as soon as we get out of this alley."
~~~~

He stepped out from under the awning jutting out over the doorway in the alley where they'd hidden and grabbed her hand. Ty led her out into the rain. "Stay as close to the wall as possible."

The rain felt like tiny pins slamming into her face as Ty shook his head then rubbed his eyes. When they neared the end of the alley they headed north. Less than a half block remained before they needed to cross the street. Since the location of the parking lot offered little to no cover, Ty promised her their hideout would be a healthier choice if the Death Apostles came in search of them. That turned out to be good advice. Since there had been no sign of them, she felt optimistic their escape might prove successful.

After spotting the strobe of light bouncing off the nearby building, Cleo picked up the pace, sloshing through puddles adding to her discomfort. "Come on. Can't wait to get out of this weather." She paused to push strands of wet hair out of her eyes. "There they are," Cleo yelled against the wind and tugged free from her protector's hand. She rushed forward dodging areas she feared might be watery abysses.

Ty lumbered after her, splashing through the puddles she had avoided. "Slow down, Doc. We could be running into my boys. We don't know where they are."

He grabbed her arm then jerked her to a stop. At that same moment, Cleo saw two men peering at something ahead of them. One man lifted a weapon in slow motion.

She tried to pry his fingers from her forearm. "You said they wouldn't come after us in this storm. Let's go."

"What about your crazy Neosho? Will he come after you? He's the one I'm worried about. Maybe he won't kill you, but my life ain't worth a nickel since I took you. Best stay out of sight. Something got those two friends of yours spooked."

Even though she struggled to free herself, he dragged her deeper into the darkest area along the brick buildings as they kept moving forward. "You're hurting me," she fumed as he shoved her against the brick.

"Calm down." He squinted. "What caused those two guys to stop? Do you see anything?

"I understand this place is putting you on edge. See that guy with long hair? I know him." Her heart skipped a beat knowing Wind Dancer was at Jacque's side. He'd survived Neosho's attack after all.

"Those your friends? You're sure?"

"Yes." Something had them spooked or Wind Dancer's senses would alert him to her presence. She eased out again then charged forward, calling to them, with Ty hot on her heels.

Both men looked toward them and waved them off.

"I don't have a good feeling about any of this," Ty huffed as he struggled to keep up with Cleo.

At a crack of lightning, they cringed even as they picked up the pace. In a split second of darkness to daylight when lightning forces itself to the ground, Cleo saw them, the Death Apostles edging out of corners like the cockroaches they'd become. Another flash revealed Neosho moving forward, steady and confident, as if this was but a walk in the park. Ty tripped when he halted then stumbled and almost fell as he surged ahead to intercept Cleo.

She picked up speed when she detected an expression of panic wash over Wind Dancer's face. Before she realized what was happening, Wind Dancer barreled toward Neosho coming out of the darkness to show himself under a flickering streetlamp. Jacque held up a hand as if it might slow Cleo down while sidestepping toward her. At the same time, he raised his weapon and pointed it at Ashanti, coming out into the light.

"Get your hands up where I can see them," Jacque yelled at Ashanti.

The gang leader waved his boys off while continuing to rush forward toward Cleo.

When a gun came out of the inside of Ashanti's jacket, Cleo screamed, "Jacque."

A shot hit the detective square in the chest, knocking him backward into a puddle. Cleo watched the gravity of what the leader had done fill his bulging eyes for a split second. At the same time, Ty caught up with her and managed to shove her behind him and face Ashanti.

Even before she could scream, Ashanti spat out his verdict. "This is how Death Apostles deal with a traitor."

A shot slammed into Ty, dropping him next to Jacque at the same time a bolt of lightning made night into day.

Jacque struggled to sit up as a mangy dog lay down beside him. "Get him," he moaned.

A menacing growl began deep in the animal's gut as he rose on his haunches then lunged forward at Ashanti.

CHAPTER 25

Jacque struggled to his feet, thankful he'd slipped on the protective vest he kept in the trunk of his car. Even so, his chest would be sore as hell, not to mention his butt from hitting the pavement. Cleo bent down beside the kid before raising her face to him. The sound of the dog tearing into Ashanti and the screams of terror drew several other Death Apostles out into the open with guns drawn. He reached down and picked up his weapon from a puddle and for a split second wondered if it would jam.

"Dog!" he yelled through the sound of rolling thunder, which brought the animal to heel at his side. Jacque unconsciously reached down with his hand and touched his scruffy head. The mutt was as wet as the rest of them. Ashanti rolled on the ground before he pushed himself up so fast he appeared to have embedded springs in his legs.

"Jacque?" Cleo stood and stared at the gang leader who rolled his red glowing eyes toward Wind Dancer and Neosho still struggling to gain advantage over each other. "I think the skinwalker took a new body."

The dog whimpered as he cowered behind Jacque. "Let's get this kid out of the rain. Help me get him in the car."

Ty moaned, lifting a bloody hand from his shoulder and staring at it in horror. The detective kept an eye on the new skinwalker as he moved very much like a dog stalking its prey.

The other gang members disappeared into the darkness.

"Joseph!" Jacque's voice seemed muffled as a bolt of lightning hit the top of a nearby building, followed by an explosion of thunder.

He watched Wind Dancer knock Neosho to the ground as Neosho leaped to his feet and escaped into the night at a speed unlike a normal human's.

Ashanti lifted his hands close to his face as if examining them for the first time then felt his body.

Jacque made exaggerated gestures so Wind Dancer would skirt the new Ashanti with caution. Wind Dancer nodded then moved toward Jacque and Cleo.

"Wind Dancer!" Cleo called as she ran toward him.

He caught her up in his arms, drawing her to his chest. "I thought I'd never see you again." The rain dragged strands of her hair across her eyes as Wind Dancer captured her mouth with his.

"Let's go!" Jacque hurried around to the driver's side of the car as he continued to watch Ashanti standing beneath a streetlamp that flickered like heat lightning.

Cleo and Wind Dancer took the backseat to help with Ty as the dog jumped into the front seat ahead of Jacque. The canine pointed his nose over the seat and eyed the three.

"The skinwalker has left his body, Jacque." Wind Dancer rubbed the dog's ear. "We need to return to the museum. It is almost dawn."

He drove the car out onto a flooded street, not sure they would be able to plow through. "That was close. At least there is some good news. How's the kid?"

"I hate dogs. Tell him to stop staring at me," Ty whined. "Take me to the hospital."

"I don't think you want to do that, kid," Jacque warned. "Suspicious cases of a mysterious illness have started showing up at several local hospitals. Probably smallpox. The Feds, Chicago PD, and who knows who else won't give a damn about what we're doing here. Cleo can fix you up." He glanced up in the rearview mirror. "Cleo," he snapped. "Can you fix him up?"

She was pale and trembling but she nodded.

"You okay? Did they hurt you?"

She shook her head as Wind Dancer touched her neck where

Neosho tried to choke her.

"I will kill Neosho," Wind Dancer growled, not so different from the skinwalker, as he withdrew his hand to stare straight ahead.

~~~~

The two security guards hesitated at letting the three bring a bloody guy who wore gang colors and swore every other word into the museum. This time they did comment on the dog. Jacque guessed it was because the animal no longer carried the soulless skinwalker inside him. They protested until he gave stern orders to stand down. He puffed out his chest like a five-star general as he shoved them aside to let Wind Dancer carry Ty inside to the coffee shop. Several of the Pawnee delegation came out of the Native American wing to help Cleo ram tables together. She suggested where the most likely niche for first aid supplies would be kept then relayed what she needed to Jacque. He ordered the security guards to take him there.

He returned to find several Pawnee wiping down the tables with bleach towelettes as Cleo scrubbed her hands in the kitchen sink. He cringed as Two Feathers lifted a bottle of bleach then poured it over her hands. Even from ten feet away at the coffee shop opening, the smell of the chemical burned his eyes. He dug through the supplies and found some disposable gloves for her as she used paper towels to dry her hands.

"You're a good man, Jacque," she said holding her hands up for him to help her, although he had to let her do most of the work.

"What can I do, Cleopatra?" Wind Dancer's forehead creased.

She picked up a scalpel-like instrument and removed the sterile packaging. When she held it up to the light, a boom of thunder followed by the lights flickering, reminded Jacque of Dr. Frankenstein. Her face appeared void of emotion or concern, which also gave him pause.

"What the hell you gonna do, Doc?" Ty squirmed as he talked through chattering teeth.

"Joseph, I need you to hold this guy down because I'm going to do a little exploring and he won't like it." She nodded to Two Feathers. "You might need to help, too, Jacque. Are you
~~~~

squeamish?"

Of course, he was squeamish, but admitting it didn't occur to him. He hated crime scenes but liked solving the mystery. "No. I'm good. Do what you gotta do."

"Explore? What you mean?" Ty tried to scoot away as Wind Dancer ripped off his shirt and threw it to the floor. "My best shirt. You better get me another one because…" The Pawnee managed to pin Ty's arm so he couldn't move.

"Hey, Doc, you can't cut me. We've been through too much together."

Jacque cringed as an evil smirk played at the corners of her mouth. He wondered in that moment if she worked in the ER because she enjoyed this kind of thing. The woman appeared steady and unaffected by the blood, storm, and possibility of falling into another universe any minute; very different from the woman he'd observed an hour earlier. The confidence in her eyes as she suspended the knife above Ty made Jacque ponder whether she could be one of those doctors with a god complex.

"Stop moving, Ty," she said.

His eyes bulged, and he showed no signs of being still. "I can't work like this."

Jacque stepped up and wacked the man in the forehead with the butt of his gun. Ty's eyes rolled to unconsciousness. Except for Cleo, the others stepped away with shock showing on their faces.

"Let's get on with it," Jacque said as he slipped his gun into his holster. "Tick tock, you guys."

"Thank you, Jacque. Not my usual sedative, but very effective nonetheless."

Even before she stopped talking, she managed to disinfect the area around the gunshot wound and started poking around in the hole. The detective stepped away and pretended to check his phone so the others wouldn't know he felt faint. He didn't want to be the cop who had to put his head between his legs to maintain consciousness.

"Deep breaths," he mumbled as the scruffy dog sat down beside him. "What are you staring at? Not my fault some skinwalker took advantage of you. And stop following me." He dialed Agent Farentino. "Yeah. It's me."

He filled the FBI in about the doctor and Ty but conveniently left out the part about the skinwalker who might be leading a notorious gang. He wanted to keep his job, not be admitted for a twenty-four-hour hold at some psych ward. The information about Cleo vaccinating the gang members and the lack of signs of infection among the group drew a relieved sigh on the other end of the phone.

"I'm thinking they're headed this way. Neosho wants the doc to cross over with him."

"How do we know this parallel universe will open or even if it will be today?" Agent Farentino gave an exasperated chuckle.

"How the hell do I know? All of this is way over my head. I'm keeping you up to speed. I've got a wounded gang member here and a bunch of Pawnee who think they're getting ready to go to the Little Bighorn."

"That was a different tribe and time."

"Excuse my historical faux pas," Jacque growled.

"Another pretty big word for you, a Chicago cop. And here I planned to get you a thesaurus for your birthday."

"Not surprised since all your experience over at the Bureau tends to be out of a book. Thanks just the same." Jacque clicked off realizing the FBI agent got under his skin, even though he seemed like a professional with a decent head on his shoulder. He didn't like the FBI getting in his way or psyche. They sometimes got credit for work his guys did.

"Everything okay, Jacque?" Wind Dancer dried his hands on a paper towel.

He slipped the phone in his pocket and unconsciously reached down to pat the dog on the head. The dog panted and wagged his tail as Jacque continued. "Yeah. Done?"

"Cleopatra found the bullet and patched him up. She thinks he'll be good. I mean okay." He gave a thumbs-up sign and grinned. "He is trying to wake up. Cleopatra wants him to sleep. Would you like to hit him again?"

"I think Cleo would object to my method a second time." He nodded toward the coffee shop then headed in that direction. "Where are the others?"

"Preparing to cross if the opening appears in the earth lodge. They have supplies, pictures, cell phones, and gadgets I don't understand. I'm not sure what it means, but they have downloaded maps to take, too, as well as extra-charged batteries for these phones. Something about solar cells."

Jacque chuckled. "You've a lot to learn. I'm guessing they're taking all those things to prove they've been here."

"Yes. I spoke into their phone to record a message to Cleo's father and to my people in case something happened to me. They must believe in the danger and the mission of these good men who cross over to help them."

The thought occurred to Jacque he might wake up someday, discover on the morning news that the President of the United States was a Native American and everyone could speak English and some other tribal language. Could this even be possible? Would these Pawnee change the world as he knew it, and would it be for the better?

Two Feathers covered Ty with a tablecloth as Jacque and Wind Dancer entered the coffee shop. He spotted Cleo cleaning up and a discarded bloody lab coat half-in and half-out of a large trash can near one of the decorative pillars. The kid moaned even as Two Feathers laid a comforting hand on his head. The old Pawnee lifted his eyes to meet Jacque's and bobbed his head in what he guessed meant reassurance.

"I think he's good for a while, Jacque." Cleo put her hands on her hips and stared down at her patient. "We're going to need to get him to a hospital, though. If he starts bleeding, I can't really do anything to help him here."

He glanced from the kid to Cleo and realized how pretty she looked standing there appearing so unconcerned after all she'd been through. Once the amount of excitement in her life dawned on her, that confident, in-charge swagger would evaporate. Now he found it way too pleasant to take in her pale skin with the freckles trailing across her nose and the strawberry-blonde hair curving around her chin. He guessed her to be a bit younger than him but not much, although the mirror suggested otherwise. Maybe if Wind Dancer had remained in the museum case instead of crossing over, this scenario would end differently. But, damn if he didn't like her spunk. Smart and pretty. Not one of those women who fussed with her appearance all the time. She reminded him of a Dove soap commercial.

"Jacque, what's wrong?"

Cleo snapped him out of his reverie as she moved up to touch his forehead. He immediately swiped at her hand. "I'm good. Thinking is all." Good thing he didn't embarrass easily or his face would be red as a beet.

She stepped toward him again with concern etched around her eyes as she touched his cheek with the back of her hand. "Are you sure? You're a little flushed."

"That's because everything has gone into the toilet," he quipped as he walked away toward the grand foyer. Her light laughter at his attempt of a joke made him feel even worse about his carnal thoughts. Wind Dancer followed him after saying something to Cleo.

"I need to ask you a favor, Jacque."

Jacque continued to walk until he entered the Native American exhibit. He forced himself to focus on the platform where the sacrifice for the Morning Star should take place. Of course, it never did for the tourists and school kids, or at least so he'd been told. He had actually never seen it. For all he knew, these guys slipped into the museum after hours and did the deed illegally. *Creepy.*

"Okay, shoot."

Wind Dancer stepped in front of him and halted with a frown of shock that creased the lines near his eyes. "You want me to shoot you? I cannot."

Jacque took in a deep breath then released it as slowly as he could manage. "Shoot is an expression. It means talk to me."

"Oh. Of course. I misunderstood." He seemed as if he might be storing the words for later use.

Jacque's jacket opened when his hands rested on his hips. The feel of comfort entered his body as his hand touched the hardness of his weapon. "What favor?"

"Can you take care of Cleopatra if I cross over with these warriors?"

The detective dropped his hands to his sides. "No. I'm not a babysitter. You've wanted to be with her"—he rolled his eyes—"forever it sounds like. Why would you leave? She's crazy about you and there isn't any mystery about how you feel." He lowered his voice. "The woman is something else. I'm not sure why she's single, but I'm not going to protect her honor while you play superhero to a bunch of Indians." A deep breath. "And, besides, what makes you think you can trust me? Maybe I got a thing for the doc."

"Something else," he repeated slowly as if deciphering the meaning. "But I do trust you. If I don't return I want to know she is safe from this dangerous world. I would take her with me, but it is too hard a life for someone like her." He shifted his gaze to the sacrifice platform. "We can't let Neosho find her."

"Not going to happen here. I'll put a bullet in his head if he shows up again. And, as to the skinwalker, I'll do the same with him. Can this get any weirder?"

"And, Jacque?" He placed his hand on the detective's shoulder, squeezed harder than necessary, and looked in the direction where they'd left Cleo. "I will come again. Remember this if you get a thing for her."

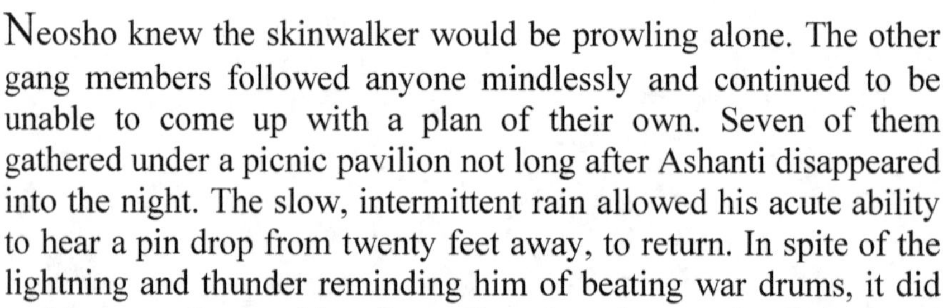

CHAPTER 26

Neosho knew the skinwalker would be prowling alone. The other gang members followed anyone mindlessly and continued to be unable to come up with a plan of their own. Seven of them gathered under a picnic pavilion not long after Ashanti disappeared into the night. The slow, intermittent rain allowed his acute ability to hear a pin drop from twenty feet away, to return. In spite of the lightning and thunder reminding him of beating war drums, it did nothing to distract him from detecting the confused body of Ashanti.

Although he didn't understand much about the spirit world or care, he pondered how the Frenchman could die and return as a dog then jump into Ashanti's body, yet he knew that he had. He'd heard Cleopatra say as much. The skinwalker would master Ashanti's body soon enough so he would have no will of his own. In the meantime, he needed to take over the remaining members of the Death Apostles.

"Neosho." One waved him over to the pavilion. "Did you see what happened, man? Ashanti shot Ty and the cop. We are in a world of hurt."

Neosho glared down at the man. "Is this world of hurt the same one as yesterday?"

"No," he said with a hand gesture indicating exasperation. "I mean we are in trouble. You don't go shootin' a cop. They will be all over us. We gotta hide where they can't find us."

"I know a place. We go to the museum. No one will search there." Neosho lifted his nose to sniff for signs of the skinwalker. He would soon double back in search of them. "There is much gold and valuables there."

"Can you get in?"

Neosho jogged in the direction of the museum. "Yes. I lived there long time."

~~~~

"We are ready, Wind Dancer." Two Feather's oldest son approached the Pawnee with caution. His slow movements and words, meant to be respectful, only managed to make Wind Dancer scowl with impatience. Jacque felt his friend somehow flipped a switch on his good nature and fumed about something.

"What the hell is the matter with you?" Jacque surveyed the area behind him, half expecting to see Neosho or maybe the skinwalker. He turned back to the platform. "So how does this work?" He chuckled and tried to make his voice sound like the narrator of a Saturday night late movie. "A booming voice shakes the museum and a bolt of lightning comes through the ceiling?"

Wind Dancer switched his attention from the detective to the platform as the younger man moved away. "Something similar. Yes."

A laugh escaped from Jacque as he dragged a hand through his hair. "This is too weird."

"The scaffold you see here represents the Evening Star's garden of the West. It is the source of all plant and animal life." He spoke in a monotone as if falling into a trance.

"You've got to be kidding me."

"The captive will be placed on the scaffold and tied spread-eagle. Do you understand this position?"

"Yeah. I've been around the block a time or two." Just as he expected, Wind Dancer flinched at the slang reference to understand, but then he shifted his interest to the scaffold.

"Two men will approach her from the East and touch her with torches then with war clubs." The son of Two Feathers returned with what appeared to be buckskins painted with splashes of red.
~~~~

Without speaking, he helped Wind Dancer remove his clothing then assisted him with the new ones.

"The warrior who captured her will come forward with a sacred bow and shoot her through the heart with a sacred arrow."

Another man named Stands Alone entered carrying a bundle, while the younger son of Two Feathers entered with several quivers of arrows. Jacque cocked his head at the group, feeling an uneasiness seep into his bones.

"At the same time, another warrior will strike her on the head with the war club from the Morning Star bundle." Wind Dancer stretched out his arms and examined the results of his traditional clothes then nodded his approval to the younger Pawnee.

"And you guys come here every year to show little kids this stuff?" the detective asked incredulously. "Geez Louise. So, is that it?"

Stands Alone removed some bows from underneath the scaffold.

"No. The elder supervising the ceremony will cut her breast open with a stone knife." He nodded to yet another Pawnee who stepped forward and smeared something red onto Wind Dancer's face near his mouth. "The elder will smear his face with her blood. The warrior who provided the sacrifice would catch some of her blood on dried meat. All the men and boys would then shoot arrows into her body, circle the scaffold four times, and return to the camp."

He impressed Jacque with having the emotional detachment of a deacon reading the Sunday bulletin to a congregation of snake handlers. No worries. Was he really hearing this right? Had someone slipped him a hallucinogenic drug? That would make everything a lot more understandable.

Wind Dancer let his gaze travel over him from head to toe as if evaluating an opponent. "The wind will blow, and we will hear thunder. Since we are enclosed, I don't think lightning will find us. But Two Feathers will know this better than I do since he does the sacrifice each year. But there must be a sacrifice or the opening in the earth lodge remains shut."

"But there wasn't any sacrifice the other day when all hell broke loose, only a storm."

"A storm will not guarantee the opening will appear. We know the combination of the sacrifice and the storms can force it open. We believe this may be one of the reasons the white man's president made us stop."

"So this is for real? Bet the conversation around the Thanksgiving table at your place is a hoot." Jacque felt the hair stand up on the back of his neck. "Where do we get a sacrifice?"

Two Feathers entered the room, leading Cleo by her elbow. "I have brought one."

~~~~

The night became calm, its sticky kind of warmth drawing beads of sweat to Neosho's forehead. A few delivery trucks plowed through standing water, raising walls of spray. Neosho stopped in the middle of the street to watch the spectacle of such mammoth machines, agile enough to dodge him. Buffalo, not quite as big, would have stampeded him into the ground. This world, or parts of it, amazed him. How would his people ever survive here? How would he survive? The smells, the sickness of the skin, and the noise of life, momentarily drowned any reasonable thought of survival. Horns blasted as they sped past him, over and over, yet he continued to stare at the chaos around him, both fascinated and horrified.

Confused as to why the night felt void of life yet continued to breathe, he stumbled toward the curb. The gang members rushed past him, dodging cars and lifting their middle fingers when a bulky man yelled at them through the window opening in his door. The truck, as he'd heard them call it, disappeared down the street void of life other than the gang.

"We need to get goin', Neosho." One of the men checked his phone and shook his head. "The weather radar has a big thunderstorm headed this way."

At the sound of tornado sirens exploding in the night air, Neosho cowered for only a second then slowly stood to survey the area around him in search of the piercing sound. "Is this sound the weather radar you speak of?"

Nervous laughter rippled among the remaining gangbangers, even as Neosho glared at them in impatience.

"No, man." He rotated the phone to show the Osage, but
~~~~

Neosho turned away and sprinted the final distance to the museum.

Neosho didn't understand many of their words, body language, or their small machine that fit in the palm of a man's hand. He'd lived on the prairie long enough to know how to feel in his bones when a dangerous storm approached. The need for a machine to tell him what his next move should be convinced him that this time managed to rob man of his natural ability to predict the weather, danger, and how to survive both.

The others, one by one, trotted after him, spewing complaints until the Osage glanced over his shoulder like an angry buffalo in need of goring someone. In spite of their youth, their bodies could not compare with Neosho's ability to feel no pain. The jog switched to a brisk walk as the Field Museum came into view. Before crossing the empty street between the stadium and museum, the men stopped to catch their breath. Neosho watched them gasp for air as some stretched out their legs, rubbing them and grimacing.

"This can't be good," a skinny, pock-faced man said, pointing to the top of the museum.

Neosho watched as clouds filled with lightning, swirled overhead and rumbled like buffalo pursued by warriors. In the first dappled rays of morning light, he could see the storm clouds billow to mountains of gray and black. The wind touched the nearby trees then rushed toward them as if it meant to halt their movements. He stopped for only a couple of seconds, contemplating the madness in entering a place filled with his enemies.

Then he caught her scent. Cleopatra. The woman who would either become his source of revenge once and for all, or the forever mate to bear him sons and daughters. She would be powerless to refuse either option. Either choice would be a fitting end to the hate he held for Wind Dancer who had destroyed his way of life and family.

He could also sense others; Pawnee moved about the museum. They all smelled like Wind Dancer. They must be the group who returned to the museum each year at this time. It took him a minute before he could distinguish the adrenaline and heartbeat of his enemy.

He found the door he knew would be hidden from eyes of the public.

"Probably locked?" one of the gang members said as he rattled the handle then tried to tug on the door until a beefy friend moved him aside and jerked on the door.

He looked at his friends and shrugged his shoulders. "Not happenin'. If I can't do it then it won't happen."

Lightning crackled overhead as the streetlights exploded and rained down into the street. The gangbangers cried out and slammed up against the wall.

Neosho waited until they looked to him in defeat before he reached out with one hand and jerked the door off its hinges. "No security alarm now with storm."

He met the surprised expression of the beefy man who tried to puff out an already-inflated chest. "I loosened it up for you."

A demonic smirk toyed with the corners of the Osage's mouth. "But, hey, you the man!"

Neosho raised his chin as he stuck his head inside. "Yes. I am the man." He stepped into the museum. "Follow me."

~~~~

"What do you mean you 'brought one'?"

Jacque could feel his forehead do the thing where it becomes so pinched your eyes squint, sometimes even twitch with unexpected pain. His finger darted to the spot as he rubbed in a slow circular motion. He noticed the old man pat Cleo's forearm, which bore a large bandage.

"I'm the sacrifice," she said simply as if she'd said, "Sure, I'll go to the mall with you." But, to him, what she said meant, "Sure, I'll go play in traffic during rush hour." All this time, Jacque thought she might be the levelheaded one. "What happened to your arm?"

"I cut her," Two Feathers said softly as he lifted a small Styrofoam cup. He withdrew his touch from Cleo's arm and dipped a finger inside the cup and withdrew a bloody finger that he smeared around his face.

"Okay. This needs to stop. There isn't going to be any sacrifice." Jacque waved his index finger at the gathering tribe like a loaded weapon. He stepped toward Cleo and forced her behind him. "Are you nuts?"
~~~~

"Jacque, it has to be done," she pleaded as she tried to step around his outstretched arm. "The storm, along with the sacrifice will guarantee the earth lodge opens to Wind Dancer's time. I know what I'm doing. My father would approve."

"Let her go, Jacque." Wind Dancer faced him and extended his hand toward the woman he claimed to love.

The lights flickered as thunder boomed outside, rattling the entire building. It almost gave the impression of lightning flashing inside the museum. Then lights went out completely except for a couple of emergency security signs. The two guards quickly appeared with their LED flashlights on bright.

Jacque swung his hand back to feel for Cleo only to find her gone. When he whirled around, he saw Wind Dancer lift her in his arms and carry her toward the scaffold. Why didn't she struggle to be free?

~~~~

"Are you afraid?" Wind Dancer moved in slow motion as he held Cleo to his chest.

She lifted her hand to his face and slid it down his scarred jawline.

"No," she whispered as another rumble of thunder shook the museum. "It is my honor."

Wind Dancer tried to smile as he lowered his mouth to hers and captured one last kiss. As he laid her on the scaffold bed, the sound of Jacque's rage reached his ears. Wind Dancer commanded the others. "Restrain him." The words came out calm, but there could be no mistake of his resolve.

Before Jacque could draw his weapon, two Pawnees grabbed his arms and tied them behind his back so fast it felt like a magic trick. The two security guards made a move to unholster their Tasers, but Two Feathers slammed a club behind their knees, knocking them to the floor. Their rotund bodies prevented them from springing up as they tried to use their hands to rise. Another Pawnee swiped his foot under one to flatten him down while another did the same to the second guard. They were secured in short order then dragged to the side. When they complained, Two Feathers popped them again on the head, knocking them
~~~~

unconscious.

"Was that necessary?" Jacque squirmed against his restraints. "What? Am I next?"

When Two Feathers lifted his eyebrows and smirked, the detective took a step back.

~~~

Wind Dancer let Stands Alone secure the restraints on Cleo's feet. He stroked her face and hair then set about fastening her wrists to the edge of the scaffold bed. "Not too tight?" He took another moment to gaze upon the woman he'd fallen in love with as a young man.

Once, as a child, he'd found the opening into the earth lodge and seen Cleopatra reading on one of the buffalo hide beds. They'd played until he fell back through the opening, only to have it close again. Somehow he made it home. When he told his father and the village all he'd done, everyone agreed the young Pawnee had had a vision. From then on, he'd been called Wind Dancer. Although he could never find his way to the earth lodge in the museum again, he found the display case where he watched Cleopatra Sommers grow up. After befriending the Osage and showing him the way into the museum cases, he worried his actions might lead to disaster someday.

"Joseph!" Jacque yelled so loud it turned everyone's head. "Let me go. This is insane."

"My name is Wind Dancer." He refocused on Cleo. "I am glad we finally met, Cleopatra Sommers."

"We still have time. This will soon be over."

"No. I must say good-bye to you." His hand trailed down her face until he reached her parted lips, where he ran a finger across their firmness. "There will never be enough time for us."

"Wait." She fidgeted nervously. "What are you talking about?"

"You are the sacrifice and I cannot live knowing I am the cause of destroying what I hold so close to my heart."

"Joseph." Her voice was panic laced with gasps as she struggled against the restraints binding her limbs. "Wind Dancer. Please. Don't do this."
~~~

Jacque tried to run toward the man he had begun thinking of as a friend, but two other Pawnee caught him and hauled him from standing so close.

"You love her," he pleaded. "Stop and think about this barbaric act." He struggled again unsuccessfully as he sought out the elder Pawnee. "Think about what you're doing to these other men, your sons, for crying out loud. This hocus pocus is a thing of the past. There's no guarantee you'll be able to cross over by doing a human sacrifice. Then what? You willing to go to jail for assaulting a police officer, kidnapping, and murder?" His eyes went to Cleo who appeared to quiet as Wind Dancer kissed her again. "Tell him, Cleo!" he begged at the top of his lungs.

"It's too late, Jacque." Wind Dancer straightened and glared at him.

Wind Dancer jerked around, alert to something no one else could sense. But the dog raised up on all fours from the floor where he'd been observing the circus of chaos. A dangerous growl emitted through exposed teeth as he allowed the Pawnee to come up beside him.

"They're here," he said in a quiet voice.

"Who?" Jacque rammed his shoulder into one of the men who decided to move away and stand behind Wind Dancer. "Neosho? Then he's probably got the Death Apostles with him. You guys aren't equipped to handle them."

Stands Alone passed out bows and arrows like they were the latest weapons for the Navy SEALs. No one seemed concerned about their prisoners.

"Cut me loose, Wind Dancer. I can help. What do you think you're going to do with those?" He moved to intercept his friend. "Unless those hold some kind of magic I don't know about, you're going to get yourself killed. The whole reason you lost this country was because guns beat arrows."

Two Feathers patted Jacque on the back. "We lost this country because the white man lied to us and broke their promises."

"Blah. Blah. Blah. Sour grapes."

New terms always got Wind Dancer's attention, and this was no different.

"Sour grapes?" He looked to Two Feathers.

"It means the past is bitter in our mouth. We cannot change

the taste because we chose to take the grape."

"Ahh." Wind Dancer nodded then shifted his narrowed gaze to Jacque. "This I understand."

"Great. So, untie me. We'll work this out. Promise."

Wind Dancer moved to stand before him. "I do not want more sour grapes. Blah. Blah. Blah."

"And what about the skinwalker. Who is going to be keeping an eye out for that guy—or whatever he is?"

Wind Dancer motioned for the others to return to the scaffold. He then closed his eyes and cocked his head. "He is here." Reaching down, he patted the dog's head. "Stand guard." Except for a slight wag of his tail, the animal continued to growl and stare out into the darkness of the grand foyer of the museum.

The Pawnee waited until his fellow tribesmen sang an ancient song and moved about the scaffold before he slipped off into the darkness.

CHAPTER 27

The lightning continued to flash, causing the museum to periodically brighten for seconds and sending an eerie glow to spill across the scaffold bed. Although quiet, Cleo moved her head back and forth, watching the Pawnee circling her with their chant-like songs as they lifted their arms up toward the ceiling. Jacque thought for several seconds he felt something powerful flowing through him but shook it off, fearful it could be the skinwalker trying to pick up where he left off.

The detective inched toward the unguarded foyer, the others oblivious of his escape. In spite of the darkness he spotted the coffee shop, lit by red exit signs and a few in-wall emergency bulbs near the floor. He stumbled only once, tipping over a chair that seemed to echo like thunder in his ears when it hit the floor. He whirled around to see if his absence had been discovered, only to see the Pawnees run out of the Native American wing with bows and arrows in hand. Soon the darkness swallowed them as they darted toward the noise coming from the other end of the museum.

Something brushed up against his leg causing him to yelp and jump into a table so hard it flipped over with a bang. The scruffy dog whined then barked as he kept looking toward the exhibit room.

"You just took ten years off my life, you mangy mutt."

Ty complained about the pain as he rolled to the side of the table then promptly fell off.

"What a doofus." Jacque backed up toward the counter where he'd seen a paring knife earlier, managed to grab it, and returned to Ty. The man groaned with such exaggeration as he stood, Jacque wondered if he could fall into him with the open blade to shut him up once and for all.

"Take this and cut me loose."

Ty relieved him of the knife and sawed slowly through the restraints.

"Come on! I don't have all day!" Jacque grumbled through clenched teeth.

"I'm hurtin', man."

"What a baby. I took a gunshot to the chest once, along with one in the leg, and still managed to bring down two bank robbers." Jacque felt the bands fall away. "Thanks." He hobbled out of the coffee shop, the lingering pain from the leg wound he'd discounted returning with the bad weather. Cleo had told him the Frenchman limped as well.

"Hey! Where is everybody?" Ty called after him, cursing as crashing noises accompanied his cried. Stumbling over furniture couldn't be helping his injuries. "You can't leave me here."

The dog trotted at Jacque's heels, providing a strange feeling of comfort. The Pawnee left his weapon holstered so this, too, increased his level of confidence as he barreled into the exhibit room. Stumbling over one of the downed guards propelled his body toward the scaffold.

One of the LED flashlights on the floor provided enough light for him to discover the sacrifice scaffold was empty. He peered beneath it, calling her name then whirled around, pointing a flashlight in several directions. Cleo had disappeared.

~~~~~

Cleo tried to squirm free as Neosho dragged her away from the far exit of the Ancient America. He had found her in the darkness and jerked the restraints from her hands and feet. A red exit sign highlighted his troubled face enough for Cleo to suspect he had become disoriented. His eyes glanced around as he held her squirming efforts to escape with ease. She watched him sniff the
~~~~~

air then pull her in the opposite direction of the earth lodge. She winced at his grip on her bandaged arm, but it didn't stop her from pounding at him or digging her nails into his skin.

The Osage was naked from the waist up. If the situation had not been so dire, Cleo realized she would have thought him a beautiful specimen of male strength. The bottom half of his chiseled face was painted black, and some kind of red adornment, attached to the strip of hair on the middle of his head, created an even more menacing impression. But the glare of pure evil filling his hooded eyes erased any fleeting admiration. The fever in his skin alerted her he was indeed sick, probably with smallpox. He'd received the vaccine too late to protect his body from what already brewed deep inside him.

He must not be allowed to cross over to his world, his time. Such an event could be catastrophic for all populations of man. Where would it stop? What would be the geopolitical ramifications of such a disaster? It wouldn't take long to spread to other parts of the world, possibly causing a pandemic making the Black Death seem like a head cold. She needed to convince him or stop him.

"Neosho. Let. Me. Go." Her voice rode on the thunder rattling the walls. "I won't run away."

He halted, jerking her in front of him. "You lie. You run away before, while I rest. We find a way to my time."

"Only because I was scared of those men. I hated the way they watched me, and Ty said they would hurt me if something happened to you. Besides, the earth lodge isn't this way." Cleo stole a glance over her shoulder and thought she saw someone moving in the shadows. Was it Jacque or Wind Dancer? If she could get him turned around, maybe help would be close by.

"Where are Wind Dancer and the others?"

"Searching for you. They planned to sacrifice me, Neosho, to the Morning Star." She did her best to pucker her lips and sniff back a tear before falling against him. Circling his body with her arms, Cleo realized he was bigger than Wind Dancer and maybe stronger. The beat of his heart intensified as he relaxed enough to return the gesture.

"Do you wish to be free?"

Staring up into his cold dark face, she added a catch in her voice. "Yes. Please. Don't let them kill me." She stepped away enough to feel his embrace withdraw, but close enough not to make him feel threatened she would escape. If he knew of another entrance to his world, then all would be lost. "The earth lodge will open soon. You must know this from watching from the display case so many years."

"There are other openings. We go there. Safe to go. The Death Apostles will come and fight Pawnee. They have guns. Come."

Neosho grabbed her hand and tugged her after him but whirled around when Cleo resisted and protested with a no.

His face darkened with rage.

"I'm afraid, Neosho. Please. Let me give you more medicine to make you strong. You are sick. Your eyes are full of fever and"—she pointed to his neck— "the blisters are starting. If you cross without my medicine, everyone will die, even you and me. This sickness changes each time a person crosses over. It gets stronger. No one can survive."

She hoped the pause meant he processed the scope of what leaping to his world meant. He cocked his head toward her, his eyes narrowing suspiciously then he glanced at his shoulder. "I see nothing."

"I'm a doctor. I'm trained to see the start of sickness." She gently touched his face with her hand, which he grabbed and squeezed until she cried out. "I only wanted to touch you, Neosho. We have been friends for too long."

"Friends?"

"Yes. Friends. Like Wind Dancer, you watched me grow up. I had no way of knowing either of you watched and listened to me. I knew little about the Osage because my father taught me only about the Pawnee." He relaxed his grip, but she didn't withdraw but laid her other hand on his. "When I found out what Wind Dancer and the Frenchman did to your family, your people, I hated that I wasted so much time for so many years." The forced smile, although weak, drew his gaze to her mouth. "I feel so foolish."

"The sacrifice is strong medicine. I have seen it. The white man doesn't like for the Pawnee to do this, and most do not. If Wind Dancer wants this strong medicine to take to his people, to save them from more white man trouble, he will sacrifice you to get it."

The lightning and thunder rattled the building as hail

pummeled the museum so hard the sound of glass shattering somewhere caused them both to cling to each other then turn their eyes to the second floor balcony. The moment of weakness evaporated when Neosho grabbed her forearm, dragging her toward the exhibit hall where hundreds of animals remained encased, like he had been days earlier.

All of the animals sprang to life. Lions lunged at the protective glass as hyenas snarled and snapped at them when they passed. Freed of their trophy status, the beasts prowled back and forth in their enclosures.

Neosho slowed, taking it all in until he came to a buffalo grazing peacefully on something that mimicked grass. He released his grip on her arm, stepped forward, and laid a hand on the reinforced glass, drawing the attention of the beast.

The bison lowered his head and charged, ramming his head into the glass so it split like a spider web. She fell backward to the floor as a scream escaped from deep in her throat. But Neosho retreated slowly, showing little concern toward the beast.

"Go to sleep, old friend. This is not your day to be free." He reached down, catching Cleo by the collar, and jerked her to stand on wobbly legs. "They're coming."

The Death Apostles slunk in with their drawn guns, gaping at the moving creatures inside the maze of display cases. With open mouths, jerky movements, and the occasional stumble, they stopped by several cases to stare at the animated movements of the beasts. They reminded her of the almost-childlike surprise of children seeing Disneyland for the first time.

She prayed they wouldn't start shooting. Random bullets would destroy priceless collections in a matter of minutes.

She tried to hide behind Neosho. Their scowls morphed to bulging eyes and shoulders. Did they blame her for Ty's defection or for their leader, Ashanti's, disappearance?

"Where to, Neosho?" the sour-faced man closest to them asked. "This place still has people inside. I saw a bunch of Indians carrying bows and arrows."

"Yeah. They like you?" Another man whispered.

"Yes!" Cleo shouted, hoping someone would hear her above the raging storm shaking the building. "And they will destroy you. This is not a safe place."

"What she talkin' about?"

Neosho returned to the great hall but stopped to peer into the darkness lit by occasional flashes of lightning.

"You should stay close," was all he said to the gang as he dragged Cleo by the hand so hard she stumbled several times.

The Death Apostles followed, swinging their weapons around like squirt guns at a Baptist church picnic on the creek. Their fumbling in the dark as they crashed into each other made their progress louder than it should have been. They rushed in to an exhibit area to find shadowy figures waiting for them. Cleo realized they'd entered the front end of the Native American exhibit. Finding her way in the dark here was second nature to her. This was home.

"What is this?" They bunched up near Neosho who observed the shadows with the calm of a displeased father with his children.

"Nothing. Do not be afraid."

Cleo jerked free and whirled around. "Oh. You'd better be afraid because the Pawnee will destroy you. You are nothing compared to their skill."

Wind Dancer stepped out, the blush of a safety light, giving him a demonic red glow. "She is right. If you want to live another day, you must go into the night."

"All I see is a bunch of Indians with bows and arrows." The chubby gangbanger chuckled as he peered around at his buddies to gain their amused support. "I think revolver trumps some kids' toy bow and arrow. Right, Neosho?" When Neosho didn't answer, they all directed their attention to him.

Neosho stood rigid, silent with his legs apart and his arms out from his sides. The Death Apostles fanned out in nervous jerks then positioned themselves in a similar posture to his.

Cleo stepped forward as she took in Wind Dancer with one foot in the past and one in the future. In spite of the lack of emotion on his face, smeared with some kind of red and black paint, creating a sinister vibe, she remembered his warm embrace and the press of his kiss that seared to her very soul. His boyish expressions and inquisitive nature had morphed into something more lethal and terrifying, but she chose to remember how he'd saved her the first night with Neosho in hot pursuit.

"I want Cleopatra to come this way." Wind Dancer's voice

became void of emotion except for the coldness characteristic of a resolute heart. Gone was the rugged beauty, replaced by a hardened look of a dangerous warrior.

Neosho switched his stare from Wind Dancer to her.

She took a chance and lunged forward, only to feel Neosho's arm fly across her chest. He elbowed her, knocking the wind from her lungs as she sprawled across the floor. In the second when she gasped for air, she noticed Wind Dancer take a step in her direction, only to stop when Neosho faced him again.

"I will not release her," Neosho growled deep in his throat as he motioned toward his gangbangers to spread out around the room.

"She will not survive in our land." Wind Dancer's voice continued to show little emotion. "She must heal the sickness you brought to this place. If you return, more of our people will die. This sickness you carry is much worse than what I or your family suffered."

"I no longer care. Cleopatra and I will start a new life in the mountains to the west, where the air is cleaner and the water clear. Our children will grow strong while you struggle to find your way home."

"I will not let this happen."

"Then I will kill you."

"No!" Cleo stammered as she struggled to her feet. "I'll go with you, but don't harm Wind Dancer or any other Pawnee. I'll go." She grabbed his arm and felt it flex beneath her fingertips.

"She's not going any place with you," came a voice from out of the darkness. Jacque slid from the doorway to stand next to Wind Dancer, holding his weapon as if he'd fire any second. "Drop those guns right now."

The Death Apostles exchanged glances then and broke out in laughter as they aimed their pistols. The heavyset man pointed his at Jacque.

"I said drop 'em or you'll be my first target, fat boy," Jacque said, lifting his weapon a little higher.

An arrow whizzed by the detective and straight through the right shoulder of the Death Apostle, which burst into flames. He screamed and ran out into the grand hall.

Jacque cringed as Two Feathers stepped forward from the

darkness into a security bulb's pool of light. "I'm a little rusty. I aimed for his heart. My bad."

CHAPTER 28

Thunder crashed, followed by a breeze, before it picked up like tornadoes do before they eat the world around them. Gang members gawked at the display cases holding other examples of Indian tribes as they came to life and began pounding on their enclosures to be set free. Their cases, now brightly lit, gave off the needed light for Cleo to watch things unfold. She could only imagine the gangs' fear, much like the first time she'd witnessed it a few short days earlier.

Other destructive sounds echoed outside the North American Indian exhibit. Perhaps a tornado had dipped down to rip away part of the museum. The gangbangers crouched near her when the Pawnee delegation let lose their arrows at them, barely missing her as she fell behind a statue of a bear.

She could hear them calling to Neosho for guidance, but in her heart, she knew he only cared about the revenge he needed to inflict on Wind Dancer. Cleo realized his lack of concern for their welfare might lead to a speedy surrender.

One of the gangbangers edged close to her and shoved her out in the open so she became completely exposed. Here she could see that with each man who took an arrow, it burst into flame. Guns, too, expelled their death with little success, driving even the Pawnee to take cover behind built-in seats, and other freestanding walls the height of a man for protection.

The two security guards stirred, but Cleo yelled for them to stay in place below the flying arrows and bullets. She watched in morbid curiosity as the other gang members moved in slow motion until their movements stopped altogether like the night Wind Dancer crossed over into her world. Their eyes held confusion and terror as if concrete encased their feet so they could no longer move. Cleo felt paralyzed with fear, even though her body remained free from the powerful forces manipulating the evil in the room.

The Osage reached down to remove a Taser from the belt of a security guard, and Cleo dodged for cover as he eyed the new machine in his hand. In two steps, he'd reached her and jerked her in front of him as he wrapped an arm around her neck. Trying to escape only caused him to tighten the hold.

The swirling wind failed to remove the smell of burning flesh and gunpowder as Neosho dragged Cleo in the direction of the earth lodge. His skin had become searing hot, dripping with sweat that rubbed into her hair and through her clothes. She could smell his breath, raw with the pungent odor of death.

When they reached the sacrifice platform, he used only one hand to toss her onto the surface. Wind Dancer and Jacque took a chance and lunged forward, but another man jumped into the fray.

Cleo crabbed crawled away as Ashanti batted both men aside like pesky flies. She realized the Frenchman turned skinwalker had taken over the gang leader, Ashanti's, body.

"I will kill you for the evil you've become, Neosho." The voice came out of Ashanti in a French accent but sounded hollow, almost wistful. He took a determined step in his direction.

Cleo watched Neosho glance her way and tried to escape off the opposite side, but he caught her foot to pull her back to him. In one swift movement, Neosho snatched one of the arrows that landed on the scaffold and jammed it into Cleo's arm. She screamed, the sound of Wind Dancer's voice fading on the wind as a flash of fire rose up from her wound. She cried out in agony, drawing the buffalo hide over her burning arm to stifle the flames. She fell back just as the Osage jammed the Taser into the skinwalker.

Ashanti convulsed violently. Was the skinwalker finally eliminated? But no sooner had the body dropped to the floor than

Jacque sprang to his feet, eyes red with the rage of a possessed being. He tossed his head and rolled his shoulders, shuddering.

Wind Dancer raced to Cleo's side and tugged on the shaft enough to free her from being pinned in place, although the arrowhead remained in her arm as he gently lifted her to place her on the floor beneath the scaffold.

She reached for Wind Dancer, but he slipped away to join in the fray. The wind increased enough to force the members of the Pawnee delegation to grab on to something to keep from being tossed like a child's toys against a wall. As currents of air lifted her body, she wrapped a rope around her good arm.

The clatter of weapons being tossed against the cases gave Cleo enough concern that she stuck her head out in the open to locate Wind Dancer and Jacque. Even the characters in the enclosed cases hunkered down as if they could feel the momentum of the storm. Only Neosho, Wind Dancer, and Jacque remained standing, unmoved by the wind.

With the cry of a warrior, Neosho beat his chest then shook his head. He pointed his club toward her threateningly, but the sound from within the earth lodge drew his attention. A large portion of the back wall ripped open. Cleo had an overpowering urge to jump up and run toward it, in hopes of leading the Osage away from the man she loved.

Then the skinwalker bounded toward the Osage with the screech of a demonic being, fist raised in a final act of revenge. Neosho's eyes widened, but he met the skinwalker with his own lunge of anger. They crashed into each other like Titans, each stronger than should be was possible.

Jacque fell under one of Neosho's hammer-like punches. As Jacque went down, Neosho grabbed another weapon strapped on the calf of the detective's leg.

"Wind Dancer, he has a gun!" Cleo screamed into the wind.

The Osage leveled his weapon at Jacque, but Wind Dancer grabbed the barrel as he fired, sending the shot into a piece of priceless pottery. Neosho fumbled the gun, which scooted across the floor toward Cleo.

Before she could get to it, Neosho grabbed the gun, slamming it upside the Pawnee's head hard enough to send him reeling. Jumping to his feet, he leveled the gun down at Jacque again as he rose from the floor in slow motion, eyes fiery red. Neosho pulled the trigger several times, sending the creature against the wall with a tortured cry.

In that instant, the wind stopped completely, causing the rest of the Pawnee to stumble out into the open.

The encased Indians remained animated, banging on the glass for release while the gang members remained frozen, except for their eyes that seemed to follow the activities unfolding around them. Several men moaned as the exhibit hall filled with one more sound. Cleo motioned for the tribal members to stand back behind a chest-high wall and held her finger to her lips for silence.

The buffalo meandered into the exhibit, snorting beasts of the plains. Jacque slid down to the floor once more, grasping his blood-soaked pant leg. Cleo wondered how he lived as blood oozed from his neck and upper arm where he'd taken a bullet from his own gun.

The Osage slowly refocused on the buffalo that eyed him with glowing red eyes and pawed at the floor with impatience.

Neosho sprinted toward the opening in the earth lodge as the buffalo slammed him into the wall with his head, over and over until he fell to the floor. The buffalo stomped him while Wind Dancer shot arrow after arrow into the beast, each bursting into momentary flame when it landed. Finally, the beast fell to its knees and turned his head to gaze at Wind Dancer. The Pawnee approached him and laid a hand on his head as his eyes faded red to brown.

Cleo stumbled to his side as he spoke. "Go on to the next world, my friend, and be with your family."

The buffalo took its last breath and collapsed on its side.

"Wind Dancer!" Two Feathers pointed to the opening in the earth lodge. "It is full circle. We must hurry before the sun breaks through above the horizon."

Several of the Pawnee had clubbed the Death Apostles into unconsciousness or pinned them with arrows before the magic of the universe subsided. Several others had been hit by flying debris so they couldn't move if they wanted to.

"Grab your things. It's time." Two Feathers motioned for them to hurry.

Wind Dancer reached Jacque and picked him up like a fallen

toddler, blood seeping from the parts of his body the protective vest hadn't covered.

"Put him on the scaffold, Joseph. I can keep an eye on him until help comes." With the burn in her arm, she wouldn't be able to help more than that.

"Remember what I said, Jacque." Wind Dancer removed his shirt as he sat him on the edge.

"Yeah. Yeah. Got it."

Cleo felt like she'd been left out of an important conversation. "I don't understand. Everything is fine now. You aren't leaving."

Wind Dancer pushed her hair away from her face, even as the others called to him. He kissed her as if there would be no tomorrow. "You are the only one I've ever loved, Cleopatra. I hope our paths cross again in the future."

"No. Wait." Tears streamed down her face. In spite of his injuries, Jacque slipped off the platform and tried to prevent her from stopping the Pawnee. Wind Dancer jumped through the hole as it began to close. The detective held her against his bloody chest with his good arm. They waited longer than necessary, as if the night might still expose surprises they didn't understand.

The mangy dog crept out from under the scaffold and crawled to their side, emitting a growl as he seemed to observe the exhibit room now in shambles. "Some watch dog you are," Jacque complained as the animal wagged his tail.

~~~~

"And that's it, Agent Farentino." Jacque finished retelling the whole story once more. The only thing left of Neosho was a smashed mannequin the museum staff had tossed in the trash. Poetic justice. Since the FBI had been in on the whole parallel universe thing, he didn't need to make anything up. They would handle the details and the media coverage. People continued to be more freaked out about the smallpox outbreak than a storm tearing through the Field Museum the night before.

The ramblings of a bunch of gang members about monsters, powerful magic, and flaming arrows got them a night in jail then booked on weapons charges, breaking and entering, and attempted murder along with a number of drug offenses. The cherry on top
~~~~

for Jacque was the additional charges of assaulting a police officer and animal cruelty.

"How's Dr. Sommers?" the agent asked as they stepped over the mess. When the detective frowned, he continued, "And you, of course. How're the arm and leg?"

Jacque adjusted his sling. "Didn't hit anything important. Cleo, I mean Dr. Sommers will be okay, too. The burn on her arm gave them concern at first, but she should be good as new before too long."

"Tell her if she needs anything to call."

Jacque rolled his eyes. "If she needs anything you will be the last person she calls."

"So Dr. Sommers told me at the hospital she wasn't in any real danger from Wind Dancer. Care to explain? I thought he planned to sacrifice her."

"Yeah. So did I. Turns out those nerves of steel I thought she had were really all because of a story Wind Dancer told her."

"Take more than a story to calm me down if I thought I was a sacrifice." The agent chuckled.

"Well, the story goes that some Pawnee who planned to sacrifice a Comanche girl to the Morning Star decided that wasn't such a good idea. On the morning of the sacrifice, he rode in and rescued her."

"Rode off into the sunset, huh?"

"Sunrise in this case. Apparently, it was the beginning of the end for the sacrifice thing." Jacque picked up a piece of broken pottery and gently laid it on a folding table brought in to place artifacts.

"So Cleo thought they wouldn't actually go through with killing her?"

"She was more upset about Wind Dancer leaving. But participating in the role of sacrifice apparently got the Morning Star, if you believe in that sort of thing, juiced up enough to open the hole into their world."

"Are you two…"

"No. Don't be an idiot. We're friends. And." He jabbed a finger in the agent's chest. "I know about your propensity to love 'em and leave 'em so no taking advantage of a bad situation."

"Propensity? Another big word for a Chicago cop."

"Yeah, well, that is the last one I know so stop feeling so inferior."

The agent laughed good-naturedly as he swung the door open to meet the press at the bottom of the steps of the Field Museum. Colonel Jefferson from the Pentagon stood with stoic resolve as he waited with a few other military personnel. Their presence made sure everyone stayed on script. "Well, let's see if they'll buy the story we've made up."

EPILOGUE

One year later

Cleo removed the disposable gloves then dropped them in the appropriate container. The clock brought her awareness she'd worked two hours past her go-home-at-five-o'clock-no-matter-what deadline. She'd promised the head nurse, who she'd nicknamed helicopter, because of her constant hovering, to cut down on her hours. But she didn't have a family or even a cat to go home to at the end of her shift, so she often times let someone else leave. Besides, then she wouldn't be thinking about her father, and the little brother she'd never know. Her memories did a flip-flop as she scrubbed her hands. She wondered if Wind Dancer continued with his studies with her father when he returned to his village on the prairie. Was he well? More importantly, did he miss her, still love and long for her body as she did his?

Two weeks earlier she'd driven out to where she thought his village may have been in Nebraska. She found a subdivision and strip mall. She parked her car and wept for a love she'd never know. With a broken heart, it became easier to bury herself in being a doctor. Others needed her and, at this point, she needed to be needed.

The smallpox outbreak a year earlier had nearly gotten away from them. Fortunately, it had been contained to the Chicago area. Seven hundred cases diagnosed, another thousand quarantined, and two million vaccinated. Only three died, and they'd compromised immune systems already: one elderly man, a woman with cancer, and a teen mom who lived with Ashanti.

"Hey, I thought you'd be ready to leave." Jacque strolled into the locker room of the hospital. "The museum staff are anxious for you to see the exhibit before it reopens in the morning." She slipped on a denim jacket and lifted out her hair over the collar. She had decided to grow it long in the last year.

"Ty dropped me off this morning because he took my car to the shop to see about the knocking sound. Can you take me home so I can shower and change clothes?"

"I wondered why you wanted me to drop by. Ty has done pretty well for himself in the last year."

"Yes. I'm proud of him. So, can you take me home first?"

"Women. I guess, but don't take all night. I got a date later."

She stood on tip toes and kissed his cheek. They'd become the best of friends. They went to dinner at least once a week and phoned each other on the weekends. Several times, Cleo had thought maybe something would happen between them, but it never did. Those moments she felt most vulnerable and alone.

"Did Mangy Dog survive his manhood surgery?" She grinned.

Jacque placed his hand over his face. "Let's not talk about it. I feel guilty as it is. Poor guy. You should see him walk."

Cleo slipped her arm through his. "It's for the best. You'll see."

Once at Cleo's, Jacque made himself at home with the Weather Channel as she hurried to get ready for the private showing of the North American Indian Exhibit. She came out dressed in a flowery dress and for once wore a little makeup she thought brought out the peaches and cream in her complexion. He wolf-whistled as he clicked off the television.

"You are really a doll, you know that?"

"So you think I'm a stuffed idiot?" She pretended to fume as she grabbed her purse.

He shrugged. "Yes. A pretty stuffed idiot."

This made her laugh.

The drive to the Field Museum went slower than usual because of the rain pooling on the highway. A low rumble of thunder followed as distant clouds flickered with lightning. They stopped to gaze out over Lake Michigan; huddled under an umbrella, Jacque found in his car.

"Ready?" He sounded as unsure as Cleo felt. She knew the case where Wind Dancer stood had been removed. The whole room had to be reconfigured because of the damage. Some of the old things had been replaced with other artifacts, but most of the cases with mannequins would remain. Donations had poured in at unprecedented amounts, making it possible to restore one of the most popular areas of the museum. A buzz had been generated by the media about the reopening the next day. The staff wanted Cleo to be the first one to see it though because of her father's life's work.

"Thanks for coming, Dr. Sommers. Can I give you a quick tour?" The curator shook her hand then Jacque's.

Before she could answer, he began pointing and directing her attention to various changes. Jacque kept an appropriate distance, letting the curator have the show. Cleo appreciated his efforts to pretend he enjoyed himself. She knew the place still made his skin crawl and that he remembered being possessed by a skinwalker for a short time. He never talked about it, not even when Cleo tried to draw him out. After several months, she'd dropped it. This was hard for her, too.

"And finally I'm going to let you go into the next section where we've restored several tribal displays. The Pawnee section is the last one before the earth lodge."

Jacque stepped up next to her and jammed his hands onto his waist, forcing his sport coat back to reveal his badge and weapon.

The curator's eyes fell on it then moved toward the inside. "Please take Detective Marquette. I know he is responsible for saving much of what we still have here. I'm going to check on a few things. A storm is rolling in, and I want to make sure everyone did their due diligence about surge protection in the lab." He pivoted to make a quick exit but added an afterthought. "Take your time."

"Thank you, Dr. McGrath," Cleo called as she grabbed Jacque's hand and tugged him into the dimly lit area where she used to steal away in search of Wind Dancer.

"Let's get this over with," Jacque mumbled under his breath.

"You're limping again. You need to have that knee checked

out. Might be something other than the weather causing the soreness."

"I'm fine. This place just gives me the heebie-jeebies."

She hugged his arm then released it as they entered the area where the display cases stood.

"I see the tribes aren't restless tonight," Jacque mocked as they stopped in front of several Sioux females holding babies, standing next to their husbands. "Hmm. Guess they do more than make war on the white man."

Cleo shoved him aside and smiled. "Stop it. Your bad jokes aren't fooling me. You're scared." She continued to move along the row of cases, admiring the beadwork of the Cheyenne and Cherokee.

"Damn right. Any of these mannequins give me a thumbs-up, I'm going to be the most trigger-happy cop in Chicago." To prove his point, he unsnapped his holster.

"I think it's in here, Jacque." She saw the case covered in a white sheet. It stood in the same spot she used to visit Wind Dancer and Neosho when she was a child.

"Will it be him?"

Cleo shrugged. "They didn't say, only that I would be surprised." She hesitated as her fingertips touched the white covering. "Here goes." A gentle tug started the slow, downward drop of the sheet-like covering, revealing the new occupants of the enclosed display case.

Cleo sucked in her breath as she fell against Jacque, who caught her by placing his hands on her waist.

"Who is it?" he asked.

"My father!" Cleo touched the glass, seeing him for the first time in years. He wore buckskins and his hair fell down his neck, making her laugh. He kneeled as if he searched for something with his hand nearly touching the glass. "Oh, Dad," she sighed. "I love you so much." She raised her hand, pretending he might be able to see and feel her from another universe.

"Who is that with him?" he asked, coming up next to her.

Cleo chuckled as she turned her face to Jacque. "Wind Dancer's sister and my stepmother." A little boy stood next to her father with his little brown hand on his shoulder. "And this is my baby brother. He's beautiful."

"I think you have a baby sister, too," he said admiring the chubby baby in its mother's arms.

"Dr. Kuzma said he and Wind Dancer had a long talk about my father the day they met. I guess the good doctor filled in some gaps for the museum."

The lights flickered as a boom of thunder rocked the building. "I hate this place. Are you done?"

A breeze moved through the room, toying with the hem of Cleo's dress. She looked toward the earth lodge. "No. I want to stay. I want…"

Before she could say another word, a great wind rushed by them. Jacque grabbed her arm and spun her around to see her father's case.

"Dad!" Her father stood as she rushed forward. "Dad! I love you! Dad!" He dropped his hand to the head of the little boy who stared up at him with admiration. He rested his palm against the glass as the wind suddenly stopped. She placed her hand against his and smiled. "Thank you for coming, Dad." He nodded then pointed at something behind her and Jacque.

As they stepped sideways, a silhouette of a man appeared in the earth lodge. At first he didn't move but stared out at them as if calculating his next move. Both Jacque and Cleo moved to completely face the earth lodge.

The lights behind him extinguished as he stepped through the opening toward them into the dim light.

"Wind Dancer." His name caught in her throat as she rushed forward.

He caught her up in his arms then buried his mouth against hers. "I tried so many times to get here." He placed her feet on the floor as Jacque approached. Wind Dancer cocked his head at him. "You have protected her. Thank you."

They clasped hands and held tight for a few seconds, each measuring the other for weakness. "I see you're still strong as a buffalo."

"And you still are going to give me advice." The Pawnee crushed Cleo to his chest. "Am I right?"

"My advice to you," he said, eyeing the two of them, "is to get a room."

ABOUT THE AUTHOR

Tierney has been in education for over thirty years. She recently stopped teaching World Geography for a nearby college to pursue her writing career. Creating a workshop for beginning writers, speaking at schools and serving as an officer in the writing group Sleuths' Ink, are some of the things she does when not writing. With the creation of *Winds of Deception,* Tierney is now working with one of the crew members of USS Liberty in hopes of obtaining the Medal of Honor for him.

Besides serving as a Solar System Ambassador for NASA's Jet Propulsion Lab and attending Space Camp for Educators, Tierney has traveled across the world. From the Great Wall of China to floating the Okavango Delta of Botswana, Africa, she ties her unique experiences into other writing projects such as the action thriller novel, *An Unlikely Hero,* the first in the Enigma Series. *Rooftop Angels* the third in the Enigma series. Living on a Native American reservation and in a mining town for many years fuels the kind of characters she never tires of creating.

Along with teaching and writing, Tierney enjoys family, gardening, reading and music. Other pursuits involve learning Hebrew in hopes of incorporating the knowledge in future volumes of the Enigma Series. She likes to research and sometimes that has involved learning new skills, such as being certified with various weapons.

She has settled in the beautiful Ozarks, but there's never a dull moment in Tierney's life. And that is just the way she likes it.

OTHER PUBLICATIONS
by
Tierney James

The Enigma Series

An Unlikely Hero
Winds of Deception
Rooftop Angels

Children's Books

There's a Superhero in the Library
Zombie Meatloaf
Mission K9 Rescue

Education Books

African Safari: A Thematic Lesson Book for Teachers

Other

The Rescued Heart
Dance of the Devil's Trill
Dark Side of Morning